WHEN THE
POUI
BLOOMS

Good Seeds Book 1

NATASHA COKER JONES

upstream publications

Published by Upstream Publications Limited

Printed in the United States of America

ISBN: 978-976-95875-1-9 (pbook)

ISBN: 978-976-95875-2-6 (ebook)

Author's contact information:

P.O. Box 9717 National Mail Centre Piarco, Trinidad, West Indies

www.natashacokerjones.com

Cover illustration Copyright© 2016 by Natasha Coker Jones

Cover design by Revelino Guevara

Author photography by Michelle Greaves

Lyrics of David Rudder's "Madness" used by permission.

DEDICATION

To my parents

ACKNOWLEDGMENTS

First, I give thanks to my Lord and Savior Jesus Christ for placing within my heart a love for people and a passion to create using words as my building blocks. I also thank God for providing all the resources I needed to complete my debut novel.

It's clear to me that my parents, Franklyn (deceased) and Alfreda Coker, raised a bibliophile. Mummy, thank you for your unwavering support in general and toward this project in particular. To my loving husband, Klenworth, thank you for giving me the space to pursue my "flights of fancy." Ever so often, I needed to stop and play, and my son, Kibwe, ensured that my play sessions were well spent!

To my editor, Dexter Webb, much thanks for your candor, keen eye, enthusiasm for the project, and insightful suggestions. My Jamaican language guides Marlon Dyce and Camille Reid— thank you for your patient help with the patois. And to Simone King for the quick lesson in speaking Bajan.

Arlene Lynch and Dana McLeod—two of my best friends— you fed me with your words of encouragement and willingness to provide feedback when I needed it. Thanks also to Michelle Soodeen for your prayer and platform-building assistance and Revelino Guevara for your inspired cover and internal design.

Special gratitude to the medical student and doctors who agreed to be my sounding board for the medical details used in various parts of the novel. Also, thank you to David Rudder who granted permission to use his lyrics.

Finally, I want to thank my pastor, the Reverend Alister Alexander, and his lovely wife, Lula, for inspiring me to swim against the tide. Your example, coupled with your call to action for the glory of God, has found fertile ground in this heart. To my Daybreak Assembly family, *I love you*. It's largely in your midst that I was graced with opportunities to express the many facets of my creative self.

So the book is here, and I've only just begun. To all my family, friends, well-wishers, and supporters across Trinidad and Tobago, Jamaica, the rest of the Caribbean, the United States, the United Kingdom, and beyond, hope you enjoy the read. Be sure to let me know what you think.

PART 1
Away From Home

CHAPTER ONE

No one could accuse him of being judgmental; he was certain of that.

For the past five days, Malachi had been careful to offer nothing more than a dash of noncommittal responses anytime freshmen felt compelled to rant or make an off-putting remark about the place that they were now expected to call home.

Remarks like the one he'd bought on Tuesday. Literally. He'd purchased lunch for a girl named Wendy—a fellow Trinidadian and a real looker. The combo of beauty and geographic familiarity worked him like a potent elixir, causing Malachi to dig deep in his pocket and part ways with money he knew he should hold on to. But the regret wasn't immediate. It came minutes later when the two were seated at a table in Turner Hall Dining

Room, and his lunch date shrilled, "Where dem get this bright yellow curry from?"

He didn't need to look around to confirm the dark looks trained at the back of their heads. Malachi rewarded his compatriot with a half-smile and pretended to check his watch.

Note to self: dine alone or with larger groups.

If the past couple of days had taught him anything, it was that it was better to err on the side of caution when dealing with sensitive cultural matters. When the Jamaicans bashed themselves, Malachi found it best to remain silent. If they needed his help, they'd ask. He was a visitor in another man's country, his dad had warned him, and you just never know what edits some confusion-maker could put on your comments.

His dad had said it on Sunday—the day before his only son was due to leave for university. Church had long been over, so it was just father and son. No pulpit, no chorus of "amen," no videotaping. At the time, Malachi was transferring toiletries from his dresser to his travel bag. His dad was leaning against the doorjamb, his hands immersed in his pockets. The admonition had been the one piece of advice his father had offered up recently that hadn't gnawed at the young man's nerves.

But that was then. On this Saturday morning, Malachi was through dodging cultural minefields. His Jamaican roommate's latest tale about the Barbadian Freshman who supposedly cried herself to sleep every night since she arrived, set something off inside of him.

Malachi punched his pillow and tucked it under his head again. It wasn't about empathy, he told himself as he lay supine on his new bed. Personally, he'd missed home far less than he'd imagined. Whether that made him lucky or pitiable, he still wasn't sure.

"Me get it direct from her roommate," Hopeton said as he lifted the lid on the jar of guava jam.

Malachi fixed his gaze on the water stain on the ceiling above his head. Someone, probably a handyman, had tried to conceal it with an overlay of paint.

A knife fell. Malachi's eyes darted to where Hopeton stood preparing his pre-breakfast snack. He saw his roommate pick the knife off the floor, wipe it against the knee of his jeans, and dip it into the jar again.

"Last night, she tell all the first years when we were playing dominoes. You know…," he started, and paused in mid-sentence to give his thumb and index two quick licks. "Some of the seniors not so bad, you know. They just pretend to hate we guts."

Malachi ran his hand across his face, lingering on his hairless chin. His mom had often told him that he had inherited her skin, never mind he was the spitting image of his dad—a darker, taller version, right down to the dimples.

"And she pretty, pretty, pretty…" Hopeton's lips made a smacking sound as they connected with his fingertips. "S—weet browning. You know what a browning is? Them nice high-color girls you see in ads. And is the roommate me a talk, not the crying Bajan."

Malachi continued to gawp at the ceiling. Only when he realized that Hopeton had returned to his meal prep did he steal some furtive glances in his roommate's direction. Churlishness, Malachi's mom had told him, was never becoming. But neither was listening to drivel, and his roommate, Malachi had noted from day one, was capable of dishing out an unending supply if encouraged. Today, however, Malachi simply wasn't in the mood to hear it.

"Not that she as nice as my Petrina, of course, but she alright," Hopeton continued, his facial expressions mimicking the variety of a gifted storyteller.

"Brains and money too, you know. She related to some rich people in Beverly Hills. In med like us. Jamaican, full schol. Not that she need it if her family is rich people. Better she did give we. Nuh true?" The question was almost muted by the half-a-sandwich swishing around in his mouth.

Malachi faked a yawn.

"You know, some people only sleep in dem own bed," Hopeton continued, as he smothered another hack of hard dough with guava jam. "You want one?" He turned his head to where Malachi lay and pointed the butter knife toward the slice he held. "Me have bread, and I see you never buy."

"No thanks."

Hopeton shrugged. "More for me," he said under his breath and resumed the tasks of slicing, smothering, cementing, and licking. "Me know this leaving home business is very traumatic for the young female dem. Me feel sorry for her."

"For real," Malachi finally quipped, a little louder than he'd planned. "Imagine having to spend a whole year with a roommate that would rat me out like that, mon. Cha!" Even before the last word was out, Malachi knew he'd earned an F for his efforts at sounding Jamaican.

Hopeton paused in mid chew and guffawed. Bits of masticated food somersaulted from his mouth and landed on the terrazzo. Malachi winced when he saw that a stray chunk of sandwich matter had attached itself to Hopeton's copy of the *Grant's Atlas of Anatomy* on his study desk.

"Yuh real different yuh know," Hopeton said, still trying to rein in the chuckles. "'Like that, mon.'" His imitation of his Trini roommate spot on. "How come everybody think Jamaicans just go round saying 'mon this' and 'mon that?' I seriously have to teach you some patois. Next time me go back home, me ah go bring one copy of *Old Story Time* fi yuh, and you have to read it. You can't go back a Trinidad sounding like that! Don't worry, we have a whole year together. You bound fi pick it up."

A sound escaped from Malachi's lips as he pulled the covers over his head. It was moments like these that reminded him of the one thing from home that he truly missed: his own room.

Malachi's room on hall was nothing like his bedroom back home in Trinidad. For one, it was twice the size, although if he took into account that, technically, only half the room was his, it was about the same.

The new accommodations also contained a hodgepodge of furniture that reflected someone's version of essentials for a success-

ful student life: two single beds, two oak-stained wooden ward-
robes, two four-drawer chest of drawers, two mahogany-stained
study desks and chairs, two four-shelf book cases, two lounge
chairs, and two lamps. Depending on how the room was divid-
ed, one occupant would have to contend with a slightly smaller
space due to a built-in toilet and bath, so compact, that Malachi
seriously felt it discriminated against the obese.

But of all the differences between his room back home and
his new one on hall, the biggest to his mind, could be summed
up in one word—light.

Everything about the room was engineered to welcome it:
walls painted the lightest shade of eggplant, and wainscoting
that interrupted itself to form double doors that tumbled out
onto a balcony. It was all a stark contrast to the cavern he'd cre-
ated back home with its dark gray walls, thick burgundy drapes,
and matching burgundy and beige-checkered rug. Back home,
when night fell and the lights were off, he could barely see his
hands in front of his face. On hall, light assaulted him at every
turn.

Malachi recalled how surprised he was back in high school
to learn that his dad had spoken to his form master about what
they incorrectly assumed was a case of photophobia. Some of
the boys in his class had begun experimenting with the goth
subculture, and his father was concerned that Malachi might
have been drifting in that direction. Malachi had had a task convincing the man who had given him his first name, as well as his
last, that his preference for muted tones had no sinister subtext.

Nevertheless, at one time, all that had been left to render his room back home fit for hibernation was to have sealed off the fancy bricks over his window.

His dad had refused to allow him to plaster it over with cement. His rationale was that folks in America and England would trade their first born for the fresh air that those ventilation blocks permit. But as far as Malachi Williamson Junior was concerned that argument wasn't worth the air it floated out on. Sure, he couldn't speak with the authority of knowing firsthand. Through no fault of his, until now, he hadn't stepped foot anywhere beyond Charlotteville—his favorite vacation spot located on the northeastern tip of Tobago, the smaller of the twin-island Republic of Trinidad and Tobago. But common sense told young Williamson that not having the fresh air that comes on account of ventilation blocks was actually a plus for those in temperate countries who have to face winter. But arguing his point, he knew, would get him nowhere. Instead, he decided to improvise.

Malachi had stayed up late one night stuffing brown paper in the grooves. The next day he could only shake his head in admiration at the jagged streaks of morning which, despite his best efforts, had dappled his bedroom walls.

Light, he discovered, was not easily silenced.

Hopeton had arrived on the first day of orientation, a day before Malachi, and had taken first dibs on the good furniture. One of the brass handles on Malachi's wardrobe was missing while both of Hopeton's were intact. The shade on Malachi's lamp was also missing—a situation which was remedied after a quick trip to the block rep's room. Even the lounge chair that was left for Malachi to claim didn't look quite as sturdy as his roommate's. The only item that appeared equal was the chest of drawers. At least that was Malachi's assessment until two days ago when he caught Hopeton struggling with the drawer slide on his bottom drawer. The discovery made Malachi smirk.

"So, any more nightmares?" Hopeton's voice snapped him out of his early-morning reverie. "Me realize you never wake up screaming and cold sweating like the first two nights. What you did scream out?" He snapped his finger hoping to jog his memory.

"Nope. No nightmares. Told you it was the cucumbers."

"What meh did tell you seh? Let me talk properly so you could understand: what did I tell you? Lay off the cucumbers then: no cucumbers, no nightmares. Simple."

"You said it."

Malachi knew he sounded ridiculous blaming cucumbers for his nightmares. But what else could he say. He sure wasn't about to admit to his roommate—someone he'd known for all of five days—that he'd fallen prey to the cliché of culture shock. No way, not in Jamaica. But the symptoms were undeniable.

Hadn't he read somewhere that the body stages a kind of coup d'état when faced with the unfamiliar. Sleep, for instance, cuts its own spare key and starts coming and going as it pleases. The olfactory nerves and salivary glands become cagey—jealous even—of the dark new aromas that cavort with the senses. In extreme cases, depression rolls in with its artillery of gloom, grinding everything to a colorless halt.

This was par for the course apparently in the world of ex-pats, and to a lesser extent, students, especially those who trade the comforts of the First World for the hard-luck zones of the Third or vice versa. He'd heard stories of former classmates, now at university abroad, who floundered at the mercy of heat waves, blizzards, bland food, and the still-too-frequent case of xenophobia.

But this was Jamaica—the girl next door.

Yet from his first night on the island, Malachi had been plagued with what could only be described as a spate of medical dreams. He reckoned they weren't nightmares in the strictest sense of the word, but they disturbed him nonetheless. In almost all of them he wallowed in some insidious stream of body fluid.

The first dream saw him swimming through pulmonary veins on his way to the heart. He had no idea whose heart he was swimming toward or how indeed he had got there, but there he was treading the viscous fluid as if life itself—perhaps his or the person in whose veins he was swimming—depended on it. Hopeton shook him out of it that first night, and out of a sense of obligation, Malachi had shared about the cucumbers. His dad had a theory that where nightmares were concerned, eating cucumbers after six was just asking for it. That stuck with him, and even now, with as good a scientific mind as any, he still wondered if there wasn't a smidgen of truth to the hypothesis. In any event, it made for an intriguing explanation for a nightmare, and to Malachi's surprise, Hopeton lapped it up.

The next night, cucumberless and without warning, it happened again. It was synovial fluid this time, and again, Malachi found himself making laps, desperately striding toward some mysterious target.

This morning's dream was different. For one, it didn't disturb his roommate. He was grateful for that. Secondly, the fluid didn't appear to be body fluid at all, but salubrious sea waters reminiscent of what he swam in just two days ago when the hall committee took the freshers, as the Jamaicans preferred to call them, to Ocho Rios in the North Coast of the island. In the dream, he floated on his back, just as he'd done that day. But instead of pellucid blue skies and clouds as light as cotton candy treats, he was staring up into the lenses of a medical microscope. Moreover, a man he presumed to be a lecturer, was beckoning the growing throng of med students around him to have a turn at peering into what Malachi somehow knew was the microbiology lab's only microscope. Like an aid truck in a refugee camp, the scene grew rowdy as scores of his colleagues jostled each other in a desperate bid to view the squiggly culture in the petri dish—the culture that just happened to be him.

Relief flooded him when he'd opened his eyes and realized it was just a dream. He'd turned his head to where Hopeton's frame rose and fell like the swell of a tropical tide. That was half past two. Sleep had split. Malachi had stared into the connecting red dots of the display on his digital alarm clock—a going-off-to-university gift from his dad. The clock was nothing to speak of. It was simple and functional, much like the giver, but staring at it was safe—much safer than allowing the mind to retrieve its pick of memories.

This morning, the clock was his answer to insomnia. He'd stared at the display until the last digit had changed. The simple act of counting down the seconds before it changed had settled him. Three more minutes of clock therapy, had put him right back to sleep.

That was how day five said hello.

When Malachi opened his eyes again, it was still much too early to be awake on a Saturday morning, and Hopeton was shuffling around his side of the room preparing his pre-breakfast snack. Realizing his roommate was finally awake, he commenced his vacuous tale about the Barbadian first year whose roommate was yapping to the world about the poor girl's struggles with home sickness.

Hopeton heard the sigh that escaped from his roommate's lips when he was finished telling the story, just before Malachi pulled the covers over his head.

"It soon done," Hopeton said with a chortle, not realizing that his roommate's groan of exasperation was directly related to his ramblings. "Don't bother fight them at this stage, Mal."

Mal. It was a contraction of his name that Malachi discouraged at all cost. His mother, an English teacher, had insisted on it, citing that mal on its own was a Latin prefix meaning bad.

Hopeton had rechristened him the day they met in the dorm room they were meant to share on Sutton Hall.

"Mal-a-chi. Wow. That come from the Bible, right? Pleased to meet you, Mal," he had said, as he pumped his roommate's hand. Malachi shot him the look that was supposed to say it all.

But it was all lost on Hopeton. Two minutes later he'd repeated the unfortunate prefix. This time Malachi chucked the nonverbals in favor of a snide remark about hating when total strangers truncate a perfectly good name.

"Yeah, that's like when people call me Hope. That's so stupid."

Malachi surrendered to the smile that tugged at his lips— relieved that his fears of being saddled with an obtuse roommate were unfounded. Hopeton then asked: "So Mal, what's Trinidad like?"

It was one of the many irritations he resigned himself to put up with until he got to second year and became eligible for a single room. Perhaps it was the downside of being an only child. He often wondered if he'd had a brother or even a sister constantly around, touching his stuff, if his private list of irritations would've been less likely to advance toward a manuscript.

He stirred under his sheets. They were still thick with the familiar smell of home. Malachi caught a movement out of the corner of his eye. It was Hopeton performing a funny jig while smearing pomade on his scalp. The jig took on interesting permutations as his roommate reached for the volume knob on his candy pink boom box, which Malachi was convinced Hopeton had lifted from his baby sister.

Malachi on the other hand had come to Jamaica with what was irrefutably an extremely decent state-of-the-art listening experience. He'd purchased it with money he'd so dutifully saved from the administrative gig he'd endured during the year he took off instead of coming straight to med school. It was his first major purchase as a working adult. The first, he resolved, in a series of sumptuous status symbols he planned to acquire during what Malachi hoped would be a long and lucrative career in medicine.

Even now, its sleek black and silver trim caught the light from the florescent bulb and gleamed down at him from its perched position on the chest of drawers. He had transferred his toiletries to his top drawer to make room for his prized asset. During the day, when he visited his room, the sound system was the first thing his eyes would seek out. And like a traveler patting for his passport, a wave of relief would wash over him every time his gaze was rewarded. He was amongst strangers after all—a fact that his block representative had reminded them of at their very first block meeting.

Hopeton turned up the volume again on Bob—the name he ambitiously dubbed the CD player after the late Jamaican icon Bob Marley. Marley was a bit of an obsession for Hopeton as far as Malachi could tell. Even now a larger-than-life Marley poster covered a decent portion of the wall over Hopeton's bed. There was also the fact that Malachi had awoken to Marley's *Rastaman Vibration* every morning since he met his roommate.

Still, Malachi had to admit that Hopeton appeared to be taking the whole orientation thing in strides. And why shouldn't he? He was in his own country, and that meant, at the very least, he probably understood everything everyone said. Besides, if any of it became unbearable, Hopeton could simply pack up and hop on the nearest bus home.

Malachi, on the other hand, was stuck.

For him the thought of facing day six of orientation week or freshers' week as it's popularly called at the University of Jamaica campus—UJ for short—was admittedly less daunting compared to his first day. He had to give the seniors credit for keeping up the charade of lording over the freshers for this long. Tomorrow, the dreaded hall induction would be behind them. Seniors and first years would be on some version of a level playing field, although Malachi still couldn't comprehend how it could ever be level. It was the utopia that every first year who indulged the ruse and ruse-makers, was coaxed to aspire toward: that great day when there would be no obligatory recall of ridiculous titles, forced errands, early morning or late night drills, vibes sessions with boisterous singing of hall songs, and random pop quizzes testing recall of meaningless hall trivia. He wondered if rush week, as his friends studying in the United States call it, was half as entertaining.

As a foreigner, Malachi reasoned it would have given him some kind of edge to arrive early. He could get acclimatized— that was the word his mother would have used. She would have advised him to use the time to check out the campus, learn the routes to the nearest conveniences, make friends, and if things were slow, she would have suggested that he go backpacking to Montego Bay, Negril, or even climb the Blue Mountain, if people actually did that. Mom would have encouraged him to do that.

Climb the Blue Mountain. Yeah right. The mental picture made him smile.

This was Malachi's first time in Jamaica, and truth be told, it was his first time anywhere outside of his home in Trinidad, but he thought it best to keep that little detail to himself.

As is customary for first years, he was roomed with a fellow freshman—a med student like himself—and a Jamaican, unlike himself.

Hopeton's eyes were closed now, and he was singing along to "Want More." Malachi had to admit that the guy was all right as far as roommates go. The fact that he was in med was a plus. Malachi had dreaded being roomed with someone in Social Sciences, or worse yet, Humanities. At least, he reasoned, this dude should have some concept of what a serious beat should look like.

Beat. He'd been in this country less than a week and already he was picking up the slang. Beat was campus lingo for a serious study session, and beat season, as the legend goes, is that season just before the poui trees bloom (naturally before exams) that signals to all that if you haven't begun to study as yet, as they say back home, *crapaud smoke your pipe.*

"Freshman Explorer, Freshman Tonto, rope out now!"

The command was accompanied by the familiar bang on the door in what Malachi was now convinced was a highly-anticipated morning ritual for the seniors, and a much dreaded one for the first years. He didn't budge. Marley's "Chase Those Crazy Baldheads" blared from Hopeton's family heirloom.

"Yow, you better get moving or the two a we in trouble," Hopeton said, his pace quickened by the rap on the door and echoes of threats from the corridor-walking seniors assigned to rouse the first years. Hopeton rummaged through his side of the room in search of one of his sneakers. Tiny beads of sweat now appeared on his forehead. Supersized versions of the same were already showing up as splotches of wet marks on his dun-colored T-shirt.

I just don't get it, Malachi thought, perhaps for the umpteenth time since he met his roommate. One would think that a burly six-foot-three, two hundred plus pound Jamaican from Rema, an infamous war zone, would be less...wimpy. But so far, all Malachi saw was a cowering freshman desperate to efface himself so he won't be picked on—a strategy that had so far failed him. And worse, when singled out, Hopeton's plan B was to try his best to ingratiate himself with the seniors, only to become their preferred errand boy. Where, Malachi wondered, was all that notorious toughness that Jamaican men are renowned for—that he'd been warned not to provoke?

Malachi smiled to himself at the memory of the earnestness on the face of elderly Sister Jack as she offered up a prayer at his father's behest the Friday before he left for UJ.

"And we bind those aggressive Jamaican spirits that would seek to destroy the heir of this man of God!" she had blurted, to a chorus of "amen" from the small prayer group.

"And forget not those Jezebel spirits that would try to tantalize, seduceeee, and corrupt this holy child!"

It had taken everything in Malachi not to burst out laughing. It wasn't that the content of the prayer was so foreign, so funny to him. He was raised to love and respect everything church. Perhaps it was precisely because of that that these brethren left him feeling like the hooded wolf at a Little Red Riding Hood family event.

His gaze darted to the direction of the thud of the bathroom door as it struck his desk. It was a crude sound that Malachi felt was totally avoidable once the user of the bathroom emerged in a civilized manner. The gentle giant erupted from the facility with toothbrush in mouth brushing vigorously.

"Alright Malachi," Hopeton blurted, having stopped in mid-brush. He was oblivious to the drool that was now cascading onto the breast of his T-shirt.

"You know if you don't come out, them will take it out on me. 'Where is your roommate, Freshman? Don't you know you're your brother's keeper, Freshman?'" he railed, in a lame attempt to mock the seniors. "Me can't take the talk, Mal. If I run any more laps I might have a myocardial infarction.

"Get it, Mal, my-o-cardial infarction? The medical term for a heart attack? Just a likkle med student humor there." Hopeton slapped himself on his thigh convulsing at his wit, the spots on his T-shirt and splatter on the floor metastasizing with every jerk.

"Oh yeah?" Malachi replied sarcastically with a roguish smile. "Thanks for telling me."

Hopeton looked down. Realizing the mess, he scurried back into the bathroom. In seconds, he was out again.

"Alright, let me go over this with you." He closed his eyes. "You're Malachi Williamson from Tuna…ah arrrr!"

"Tunapuna, Hopeton."

"I coulda never remember that word. It come in like the Periodic Table all over again. You know how long it take to memorize the whole Periodic Table?"

"Most people don't, Hopeton."

"Well I had to. What next?"

"Breds, let me make this easier on you." And for the third or fourth time since they met, Malachi told Hopeton all the details about himself that the seniors were fond of quizzing freshers on. He was extra careful today since it was the much touted S-Day—the day when they would undergo a series of dummy tests that, if successfully completed, were meant to culminate in them becoming bona fide members of Sutton Hall.

Malachi reminded Hopeton that he was from the twin-island Republic of Trinidad and Tobago. Trinidad to be exact.

"But don't forget to mention Tobago," Malachi added, and noted with amusement that Hopeton highlighted something on his index card.

Malachi reminded his roommate that he was nineteen and an only child. His father was into social work, which was kind of true. Malachi Williamson Senior was actually a full-time deacon in his church back home. His dad had a degree in social work and after working as a social worker in the public service for twenty years, had suddenly decided that his gift would be put to better use in the work of the Lord. His mother had died two years ago, but Malachi preferred that Hopeton make no mention of that. Hopeton understood. They agreed that that was basically all the seniors needed to know. Malachi could supply the rest at his discretion.

Hopeton asked Malachi if he'd remembered his specifics. Malachi assured him he had. Hopeton repeated it anyway, just to be safe.

Hopeton Fitzroy George, eighteen, was the eldest in the family, at least of his mother's children. His father was in and out of the picture. Something about prison and allegations of abuse of some kind, but that was strictly off the record. His mother is a hairdresser. He was originally from Rema but went to school in Mandeville and practically grew up there with his aunt and cousins, hence the word *Remaville* which was coined by his girlfriend, Petrina. He and Petrina found the term incredibly funny. When the crowd was a tough one, like the one he'd had to face this past week, Hopeton says he's from Rema. When it's more upscale, high society, he morphs into the mellow Mandevillian. "It's complicated," he explained.

Malachi didn't think so.

On the first of these chats, Malachi had learned that his roommate had one brother and two sisters on his mother's side. Those siblings live with his mom in Rema. Malachi was also told of half brothers and sisters that Hopeton had apparently never met on his father's side, but it was probably best not to mention that either, he reminded Malachi.

Malachi had planned to be defiant today. Many on Sutton had done it throughout the week. Some first years had ignored the quarter to five call to "rope out now!" Others simply went MIA. Malachi and Hopeton had been there every morning with twenty-something other sleep-starved first years.

Of that bunch, few dared to complain. Sleep, after all, the seniors were fond of reminding them, was a concept.

Hopeton had showed up every morning, Malachi suspected, out of sheer fright. Malachi presented himself mainly out of curiosity to see what the seniors would do and say or have the first years do or say next. He had to admit that amidst the convincing and not-so-convincing attempts at intimidation, the seniors had provided no shortage of entertainment. Fortunately, boot camp mode only lasted a few hours in the morning and at night. The rest of the day was more relaxed and fairly productive with lectures to attend, organized tours of the campus, and even off-campus trips to the nearest mall and shopping zones like the place with a name that sounds a lot like Half a Tree. He'd been to New Kingston, Downtown Kingston, and the scenic Ocho Rios. He ate jerk chicken and festivals in Boston Bay and swam in the enchanting waters of Reach Falls. Those were the moments that made up for the hazing. But this morning, Malachi really wasn't in the mood.

One look at Hopeton's face, however, disarmed him. He had to go out and face the music.

"Hope, man. Look…Give me five minutes to throw on something." Malachi sprang out of bed and did a light jog to the bathroom.

"You're a brother from a next mother," Hopeton exclaimed, his voice rife with relief.

"As the late great say, 'One Love,' my brother, 'One Love.'"

"True dat, Mal. True dat. Boop, boop, boop!" Hopeton said in agreement as his fingers mimicked a gun discharging in the air.

The simple gesture had brought out the yardie in the man, Malachi noted, as he shut the bathroom door.

CHAPTER TWO

Built in 1950, Sutton Hall straddled that delicate line between quaint and shabby.

It was the first hall of residence to be constructed at UJ—a fact which the hall trumpeted to gain a competitive edge over the six other halls on campus. Most of Sutton's original architecture had been preserved with a few modern touches to satisfy the demands of a growing student population. In the early days, for example, all the residents on a block shared facilities. The hall underwent extensive renovations in the 90s to install, among other things, built-in facilities in almost every room. The only things that remained communal were the kitchens—one for each block—and a large dining room—one to each hall. The latter doubled as an all-purpose room facilitating everything from parties to hall elections.

Many, however, agreed that Sutton's most unique feature was not the shared veranda that connected the rooms on each block, or the hint of Georgian detailing at the entrance of the porter's lodge—an echo of the island's colonial heritage under the British. It's most intriguing feature, by far, was the manner in which its eight blocks radiated from a central S-shaped pathway like legs from a giant spider in motion. This detail conferred upon Sutton a certain air of distinction, so that what it lacked in contemporary appeal, it made up for in originality. No other hall had captured the essence of its camaraderie in its architecture to the same extent—at least that's what the warden and the hall committee members kept telling them.

Sutton had long been unisex. Four blocks housed female students and four housed the males. But the seniors knew, and the freshers had begun to realize, that the division was a mere technicality, since there was a fair degree of mingling between the sexes on the various blocks. Malachi got first-hand evidence of this fact that very Saturday morning—mere hours away from hall induction.

Half an hour into the morning drill session, he was summoned out of the line by the hall secretary who ordered him to report to the porter's lodge for special duties. His assignment seemed simple enough: help a returning female senior cart her luggage from the porter's lodge to her room on Block B and get back to the line ASAP.

On Block B, Malachi ran into Super Senior Python—a Jamaican tough guy. The genuine article.

SS Python, as Malachi and Hopeton secretly called him, looked right at home in his striped three-quarter pants, white vest, and fluffy pink bedroom slippers. He was a six footer—the same height as Malachi and of dark complexion. His arms bore the definition of a natural born athlete, and he had some kind of Asian tattoo on his right shoulder. He had been sent by his companion in B38 to ask the neighbour in B37 for a roll of bath tissue.

The door of room 37 was ajar. SSPython knocked and waited. That's when Malachi spotted Super Duper Senior Desperate, who had alighted from the kitchen and was now approaching 37, balancing a breakfast tray.

The smell of breakfast wafted over, reminding Malachi of exactly how many hours it had been since his last meal. An ivory ware plate stacked with boiled yams, eddoes, and sweet potatoes lay to the left of the tray. Next to it was a gilded serving plate slicked with the excess grease from a half dozen festivals—the slightly sweet cornmeal fritters, which he tasted for the first time on his recent visit to Boston Bay. Somewhere in the middle of the plate, the oil slick pooled and merged with the gravy from the ackee and saltfish—the national dish of Jamaica.

Malachi recalled the first time he'd seen the signature Jamaican dish in the cafeteria. He'd mistaken it for scrambled eggs. A Jamaican from his block who'd stood directly behind him, had encouraged him to give it a try. When they'd sat down to eat, Malachi remembered how keenly his blockmate had studied his face, hoping presumably, to glean as Malachi chewed, a hint of his pleasure or displeasure.

"It's an acquired taste," the blockmate had finally offered when the foreigner's face had proved difficult to decode.

"And I'm acquiring it," Malachi had responded with a nod, and pressed on with his chewing. The Jamaican beamed. It had been the right thing to say. Now as he stood on Block B, Malachi wasn't sure if it was that memory, or the image of a carrot-chomping Bugs Bunny on the mug that had Malachi biting back a grin. The widemouthed mug was heaped with chunks of melon, papaya, apples, and grapes. Two plump strawberries—the imported kind—poked through like twin peaks. To the top left of the tray was a cup of tea. Malachi recognized it as chamomile and, if his nose was on the job, it was the same brand that his father was fond of—one of the few luxuries his dad hadn't completely dispensed with.

"Is for her birthday," Desperate volunteered, and diverted his gaze to the black cat that was feasting on its own breakfast from the overflowing bin at the end of the corridor. Python nodded, and Malachi wondered if he too wished he had an explanation. Slowly, the crack in B37 widened and Super Senior Passion sashayed out.

Look trouble, Malachi thought.

Alesha Foster aka Passion leaned against her door wearing a pearl white baby-T and dark gray drawstring boxers. The words "Can you handle it?" emblazoned in red, screamed for attention from the bosom of her T-shirt. Malachi averted his eyes and hiked his eyebrows. Passion noticed.

Five days ensconced in his new home and Malachi still couldn't figure out what was the deal with Passion. She was constantly picking on him when the first years assembled: asking him ridiculous questions about the human anatomy, scolding him for what he didn't know, not to mention her famous innuendos. She had done the same with other freshmen over the past days, but even Hopeton, as clueless as he could be, had noticed that Malachi was getting more than his quota of the senior's attention.

"Oh goodie, company. Are you guys coming in?" Passion asked, and batted her eyes in comic exaggeration.

The girl was gorgeous, and she knew it. At seven thirty in the morning, Passion was ready for an *Essence Magazine* photo shoot. Her dark brown shoulder-length dreadlocks with blonde highlights flattered a complexion that reminded Malachi of Julie mangoes when ripe and ready to be picked. Her eyelashes stretched out like hammocks in the shade, and her lips had a way of curling a tad more to one side when she smiled.

She shot the freshman a suggestive glance before honing in on the tray in Desperate's hand.

"Oh baby, this smells so good. You did this for me?" She lingered on the 'me,' pressing her palm against her chest. She released a gasp that no one in Hollywood would buy, and tip-toed to the balls of her bare feet to kiss Desperate full on the mouth.

SS Python stepped forward and cleared his throat. He whispered something to Passion prompting her to pivot on her toes and slip back inside. Desperate's gaze shifted to a second black cat that had joined the first in its forage for breakfast. Passion re-emerged in seconds, balancing a roll of bath tissue on her index.

Python thanked her, cleared his throat again, nodded and donned his most manly gait back over to 38.

"Oh, Happy Birthday, Passion." He looked back and muttered before turning the key in 38.

That's when Desperate's focus shifted to the smiling freshman. "Who give you permission to come on this block, Freshman?" He took a few steps toward Malachi.

Malachi inhaled deeply. He ran his right hand over his head and continued to prop up against the wall. He buried his left hand deep inside his jeans pocket and nipped at his bottom lip, hoping, as he did, to quell the ripple of irritation that the question, not to mention, the tone of the questioner, had provoked.

How daft could one person be? I'm a freshman, on a senior female block surrounded by plaid suitcases. I know everyone can't be doctors, but still...

His roommate's advice not to fight them at this stage came back to him. It was now mere hours before hall induction. Abolition was in sight.

Desperate cocked his head—a signal that he was awaiting a response.

"Hall Secretary Lollipop sent me over here, Super Duper Senior Desperate...sir." Malachi added the *sir* after a two-second delay. He hoped the nuance wasn't lost on the senior.

"He's with me, Jerome." The senior with the American accent, whose name Malachi didn't get, sauntered down the corridor, pulley in tow.

"Fanciful, ah you dat?"

"In the flesh."

"Welcome back, gorgeous. Look how you look nice and fat ee."

Passion, who up until now was imbibing the scene with her arms folded and a smug expression on her face, suddenly rolled her eyes and released a yawn as suspicious as her lashes. Without a word of greeting to the returning senior, Passion stepped forward, relieved Desperate of the tray that he was still holding and disappeared back into her room.

Desperate shrugged in a gesture meant to assuage.

"Oh no, you didn't just tell me I look fat, Jerome." The senior, ignoring the gesture, punched him playfully. "Don't say that! I know what you mean, but just don't, OK?"

He feigned being hurt by the punch. "OK," he repeated, mimicking the senior's accent.

Desperate's white smile vanished as he honed in on the freshman, who for the look on his face, could have been watching a livestream of his favorite reality flick.

"Look now, Trini boy. Don't get too cosy on this block. This is a big man block, zeen?"

Malachi thought of telling the senior: *"Funny, I thought it was a female block."* But he resisted the temptation.

Desperate continued, "You lucky you even get to see what color paint on these hallowed walls."

"For real," Malachi replied in his best Jamaican twang.

Desperate glowered, causing Fanciful to stifle a grin.

"Disrespectful."

That was the word Malachi heard the senior mutter as he reentered Passion's room.

The female senior with the accent turned out to be a second year med student. Her real name was Abigail Shaw, Abby for short, she insisted. Like her mother, she was born in the United States, which explained the accent. Her father was Jamaican. She'd lived with her parents in New York up until age fourteen when her dad, a neurosurgeon, was offered the position of Medical Chief of Staff and CEO at the University Hospital in Jamaica. The family immigrated to Jamaica, and she's been there since.

At five feet six, she would easily be considered thick and curvaceous by West Indian standards. She had brown eyes which complimented reddish brown corkscrews that fell just beyond her shoulders and curled mercilessly at the ends. Her skin reminded Malachi of the color of sand at twilight after the tide had stripped it of its paleness. She had a cluster of tiny dark brown freckles on her nose which made her appear like she'd spent the day on the beach. But to Malachi, the senior's most outstanding feature by far was a smile that could usher in a Middle East détente.

"Don't let the seniors freak you out too much," she said as she unlocked her room door. "They're just giving what they got last year. My friend in New York tells me the whole sorority and fraternity pledge thing at her college is just as crazy. Trust me you'll be doing the same thing to the poor freshers next year."

"I doubt that very much."

"What!" she exclaimed and whipped around so suddenly that she barely missed smacking him on his shoulder with her hair. "You mean after all this love from us you don't plan to live on hall next year?"

"Yeah, I plan to be here, but this is just a saucepan of silliness for no reason. I'd rather take the freshers backpacking through the Blue Mountains or something. Now there's a lesson in endurance."

Abby placed her hand over her stomach as the laughter took over. She laughed so loudly that she scared the cats away.

****

"Freshman Explorer, are you with us?"

All eyes were on Malachi. He had just slipped back into the line after his early morning trek to the senior block to help Abby with her luggage. On the senior's invitation, he had hung around for an extra twenty minutes—happy at the chance to escape the morning routine. When Abby had announced that she wanted to catch up with the hall chairman before he went off for breakfast, Malachi had pushed out his lower lip in a petulant sulk and had asked his newfound pal if she was sure it couldn't wait.

The comment had elicited another one of those laughs from the senior.

Minutes later, when Malachi and Abby walked into the Sutton Hall dining room, both could tell that something special was up. The first years were not lined up in their usual three-row formation but in a single line which spanned the width of the dining room. As Abby walked in, she couldn't resist an under-the-breath remark about déjà vu and flashbacks of the movie *Schindler's List*. Malachi had never seen the movie, but he found himself choking back a snort of laugher all the same. In fact, the struggle to rein in the chuckles as he joined the line caused him not to realize that the drill commander on the floor was actually addressing him.

"We have ten more minutes till you plebs are dismissed. But Freshman, you seem distracted this morning." She looked behind her and winked in the direction of Abby who was now seated next to the hall chairman.

"No wonder. I see you strolling in with a senior, all filled with mirth, behaving oh so familiar."

A groundswell of suggested punishment arose from the usual gaggle of seniors who made it down for the early morning sport. The person addressing Malachi was Super Senior Curry Que, a petite Guyanese national of Indian descent who also held the post of hall treasurer.

"Freshman, I was just reminding your fellow first years that tonight is the big night; the night when they become official members of this esteemed hall community. Did you know that, Freshman?"

"Yes, Super Senior Curry Que," Malachi replied.

"And do you believe you are ready for that step, Freshman?"

"Most certainly, Super Senior Curry Que. It's all I think about."

A bark of laughter escaped from one of his peers. Others tried in vain to suppress their chuckles.

"Well, well, well, Freshman. Aren't you a smart one. So if that's 'all that you think about'—your words—I suppose food is the furthest thing from your mind. Right?"

The seniors started to thump desks, chairs, and any piece of furniture they could get their hands on.

"Point!" someone shouted.

"Well uh…" Malachi started.

"Such loyalty, such devotion," Curry Que continued. "That's what we like to see, Freshman. You plebs are hungry; I can see it on your pathetic faces, but not this Freshman. Right? Surely, Freshman, you're above such base appetites?"

There it was: the hunger question. It was one that had been asked and answered every day this week before breakfast. It was a known trick question—one for which there was apparently no right answer. Those who answered "no" in the past were told, "Good so you can stay here five, ten, fifteen more minutes." Those who said "yes" were accused of being greedy, of lacking self-control and mental fortitude, and were still made to suffer it out. Malachi glanced at his fellow first years. Freshman Fraggle was rocking up on the balls of her feet and coming down repeatedly. Freshman Thundercat was shaking his head in anticipation. Hopeton had his head down as usual. It was clear.

The occasion demanded quick-thinking and gumption, and for some strange reason, Malachi felt an intoxicating surge of both.

"Super Senior Curry Que, while I always enjoy the outpourings from your superior intellect, today I'm humbled by the reality that our finite minds can't possibly take it all in." His right hand sliced the air capturing the line of first years in a sweep.

Malachi stopped short of squawking as he addressed the gathering. "Maybe it's because we're on the cusp of being inducted into the most significant community of our lives that I feel that some morning sustenance can widen our capacity to retain your poignant truths. Certainly, it will allow us to better ruminate on the substantive matters that all of our beloved seniors have taken the time to share with us this past week."

Some of the seniors began thumping the furniture again. A smiling Curry Que motioned to them to pipe down as she realized he had more.

"Please, please Super Senior Curry Que, I beg you. Don't deny us of the opportunity to make the seniors proud of us when we demonstrate tonight, once and for all, that we are indeed superior to the maggots that masquerade as first years in the other stalls of residence."

The seniors were delirious with amusement. They pushed furniture around for a half a minute until someone started a chant.

"Let them eat! Let them eat! Let them eat!"

It was one for the freshers—a big one at that.

Malachi surprised himself that he was able to keep a straight face throughout his impromptu speech. Several of the first years had broken the formation and doubled over cackling. Malachi struggled to keep the smile at bay as his peers moved across to pat him on the back. It was his grand moment for the week. Even the regular group of seniors who lined off like vultures with an insatiable appetite for folly, had joined the call to "Let them eat!"

It was a small victory for the freshers. For the first time since they arrived, they were on their way to having an early breakfast. And so it would have gone down, if trouble hadn't sauntered in.

CHAPTER THREE

"Oh, I'm sorry. I asked the gentleman at the front desk to direct me to my room, and he sent me here instead." She glanced down at the plastic key chain in her hand. "This is obviously not my room. Um, can you point me to F4?"

The British accent was the first thing that caught everyone's attention. For the week, the first years had been exposed to a cacophony of accents: Jamaican, St Lucian, Belizean, Vincentian, Kittitian, Nevisian, Grenadian, Antiguan, Dominican, Caymanian, Barbadian, Bahamian, Montserratian, Trinidadian, Tobagonian, and Guyanese. But this was the first bona fide Brit.

The second thing that stood out was her erect posture. At five nine, the newcomer stood ramrod straight with her arms arched slightly and hands clasped one on top the other in front of her like a soprano priming for the opening number. Her slender neck complemented an oval-shaped face that might have been described as angelic, had it not been for the fierceness with which her mane was lassoed into a high ponytail. Gray-green eyes honed in on the face of the one person in the room who was likely to have answers—the hall chairman. In fact, her question seemed directed to him. And even as she waited on a reply, her lips pouted up ever so slightly as if something smelled a little off. She wore a red tank top, khaki shorts that revealed strong, shapely legs, and tan flip-flops. If she wasn't a model she could easily have passed for one. But today whatever chances the newcomer had of effacing herself among the student population were foiled by the red and gold Indian silk wrap that straddled her hips and kicked out dramatically from behind her like a bridal trail as it frolicked in a tipsy island breeze.

Curry Que was the first to recover. She cleared her throat.

"Where are you traipsing in from, Freshette uh…?" She slid her index down the yellow foolscap sheet fastened against the clipboard that bore the names of all first years on Sutton. "What name were you assigned, Freshette?"

Hall Chairman Police, a burly, final-year law student, pushed off from his vantage point on a derelict desk perched midway between the freshers and the spectating seniors to proffer a response.

"Ah! This is the freshette who came in yesterday and resisted our attempt to supply her with a hall name. In fact, if I remember correctly." He tilted his head, licked his lips, and flashed a smile which revealed a gap between his front teeth. "The goodly lady called our hall-naming tradition 'a juvenile and unnecessary charade.'"

The seniors shouted; some swore and dragged desks, chairs—anything that would move.

"Is that right?" Curry Que's voice rose to a shriek as she struggled to be heard above the din.

Curry Que plopped her left hand on her hip. "Well, Freshette, Sutton Hall has many fine trad—"

"I'm actually quite impressed that you recall my ramblings," the newcomer began, ignoring Curry Que and fixing her gaze squarely on Police. A hush quickly fell over the room.

"Yesterday, I was so exhausted from my transatlantic flight that I must confess to being more than a tad miffed at your welcoming party's—um—how shall I put it? Utter lack of compassion? Truth be told, I could hardly recall half of what I said to you yesterday." She gave a light chortle.

"I'm happy to report though that I am much improved this morning—thank you for asking—and forgive me for having intruded on your little mock military…." She waved her hand dismissively toward the single-row formation of first years whose attention she'd secured. "I'm not sure what you call this—"

"Pol-ice!" Passion's Jamaican twang ripped through the hall.

"Police, you mean say you just ah go stand up there and allow this, this…." She eyed the newcomer from head to toe as she searched for a word. "This alien from the "motherland" to talk to you like that?" She said the word motherland in a mock British accent.

The statement earned a few chuckles, overpowered by a groundswell of oohs and a few hoots, mainly from the seniors.

"Lawd a mercy, look pon trouble," a female Jamaican voice from the direction of the seniors bemoaned.

The first years fidgeted. Some, like Hopeton, scanned the room for a safe harbor to berth their gaze.

The newcomer didn't miss a beat. Her smile stiffened.

"Motherland ha!" No one was sure whether the amusement was genuine or contrived. "Goodness, haven't heard that term in a while. As for alien, actually, the term is undocumented foreign national. Alien is no longer politically correct, but I honestly won't expect you to know that. Neither do I expect you to know that such terms do not apply to international students on a university campus. So, I'll chalk up your unfortunate utterance to plain old ignorance. Unless your intention was to insult all such students in the room—a possibility I've only just considered. So, was it your intent to insult all foreign students or just me in particular?"

Before Passion could respond, Abby stepped in.

"OK, this has already gone too far. Passion, I think you need to…" She made a gesture to Passion which could have been interpreted as an appeal for her to retract the offensive remark.

"Uh, nobody nah chat to you, Miss America!" Passion said, her finger pointing at Abby. "What this university a come to?" she added, flailing her arms and letting them land on her hips.

"Yes, but I am talking to you. I was trying to be subtle and give you an opportunity to correct yourself before I call you out, but you don't seem to be taking hints today."

"Ladies, ladies. Let us calm down," Hall Chairman Police said realizing that tensions were rising.

"With all due respect, Terrence, we need to deal with this now." Abby turned back to address her fellow senior directly.

"Passion. Pardon me, Alesha. What you said was out of line." The American pivoted slightly; her gaze burrowed into the senior who had made the offensive remark. Abby then turned and made three confident strides forward, stopping short of the row of freshers.

They stared at her, some with suspicious eyes. She was a new face among the seniors. This could be a well-choreographed trick. It wasn't beyond the seniors. The carrot of kindness had been dangled and yanked too many times to count since the week began.

But Abby's tone matched her guileless facial expression. "Now you guys have a right to know that the university has a strict policy against abusive behavior, including hazing. And as a peer counselor, I cannot just sit here and support gross disrespect."

"For real," Malachi found himself saying aloud.

Abby nodded without looking at him.

"Alesha, I believe you owe Ms…uh…"

"Le Blanc. Megan Le Blanc," the student with the British accent volunteered.

"Ms. Le Blanc, an apology."

Before another word could be uttered, Police cleared his throat noisily. "Um Ms. Le Blanc, let me just say, on behalf of all the seniors, I must apologize for that...um remark. Fanciful is right." He turned to face Passion who'd left her seat with the seniors and had moved closer to Abby during the exchange.

"Passion, you're out a order!" Police said with newfound conviction, then cleared his throat again.

The room fell silent. Passion turned, tsked and stormed out of the hall muttering obscenities under her breath. Two female seniors ran behind her calling her name.

"I must hasten to add that that senior is not a bona fide member of the Sutton hall committee," Police said with a pivot, addressing the audience in general.

"Bwoy, there's a lawyer in the house!" The comment from a senior elicited a ripple of laughter that diffused the tension that the incident had spurred. Even Le Blanc smiled.

Police turned to the newcomer and bowed slightly. "I hope you appreciate that we do not disrespect our first years like that."

"Of course not!" came a retort from Buck Rogers, one of the first years with a hard-earned reputation for provoking the seniors.

The laughter from the first years strengthened.

"Well, I suppose that settles it, doesn't it?" Le Blanc responded, surprisingly upbeat. "If I knew things were so lively around here, I would certainly have made an effort to stay on hall last night. Well then. Ta-ra."

Without a backward glance, the newcomer rotated her overnight bag and wheeled it past the seniors that lined both sides of the dining room entrance—her ponytail waving goodbye to thirty-something pairs of eyes.

****

"Freshman Explorer, phone call!" The voice from outside was not one that Malachi recognized.

"Malachi, that's you. Phone call." Hopeton called to him from his bed on the other end of the room, sleep still in his voice. It was Sunday morning. They were Suttonites, and everything was right in the world again.

"Yeah, me soon come!" Malachi yelled back in his best Jamaican accent.

Malachi sat up and slipped his feet into his blue and white beach slippers, suddenly conscious that it was his favorite pair from home. He marvelled at the discovery of how sentimental human beings get about ordinary stuff when they're away from home. Like the faded cotton Batman sheets he was using as a blanket just a moment ago. He knew when he packed it that it was probably too juvenile for a university dorm, not to mention old. But it had sentimental value. His mother had bought the sheet set for him on one of her crazy shopping sprees when he was eleven or twelve. He kept the top sheet.

Malachi found a football T-shirt and hurriedly pulled it over his head as he reached for the old brass door knob. He had seen many of his blockmates walk around without shirts, but his home training had not given him the liberty to do the same. Besides, it was counted among the acts of impropriety that bothered his mom.

"Hello?"

"Junior man, what you saying?" It was Caleb Olivere. He was one of the few persons who knew that his name back home was Malachi Junior.

"Hey, what's up, Trini? I real tired yuh see me here. Last night was hall induction, so you know." Malachi yawned into the phone. "Pressure!"

"It couldn't have been worse than mine. Well is pure fellas over here, so multiply your experience by three. I think the brew they had us drink had alcohol in it."

Malachi laughed. "That good for the worms man. A little alcohol won't kill you, Caleb."

"Yeah, yeah, I know. But they were extra hard on me last night. It was definitely payback for all the opposition I gave them during orientation. You know—the Christian thing."

Malachi rolled his eyes. He knew exactly what Caleb was talking about. The pastor's son was playing Christian of the Year as usual. When they'd met for lunch to swap stories after their first day on campus, Caleb had said that he told the seniors on his hall that he didn't care for a hall name—that he already had a strong Biblical name—and that the only other name he was looking forward to was the new name he was going to get when he went to glory. Right there and then, Malachi had felt the urge to reach across and clobber his blood-washed buddy.

"I don't know why you didn't come on Sutton with me. We could've been roommates."

"Nah boy. I good here. Too much temptation over there. Those girls on your hall…Wow. That's all I'll say. Wow! You better watch yourself."

Jezebel spirits.

The words popped into Malachi's head, causing a smile to creep over his face. He wondered if anyone had laid hands and prayed a similar prayer for his best friend.

"Speaking of temptation, when last you spoke with Brandy boy?" Brandy was Caleb's on-again off-again girlfriend from back home.

"Brandy. Like she trippin', boy. In fact, I really want to talk to you about that, but this phone call is already too long. Meet me for lunch in Turner Hall cafeteria. Say noonish?"

"Sounds like a plan."

There was a pause.

"You called your dad yet?"

"Nope."

"Call him nah. My dad told me to find out if everything was alright with you. He apparently asked your dad if he'd heard from you and he said 'not yet.' My dad said he felt you could do better than that."

Malachi didn't respond. Sometimes he felt that of all the best friends he could have picked, why had it been the pastor's son? And why did it still feel like Caleb had shadowed him all his life? They'd attended the same primary schools. Their fathers were thrilled when they'd passed the eleven-plus exam for the same secondary school—both first-choice picks. And here they were again mysteriously at the same university, even though Malachi had taken a year off before taking up his spot. It wasn't that he didn't appreciate having someone from home so nearby, he told himself, because he did. It was just that when he imagined university as this place where freedom was absolute, there was no best friend from home looking over his shoulder.

"Anyway, call the old man." Caleb's voice brought him back to their conversation "You're his only son. I'm sure he'll lov—"

"Listen, Caleb, I've got some laundry to take care of before we link up for lunch. It's already close to nine. Vibes you later, OK?"

"Yeah man."

Malachi clenched his jaw and hung up the handset a little harder than he meant to.

CHAPTER FOUR

At eleven thirty the line leading to the serving counter at the Turner Hall dining room was already spilling out toward the entrance. Malachi suspected that with classes starting the very next day, the crowd was the healthiest representation of the on-hall community he'd seen all week. Long before the scribbles on the white board became visible, Malachi's nose cued him in on at least one item on the day's menu: macaroni pie. His mother had always marveled at what she'd often called his keen sense of smell. Whatever it was, he had to admit, it served him well in his chemistry labs.

The menu board was visible now. The clank of pots and pans grew more distinct as the cooks busied themselves behind the serving counter. The menu, he observed a few days ago, was amended daily, probably by the same person judging from the handwriting.

Today's offering was one that no warm-blooded West Indian could refuse: macaroni pie (although the Jamaicans prefer to called it macaroni and cheese), rice and peas, jerk chicken, fried chicken, fish in tomato sauce, stewed peas, baked lamb, steamed vegetables, garden salad, potato salad, macaroni salad, yam, dasheen, plantain, and eddoes. Most of the dishes were laid out in stainless steel containers nestled in warmers.

He scanned the menu listing. He couldn't help lament the absence of the one dish he knew he would never see in all the Sundays of all the years he would spend on the island: callaloo—a delicacy from his native land. He had asked one of his Jamaican blockmates about it two days ago, but when the Jamaican version of the dish was described with spinach as the main ingredient, he knew that it was a far cry from the one-pot slow-melt of dasheen bush, ochroes, salt meat, and coconut milk, seasoned with fresh herbs and spices and blended to perfection.

Back in high school, he recalled that the American cousin of his lab partner had taken one look at his favorite dish and had asked how anyone could eat "green slime." Right now he felt like Esau in the Bible, just about ready to part with his birthright to secure a pot spoon or two of that green slime, especially if his mom had prepared it. Back in the day, his dad had dubbed her "Queen of Callaloo" as she was particularly good at cooking it. Since she passed, Malachi had been on the lookout for a close second.

Sister Marva from church back home had been bringing over her version of the dish almost every Sunday for over a year now, along with other dishes from various members. Malachi felt a fresh wave of nausea as he visualized the bright green of Sister Marva's callaloo. He often wondered if she added green coloring to her pot, and he'd come desperately close to asking her once. But in all fairness, it was the only dish from her that she failed miserably at. Her macaroni pie was flawless, and she clearly enjoyed preparing her assigned dish. Neither did she seem to mind the task of collecting dishes from the other church sisters and bringing them over. It was her way of taking care of *her* deacon, she said almost every Sunday as she arranged the dishes on the table. Malachi suspected that for the never-married head usher, it was a little more than that.

"Being a deacon isn't without its perks," his father would say every time. Every time.

At first, Malachi thought it was kind of nice: The ladies of the church fussing over their deacon and his son, but it wasn't long before it all began to feel too much like charity.

"Really, Sister Marva, isn't it your turn to prepare the chicken for poor Widower Williamson and that nerdy boy of his?" He imagined them asking, as if haranguing over the week's ushering roster.

Sunday charity was the worst.

His dad had laughed himself silly when six months after his mom died, Malachi Junior had suggested that they take a cooking course together. He had noticed that the man was losing weight. Grief perhaps, but he was also painfully aware that for someone who despised takeout, his dad had but four dishes in his culinary repertoire: eggs—boiled or scrambled; stewed chicken; rice with peas, carrot and corn (from the frozen pack); and fish broth. Sure, it was more than most men he knew had mastered, but there was more—much more to the world of food. He was no gourmand, but he couldn't understand why his dad didn't care to experience more.

Only two people were in front of Malachi now. He pulled his wallet from his back pocket and scanned the notes. It was nearly a week since he arrived, but he was still getting used to the colors of the various denominations and how much more everything here seemed to cost until he did the mental conversion to US or TT dollars.

"One rice or two?" The questioner was a young woman who could've been his age. She was holding the pot spoon in her right hand, while her left was plopped on her hip.

"Beg your pardon, Miss? I don't—"

"One. Rice. Or. Two?" The server repeated slowly as if talking to a child. Her voice and eyebrows rose in tandem.

"Nadia! What I tell you 'bout talking to the patrons like that? Obviously 'im is a first year, and you never hear me tell you that we need to explain to all the first years about the portion sizes?"

His defender was a rotund woman who could have been in her late fifties or early sixties. A warm, toothy smile lit up her round face. The mole on the right side of her chin must have been a beauty spot in her youthul days. A few strands of hair now peeped through. She wore a green and white checkered apron and a matching head tie. Her name tag read *Mrs. Taitt Manager.*

Mrs. Taitt took the pot spoon from the young server who nonchalantly moved on to the tall, stocky man behind Malachi. The freshman was mildly amused when he observed how Nadia had smiled at the gentleman in the cobalt blue coveralls and greeted him by name. She rattled off something in patois that Malachi knew he would never understand.

"Let me apologize for her," Mrs. Taitt said, in a sweet mother-ly tone. "Now this is one portion, and this is two."

She scooped spoonfuls of rice and peas onto the white plate in her hand. The demonstration had taken less than ten sec-onds. Malachi ordered two rice and peas with baked chicken and steamed vegetables.

"Now that's a balanced meal," Mrs. Taitt said with a nod of approval. Malachi returned the smile.

"Thank you, Mrs. Taitt."

"You are most welcomed, sweetheart."

"Malachi. The name's Malachi. Pleased to meet you."

"And you come from Trinidad too. Me know the accent well. You have one powerful name right there, Malachi. The last prophet of the Old Testament. Me can see Jesus all over you."

"O—K. Well, thanks again," he said with a polite smile.

Malachi paid the cashier and scanned the room. He spotted Abby, the American, and walked over to her table.

"You know the first years are calling you 'Saint Abby, Patron Saint of Hapless Freshers.'"

Abby looked up and surrendered her smile.

"Is that so? Well, I'll have to do something truly devious then to maintain the seniors' status quo."

"Sorry, Abby, induction was last night. You missed the boat."

"You mean I'm stuck with the goodie-two-shoes rep?"

"Fraid so."

Abby looked at the freshman sitting across from her. He was a looker alright with his soft eyes and perfect smile. She had heard his name being bandied by the girls on her block. A few of the comments had been crass and offensive to Abby, but most of them were benign enough; just seniors having fun.

Malachi's voice interrupted her thoughts. "So Saint Abby, I'm curious, what's likely to be the fallout for sticking up for us?"

"Honestly, I don't know. Never thought about it. I mean, if there's a fallout, I guess the question is whether there's such a thing as too high a price for standing up for what's right."

"Whoa. You sound like my dad."

"Then your dad's a very wise man."

"That's debatable."

There was a pause.

"Is that all you're eating—a growing boy like you?" Abby asked, as she looked across at his plate.

Malachi squirmed in his seat. "I had a…late breakfast. Besides, we have an old saying in Trinidad: 'Eat little and live long.'"

Abby cocked her head. "Oh yeah? Well my Trini roommate in first year never heard of it. She gained twenty pounds after her first semester—the freshman fifteen, as they call it, with a few extra for good measure."

The story made his dimples dance.

"So, tell me about med. How was first year? Honestly."

"Excruciating."

"Gee, thanks."

"You asked for honesty."

"I guess I did?"

There were those dimples again.

What would he do if I suddenly stuck my finger in it? What am I saying? Sorry Lord, that's a real messed up thought.

Still, Abby wondered if he had a girlfriend back home pining away at being deprived of her dimples. Not that she really cared of course, she told herself.

A guy in a Turner Hall T-shirt with hazel brown eyes and a week's worth of stubble approached the table, tray in hand.

"Hey man, sorry to be late. I decided to do some laundry as well. Boy do I miss my mother."

Abby tried in vain to stifle a snicker. Malachi shook his head.

"Abigail Shaw, my best friend Caleb Olivere. Caleb, Abby's from my hall."

"First year too?" Caleb wanted to know.

"Not even if you paid me," came Abby's quick response.

Caleb positioned himself next to Abby. At six foot two, he had to do a side twist to stretch out his legs.

"So what's this? Malachi. Caleb. Is there a Bible names Trini crew on campus? Are Joshua and Daniel going to show up anytime now?"

"As it turns out Daniel is my middle name, and Joshua is my younger brother, but he's not here," Caleb said. "Not much of an academic. Guess I'm the brains in the family."

"OK," Abby said, her voice humming with mild amusement.

"My dad's a pastor."

Malachi pretended to be preoccupied with his veggies as he marveled at his best friend's lack of game.

"So you're a Christian?" Abby asked, with gusto.

"Of course. Of the born-again variety. Just to be clear."

Abby tilted her body forward, placed her elbows on the table and cupped her face in her hands.

Malachi distractedly rolled his neck and cracked his knuckles. He knew how easy it would be to allow his growing ennui with the topic of church to outpace his good manners, but it didn't seem fair to his current company to do so. He silently instructed himself to make appropriate amounts of eye contact as Caleb related the story of being twelve years old when he gave his life to the Lord at a crusade in the savannah near his home church. He told Abby how excited his parents were that he'd finally made the decision. He was baptized three months later and was proud to be called a Jesus Freak.

"You know, like the band."

"DC Talk. I know of the band." Abby was smiling. Malachi wasn't sure if it was his imagination, but he thought that the lilt in Abby's voice had changed. It was smoky now, as if at any moment she would break out in song. A fleeting pang of jealousy came over him. Where it had come from, he wasn't sure.

Just then, he caught a glimpse of Megan Le Blanc before she disappeared behind the partition that led to the serving counter. She was wearing black shorts, a gray halter, and a pair of strappy sandals. Her hair was harnessed in that fierce ponytail again.

Malachi shifted his gaze to the other end of the partition, waiting to see when Megan would emerge. Caleb had wrapped up his testimony. He and Abby were now discussing churches in the area, cell group meetings, and the challenges of getting people on hall to attend.

"So are you saved as well?" Malachi shifted his attention back to Abby and Caleb who were both staring at him. Abby, the questioner, had stopped chewing as she awaited his response.

"Excuse me for a sec, guys." Malachi stood up and signaled to Megan to join them. Abby thought she saw Megan give a moment's hesitation.

Megan sauntered over, her smile planted.

She balanced a tray which had a double helping of garden salad, steamed vegetables, peas, bottled water, and a fruit bowl, something Malachi had looked at but had passed over.

"Can you believe they have no tofu?"

"Imagine," Abby quipped and immediately felt regret.

If Megan detected the sarcasm, she didn't react.

Malachi introduced himself, Caleb, and Abby. He motioned for Megan to join them. She took the vacant seat to Malachi's right.

"I simply asked, 'Do you have any tofu?' to which the rather petulant young lady serving me replied, 'Eh?'"

Light chuckles erupted from the table at the imitation.

"Are you a vegan, Megan?" Abby wanted to know after glancing at the meatless spread on Megan's tray.

"Actually, I eat fish, but the one I saw in there was languishing in some kind of horrid tomato puree. Frankly, it took everything in me not to barf at the mere sight of it."

She turned to Abby. "By the way I never got a chance to thank you properly for what you said, you know, coming to my defense and all when that silly girl insulted me. Mind you, I was quite prepared to have a go at her."

"OK, I'm lost," Caleb said, his palms in the air.

"Actually, it's a Sutton Hall thing," Abby responded.

Caleb shrugged and scooped up some more potato salad from his plate.

"Caleb, we're kidding," she said, bumping him playfully with her shoulders. Abby then proceeded to fill Caleb in on the incident with Passion. Malachi pitched in where modesty made Abby hold back.

"Wow. Where was my Abby when I was in distress on Turner?" Caleb wanted to know.

"She was probably caught in some kind of air traffic while attempting to fly over to your rescue," Megan offered in response.

Abby stopped sawing at her sliver of lamb. It was as if someone shouted "freeze" and caused her mouth and arms to stop moving.

"Sorry, but it sounds like you're suggesting that I'm some sort of witch?" Abby said, her eyebrows now hitched.

Megan coughed and patted her chest. "Goodness no. How clumsy of me. The imagery was meant to convey more like that of a flying nun, I suppose. You are religious, are you not?"

"I am a Christian, if that's what you mean."

"Right, like I said, religious." She scooped a forkful of peas into her mouth.

"Oh no, Megan, there is a big difference, but I'll leave that for another time," Abby replied, smiling.

Megan allowed her shoulders to relax and her back to arch slightly.

"Speaking of being a Christian, you never answered my question, Malachi."

"Oh, whether or not I am saved?" Malachi noticed Megan's shoulders stiffen again. She looked distractedly toward the dining room's entrance.

"Let's just say I have issues at this point in time."

"I can absolutely identify with that," Megan injected, a bit too fast. "I too have issues with the need to define oneself by religious orientation. Isn't being human difficult enough as it is?"

Caleb looked from one female to the other. He tilted forward on the table and clasped his hands. He had to try to look cool, he told himself, though mentally he had begun to rehearse the

Scriptures that would win points in this debate with this girl who was obviously an atheist. These were exactly the kinds of situations his dad had warned him to expect at university.

Abby bit her lip. She knew she had no qualms taking Megan on, but she questioned whether it was the wisest thing to do just then.

She glanced down at her watch. "You know I have a Christian Fellowship meeting in an hour. We're trying to organize cell groups on the various halls."

She got up from the table and took up her tray. "The Sutton Hall cell group meetings should start in a week. I hope you guys can visit us. It would be nice." Her eyes moved from Malachi to Megan.

"I'll be there," Caleb replied before catching himself. "I mean...to the one on my hall."

Abby's smile widened at the unexpected show of solidarity. "Hey, Caleb, if you like I can give you a listing of some of the believers who are returning on your hall."

"Sounds great." Caleb stood up. He took that to mean that he should go with her immediately. She didn't correct the misunderstanding.

Abby excused herself, gave a weak wave to nobody in particular, and left the canteen. Caleb was two steps behind.

"I'll catch up with you later or tomorrow," Caleb called back to Malachi. He didn't acknowledge Megan as he disappeared out the door of the dining room.

"That was fun," Megan said, as soon as she and Malachi were alone at the table. She stabbed a piece of melon with her plastic fork.

"I really hate when people try to shove their religious beliefs down other people's throat," she continued.

"So you're an atheist then?"

"There we go with the labels again. I would say it's a West Indian thing, but I've encountered that back home as well. I'm a nothing, if you must know. I believe in spirituality, but religion divides. Watch the news; read a newspaper for crying out loud." She pierced a grape and plopped it in her mouth.

"Where are you from, Megan?" That was Malachi's big attempt to steer the conversation toward safer topics.

"I was born in England. My mom is Jamaican by birth, left as a teenager when her folks immigrated to the UK. My father is British. He's white in case you were wondering."

"I wasn't."

"They are both diplomats. Mom more or less goes where he goes now. They met in Ghana, fell madly in love, got married. My older brother Paul was conceived in Ghana, as the story goes, but was born in England. He's five years older actually, but we're very close. He finished up at Oxford earlier this year and zipped over to the United States after the graduation ceremony. If you ask me, I think wedding bells are going to peal for our family very soon." She wiped the corners of her mouth with her napkin. "Anyway, I spent most of my childhood in boarding schools in the UK and I even lived a year in Switzerland. Boarding school was my parent's idea of stability for me while they served in various parts of the world."

"Where are they now?"

"Here in Jamaica. My father was posted here about six months ago. He hates it. Thinks it's a step down from some of the places he's been, but I'm not supposed to say that. My mom, as you would imagine, couldn't be happier. What's your story?"

"I'm from Trinidad. Do you know where that is?"

"Please, don't insult me. I think you have me confused with the American."

Malachi didn't comment. He wasn't about to indulge the jibe at his newfound friend.

Megan continued. "They are the ones who are usually oblivious to the fact that there's a world beyond the Atlantic. My father calls people like that who aren't well traveled barbarians—behind their backs of course."

"That's...cold."

"We're from a cold country, haven't you heard?"

Malachi told her about his dad being a social worker, his mom being dead, and since playing doctor was his favorite childhood game, he thought he might explore what being a real one was like.

"I admire people who know so early in life what they want to be. I wasn't so fortunate. Actually, that's not true." She looked around and in secret-agent styling leaned in; her voice was almost a whisper. "I really, truly wanted to be a ballerina, if you could imagine that. I've wanted that since I was five years old and put on my first pair of pink stockings and pointe shoes. I've attended some of the best ballet schools in Europe, and I'm actually quite good."

"So why are you here? Why aren't you in some fancy ballet school?"

"Ah. Alas, my momma said that was not a sensible profession. She sat me down and told me that despite my father's ancestry, to the world I am black, as if I needed to be reminded."

She mimicked what he assumed was her mother's cultured British-Jamaican accent. "Darling, of course you see cute little black girls running around in their tutus, but where are the black grown-up girls, Megan? Hmm, where are they?"

"What did you say to that?" Malachi leaned in.

"I told her about Janet Collins."

"Who?"

"Janet Collins. The first black prima ballerina of the Metropolitan Opera Ballet. Since that conversation with mom ages ago, I've discovered Raven Wilkinson, and of more recent vintage Lauren Anderson. Anderson's retired from performing, but I actually got to attend a ballet lecture she was having. I was so inspired! And there are men too. Carlos Acosta, another minority. Cuban by birth, I think. Saw him perform live a few years ago while in Moscow. To see them on stage, even clips of them. Well...words simply cannot describe. What I'm saying basically is that minority representation at the highest levels in ballet is still pathetic, but the folks I've mentioned have all broken serious ground for people like me. I actually have a chance in ballet, in no small part, due to people like them."

"So you've been to Moscow. Wow."

"Yes. It was all part of an exchange program at my school," she explained with a shrug.

"France, Germany, Belgium, Italy. Basically the whole of Europe. Ghana of course, Tanzania, South Africa, several states in North America, Canada, and oh, and I almost forgot, our company went on tour in Australia two years ago."

"Anywhere in the Caribbean?"

"Besides Jamaica, no, sadly."

"So what are you studying here?"

"I'm doing a first degree in International Relations. I heard the undergrad program is quite decent, and I figure here is as good as anywhere else. Besides…." She leaned in again. He caught a whiff of her perfume. He didn't recognize the fragrance, but it smelled expensive.

"I hear the university's dance program is quite good, and every good dancer looks for opportunities to expand her repertoire." She straightened up again. "So now you know my little secret."

"I knew that posture had to come from somewhere."

"Definitely ballet. I'm extremely well turned out."

"Turned out?"

"I'll explain one of these days. The posture is also a result of a bit of finishing school I must confess, and if you tell anyone—anyone—I'll kill you."

"Your secret's safe with me."

"Enough about me. What kind of doctor do you want to be?"

"A rich one."

They laughed.

"Seriously, what do you want to specialize in?"

"I'm very serious, don't mind I'm laughing. Whichever makes the most money. I haven't done the research yet, but I bet it's a toss-up between cardiology and oncology."

"That's obscene!"

"Why is it obscene? Are your parents poor diplomats?"

"No but—"

"Then why must I be a poor, starving doctor."

"I wasn't suggesting that you aim for the mendicant path, but most people see the medical profession in more…how should I put it? I suppose, in a more altruistic light."

Malachi shrugged. "And that's great. Personally, I think altruism is overrated where—."

"Altruism is wha—."

"Hold on! Hold on!" He put his right palm up. With his left, he touched her arm. "You didn't allow me to finish.

"I was saying that altruism is overrated where medicine is concerned. Or maybe I should say it like this: People think that the medical profession is much more altruistic than it actually is. The irony is that I suspect many of those who take that path, you know, the Doctors Without Borders and other medical charities and save-the-world do-gooder types are the bored progeny of rich folks who are just fed up of their toys and trust funds and are searching for the next big thing. So that giving back"—he made air quotes around 'giving back'—"I assume, beats snuffing it up their noses. Trust me, Megan, I know the type. I went to high school with some of them. I won't be surprised if I bounce them up later when I'm doing my internship or residency. They don't care about people, but it's to the profession's advantage to make you think they do." He tapped his temple.

"Wow. Whose BMW ran over your fire truck?"

Malachi shook his head in a soundless laugh. "Naw, nothing like that. It's just that for me—or for my dad might be more accurate to say—studying medicine is a huge financial sacrifice. And let's not even talk about the personal sacrifice. You're going to see very soon that the med students on this campus are always up. Even when we're asleep, we're up. Trust me, some of us even dream this stuff." His thoughts drifted to his recent dreams.

Megan smiled and took a swig at her bottled water.

She even made drinking bottled water look classy, Malachi observed.

"You smile, but it's all true," he continued. He was suddenly struck with a need to be understood. "This is no jokey profession you know. They make the program real hard...for spite. And you can't really blame them. I mean, people's lives depend on us—well them. So one day, I'll save lives like the next guy, but I intend to make a truckload of money while doing it. The way I see it, nothing's wrong with doing both."

Megan raised her eyebrows and sighed audibly. "Technically...I suppose I can't argue with your logic, even though you are making far too many assumptions about people with money. And I'm sure you appreciate that your thesis—"

"My thesis? That's rich."

"Another bad word apparently."

Malachi chuckled.

"As I was saying, your thesis, reeks of Machiavellianism. Couldn't you have allowed me to wallow a little longer in my ignorance of the medical profession? I fear that I simply won't be able to look at poor old Dr. Raj the same after today. That's my family GP, by the way."

"Oh, they make a mint."

"Stop it!"

They shared another laugh.

Malachi allowed his gaze to linger on her face until her laughter tapered off to a prissy little smile. Megan looked away—suddenly conscious of the intensity of his gaze.

She is beautiful. Wonder if she knows it? Of course she does. Women of that class always do. What is she thinking about so intently? I wonder if I gave her the wrong impression about me? So what if I did. I don't care...Do I?

Malachi bit his lip. "Well… it's early days yet, Ms. Le Blanc. Don't mind me. This is just the ranting of a med student who hasn't even had his first day of class. Right now I just want to make it through my first year in one piece. Yep. One year at a time."

Megan studied him. He was obviously very intelligent. His dreamy eyes belied his harsh philosophy about his future profession. His mouth was strong and very masculine. He had what her dentist would call a good dental display. And that dimple…

She wondered for a second if she should say what was on her mind.

"Well, I would certainly have no problem coming to you," she said matter-of-factly. "As a doctor I mean."

"Is that so? And why is that, if I should dare ask?"

"Don't take this the wrong way, but there's something about you, Malachi, that makes a woman want to… how should I say it? Expose herself; bare her soul."

Malachi allowed himself a whopper of a laugh. The outburst earned him some curious glances from patrons at neighboring tables.

"That's a first and certainly one for the books."

Megan sipped her water and shrugged. "So will you be at the highly-touted Jama party tonight?"

"I'm not sure. I have my first class bright and early tomorrow. Do we really have to come in our PJs?"

"I doubt that. I'm certain half the guys here probably sleep in boxers, if anything at all."

"Now that's a visual I really didn't care for."

"The point is I'm sure jeans and a quirky T-shirt would suffice. Come on, don't be such a stiff. All the first years have their first class tomorrow, and I'm sure they'll be out in droves."

"I take it you're going."

"Sure, it will be my first shindig on hall. I won't miss it for the world. Clubbing is an essential part of life at uni you know. So?"

"I'm thinking about it. If you'll be there then at least I'll have somebody to hang with." He looked directly at her and smiled.

Megan was sure that her mind was defying her instructions not to blush.

"Well, that's provided you get to hang with me at all," she said with a sniff. "Two—no, make that three seniors and a freshman—came to my room on separate occasions yesterday asking me if I would be attending said event. They want me to accompany them blah blah. Buy me drinks blah blah. Dance the night away. You West Indian men are actually quite talented when it comes to the pick-up lines. Beats the hackneyed ones I'm accustomed to."

So she's accustomed to suitors. Why am I not surprised?

"So what you're saying, Ms. Dancing Diplomat, is, take a number?"

"You're quick."

"Well, I guess everybody can't be doctors."

They had a good laugh at that one.

CHAPTER FIVE

"Hi, Dad."

"Hi, Dad? When were you planning to call, Junior?"

"I was waiting till classes start so I'd have something interesting to tell you. I guess you beat me to it."

"But Junior, I thought we had agreed that you would call home to let me know that you had arrived safely."

Malachi Junior snorted out a laugh into the phone. "Dad, it's not like there were any reports of a plane crash in the news this week, now were there?"

"What the jail is this! So that is why I spending all this set-a-money to educate you, so you can find creative ways to insult me?"

There it was, Malachi thought. *Why is it that every conversation with you has to include some reference to money, usually the lack of it?*

"And who is Explorer? The person who answered the phone yelled for Explorer."

"That's my hall name, Dad. Everyone has one."

"What does it mean?"

Malachi sighed.

Round two.

"The hall names have sexual connotations, Dad," he replied truthfully.

"And you accepted it? Malachi Junior, your mother and I didn't raise no lemming."

"Any."

"What?"

"Never mind."

Silence.

"Did you find out about what we talked about?"

"What's that again? It's late; my brain is a bit tired." Malachi choked back sigh number two.

"What are you talking about? It's just after ten over there. This is when you get started. Look Junior, don't play dumb with me. You know very well that I'm talking about the food stamps. Did you get any?"

"They're called meal vouchers, Dad, and no, I haven't got around to asking about it."

"That's not good enough, Junior. I told you the loan I took out is not enough to cover tuition, books, and food. Do I have to go over this again? Look, Mrs. Henry in student services said all you need—"

"Dad, why are you stressing out yourself about this? It's cool; I have a little extra money to last a bit, you know, from my job. I'll make it do."

"Malachi Junior, you don't have jack squat. You would have if you had listened to me and saved more instead of blowing your salary on that ridiculously expensive boom box or whatever you call it, or that overpriced gym you insisted on joining. I mean, who were you trying to impress, those preppy friends of yours? Are they planning to pitch in and help you through five years of med school?"

Malachi choked back the exasperated grunt that almost escaped his lips.

"So...found a church yet? Did you ask around about the churches on the list I gave you? That's good information I got from Bishop Palmer. You remember Bishop Palmer, right?—the Jamaican who preached in our church last convention?"

"Of course. Bishop Palmer. He had the place in stitches. They couldn't get enough of the accent."

"It wasn't just the accent. It's obvious the man has a powerful anointing on his life. I still remember his message on forgiveness. I can tell you it touched me in a big way. Anyway, you asked any of the locals about the churches on the list?"

"Not yet."

"Well, I shouldn't have to remind you of this, but fellowship is very important, Junior. Your spiritual survival in that place depends on it. Being at university can be warfare for the believer. I'm not asking you; I'm telling you. I remem—"

"They have UCCF here you know: Universities and Colleges Christian Fellowship," Malachi Junior, said, interrupting. "Somebody invited me already. Plus, they have cell groups and all kinds of churchy stuff on hall." Malachi squeezed his eyes shut and pinched his nose bridge on account of the words that just tumbled out. It probably wasn't a bright idea to use the term *churchy*. The last thing he wanted was for his father to call him out on his caustic tone on this subject. He'd never get off the phone, and right about now he needed to wind up this conversation so he could sort through possible wardrobe options for the party.

Malachi instructed himself to muster up all the enthusiasm he could.

"Daddy, yuh there? Wonder if I get cut off, boy?" Malachi held the mouthpiece two inches away as he asked the latter question aloud.

He knew that his father was one of those typical church folks who've grown accustomed to controlling a microphone. He also knew that his dad was adept at anesthetizing captive audiences—even if it was an audience of one.

"Ah right here," Malachi Senior finally said. "OK, well great. You still need to find a home church. But that's a good start, I guess. Good to know you're getting involved in campus ministry. So where is Caleb going? Churchwise, I mean? Maybe you and he could—"

"You know what, Dad, sorry to cut you, but class starts at eight o'clock in the morning, and I still have some stuff to sort through for my first day. Besides, this is long distance and I know how you are about the bills."

He heard his father clear his throat. "Yes...well. Just talk to someone and get those food stamps so you don't starve to death in that place. What possessed you to go and study quite over there when there's a perfectly good med school in your own country, is anyone's guess."

Anything to get away from you.

"Bye, Dad."

****

The Jama Night party was scheduled to start at ten in the Hall Chairman's flat. The flier said prizes would be given for Best Jammies female and Best Jammies male.

I wonder if it's money.

"Great, now I sound just like dad," Malachi told his reflection. He shook his head and groaned as he replayed in his mind the telephone conversation he'd just had with his father. He knew he'd engaged in subterfuge with his feigned enthusiasm about campus fellowship, which he intended to avoid. Not to mention the line about having to get things prepared for tomorrow. But what choice did he have? He couldn't exactly tell his deacon dad that he was taking his backsliding self all the way to a hall party—a pajama one at that. Malachi's strict Christian upbringing had been virtually party-free, save the occasional birthday bash, wedding, or sober church social. He'd managed to sneak in a real one under the guise of a group study session when he was studying for A Levels. But that was it.

He studied himself in the mirror on the door of his wardrobe. He had no idea that the pajamas he bought would have come in so handy. Like the sound system, the PJs were one of several "strategic" purchases that Malachi had made over the past year as a working adult. He had discovered the magical power of the word "strategic" from his immediate supervisor, who had used it to confer a veil of legitimacy on all requisitions. He saw how the corporate world had wielded the adjective to its advantage, so he thought it might be worthwhile to try it out.

The PJs were part of his strategic collection. His mother once said that a man should always have a good pair of pajamas in case he got sick and had to be taken to the hospital. He was sure that the designer brand he'd chosen would have met her approval. Just as he was sure that his father would have dismissed it as another one of his nonsense buys, had he seen the price tag on it.

Well that nonsense is coming in handy tonight, Malachi said to himself as he fastened his sandals. If there were a prize to be won, he had an above-average shot at it, he thought, as he took a final glance at his getup in the mirror. He'd whittled down his options to the Superman muscle vest he'd bought strictly for fun, which he wore beneath the dark brown buttoned down pajama top. The vest, he admitted, was a vanity purchase he'd made simply to show off his new and improved gym-crafted physique. It seemed like a good idea at the time, but somehow he'd never found the occasion, or maybe the courage, to wear it in public. His pre-gym body was OK, but he always felt he was a bit too scrawny. Having a regular cash flow gave him the power to do something about it. The fact that he had joined a high-end health club, however, had not gone down well with Mr. Frugal. With Malachi Senior, it was always about the money.

He heard the key turn in the door. Hopeton shuffled in, knapsack on his back, a brown paper bag in his hand. Judging from the smell, Malachi suspected it was the doggie bag from Sunday dinner at Petrina's home in the parish of Saint Catherine. His own stomach did cartwheels.

"Mal, like you ready for Jama Night. That PJ outfit a de lick man."

"Guess that means it's good?"

"Sorry, sorry. Let me translate. The outfit..." Hopeton gave Malachi a thumbs up.

"What can I say? When you're right, you're right," Malachi said and flipped up his collar.

They both laughed.

"Coming down later?"

"Yuh mad? That admission too dear for me. Me barely have enough for food as it is. Nope, I plan to have my own Jama Night right here in my bed. Warm up the food that me bona fide pack for me and when that done, put on Bob and enjoy my last study-free night on Sutton. Yow, want some food? She make enough for two."

"Nah, you fix yuh mix. I'll grab something down at the party."

"More for me," Hopeton replied with a shrug as Malachi strolled out the door.

CHAPTER SIX

Ten.

That's how many people Malachi counted when he stepped into Sutton's dining room. The party was originally earmarked for the hall chairman's flat but there was a last minute venue change when they realized tickets were selling out. His watch read quarter to eleven. He reasoned that because most people had their first class the next day, they would come early with the hope of leaving early. Apparently, he was singular in that plan.

Super Senior Gadget, whom he now earned the right to call Gadget, was the deejay for the night. An applied physics major, Gadget was regarded as a bit of a pedant when it came to electronics. The talk on the block was that he applied to do mechanical engineering in Trinidad and got in but couldn't come up with the tuition. He was doing applied physics with the hope of transferring to engineering eventually. Tonight, Gadget was in his element surrounded by his turntables and speakers.

Kemba, a first-year management studies major from St. Lucia, sat on a stool close to Gadget sorting through CDs. Orange kite paper covered the fluorescent bulbs giving the room a tacky amber glow.

Gadget had slipped in Marvin Gaye's "Sexual Healing" and all speakers cranked out the seductive lyrics. In less than ten minutes, the room, which just the night before was the torture chamber for first years, had taken on a different character. They came in groups: five female first years, followed by three male seniors, a group of six, followed by a steady flow of first years and seniors.

The ladies were attentive to the theme of the night. Some came in pajama bottoms and tank tops, others opted for shorts and a baby tee. Some of the ladies started dancing as Gadget changed the tune to the more upbeat Whitney Houston "My Love Is Your Love." By eleven thirty the party was in full swing. Students had made repeated trips to the bar, taking advantage of the free drinks that came with the admission fee.

Passion walked in alone at quarter to twelve wearing a lacy pink top and a pink and gray pajama bottom with a pink lace trim. She sashayed over to Malachi who was engaged in conversation with Geraldine, a third-year med student.

"Hey handsome. Why don't you buy me a drink?"

Geraldine rolled her eyes and moved toward a group of her blockmates who had walked in.

"The drinks are free, Passion. What are you having?"

"A screwdriver. If they don't have dat, a rum and coke." Malachi paused. He had very strong views about alcohol consumption and smoking. He told himself it was health-related, but deep down he knew it was probably on account of his Christian upbringing.

Just then, the tempo changed as Deejay Gadget slipped in Trinidadian calypsonian, David Rudder's, "Madness." A portion of the crowd, mainly Trinis, began jumping and waving their hands in the air. Others joined in.

"This is not a fete in here. This is madness!" they sang with gusto.

In what seemed like seconds, there was a premium on standing room as a steady flow of freshers and seniors filed into the dining room.

"If you want booze, you'd have to get it yourself, Passion. I'm a teetotaler," Malachi shouted above the music.

"A what?"

"A teetotaler; I don't drink!"

"Ah true? Too bad, things taste nicer when you drink," she simpered.

"So a where you learn all them fancy words? Aren't you a med student? Me did think you suppose to be semiliterate with all them illegible doctor scribbes," she said with a giggle.

Malachi smiled. "Hardly. I think we all had to be pretty literate to get in here, trust me. Nah it's just that my mom was an English teacher. A good vocabulary was a must."

"English teacher? You think say she could improve my vocabulary?"

Malachi pretended not to have heard the question. His eyes focused on the PJ wearing throng. But where were the extra fans? The room felt like an inferno. The whirling overhead fans were about as useful as a thesaurus in a math exam. Malachi started to feel sweat trickling down his back. He silently prayed that his deodorant was still on the clock.

Another selection had begun.

"This one is for the Bajan posse in the house!" the Deejay announced. The crowd roared.

The intro to soca musician Rupee's hit song "Tempted to Touch" caused one fan to squeal her approval. Some patrons laughed, more cheered. The mingling was now firmly in motion. Those who knew the tune belted out the lyrics. Passion seemed to have caught the vibe. She hooked her hands around Malachi's neck and began to sway, Jamaican style.

"Easy girl," Malachi said.

"Don't tell me you don't dance neither?"

"OK. I won't tell you. You'll just find out."

She released him, but not before tracing her index along his jawline. He flinched.

"Explorer, give me a likkle something to work with, nuh?" she said while continuing to sway in front of him. Through the corner of his eye, Malachi caught a glimpse of Jerome Hunter, aka Desperate. He was looking directly at them.

"Passion, I think your boyfriend might be digging a little horrors with the scene over here."

She followed his eye and tsked. "Who Jerome? Me and him nuh de again. Besides, that was never serious. Just your typical case of a first year liking off a senior. Been there, done that."

That's not what it looked like yesterday, Malachi thought.

"Him probably come to see how much fool fool likkle first years him can lure in him bed. Like father, like son." She smiled up at Malachi.

His stomach growled—a not so gentle reminder that he hadn't had anything to eat since lunchtime. He'd reasoned with himself that if free drinks were part of the ticket, then there might be finger foods, too. That theory was debunked the moment he saw the "hotdog bar" as the sign advertised, and it wasn't free. He reached into his pajama pocket. All he felt was his room key.

"Great," he said aloud as the realization that he had forgotten to transfer the fifty-dollar bill he had pulled from his wallet, sank in. He would have to go back to his room to get it. Either that or let the worms frolic.

"Hey Passion. I need to run up…uh to use the bathroom. I'll check you later, alright?"

"You promise? Sure you don't want company… In the bathroom?" she purred.

"Alesha, something tells me you are way more than I can handle," he replied truthfully.

"I'm a great teacher. Never underestimate the Faculty of Education."

"Don't doubt it."

She threw her head back and laughed as Malachi made his escape.

****

Megan observed the friendly exchange between Malachi and the ill-mannered Jamaican girl who insulted her in front of everyone that morning on hall.

If that was his taste, she told herself, he wasn't even worthy of friendship. She'd dealt with that venomous kind all her life. There was no shortage of them at her boarding schools. It was always difficult for her to fit in at the three boarding schools she had attended. She was always the student to arrive weeks after the term began, and she never seemed to stay in one place long enough to truly bond with the girls.

Megan was suddenly conscious that a group of girls standing nearby was staring at her. A round-faced girl in shorts and fluffy pink bedroom slippers whispered something in the ear of her friend with the short cotton T-Shirt and gray slacks. The latter cackled so hard that she spilled some of her drink.

"I was just about to give up on you; thought you'd changed your mind." She didn't even realize that Malachi had dispensed with his unfortunate company. He was now standing in front of her with two drinks in hand. "Do you like your sodas dark or light?"

"I'm not much of a soda lover actually and...I don't know you well enough to be accepting drinks from you." She smiled hoping it would soften her truth.

"Ouch," he exclaimed and dropped his head to dramatize the effect of her rebuff. "What can I say? You are very right and very smart. I hope one day to have girl children as clever as you."

"What? You don't know me a good two days and already you're talking children? Trying to scare us silly are you?"

Malachi laughed. It took him fifteen seconds to recover.

"I like you, Megan Le Blanc. You speak your mind. That's refreshing." Megan didn't know why the statement made her tingle.

"You look great by the way," Malachi added. "Is that silk?"

"It is, and you might be the only one who approves of my getup judging from the devious stares and whispers I seem to be attracting since I arrived. What is it about the West Indian obsession with staring at people. I don't quite follow."

Malachi surveyed her. She wore dark brown silk pajamas that were open in the front revealing a burnt orange tube and a flat stomach with what looked like a silver navel ring at first glance. She wore her hair up with some sort of clamp at the back.

I wonder how she looks with her hair down?

"If the stares are coming from the men, it's because they can't help it. If they're from the ladies, trust me, they're jealous. But unless I've read you wrong, Ms. Le Blanc, you don't seem to be the type to care two hoots what people think."

"I don't usually. It's just that…" She hesitated. "Well, I guess it's no fun not being liked all the time, and at times, I can hardly blame them really."

"What yuh mean?"

"Well just yesterday a girl on my block, I think she's from your country, actually. She came up to me and said the most astounding thing."

"OK."

"She said she just loves Colin Firth."

"The actor?"

"Of course."

"What's so astounding about that?"

"Hold on, I'm not finished." Megan cleared her throat and ventured a Trini accent.

"She said something like, 'Oh my gosh, I just love Colin Firth. *Pride and Prejudice* is my favorite movie. I am so in love with the Mr. Darcy character.'"

Malachi laughed and shook his head.

"Your Trini imitation is beyond pathetic by the way; just thought I should mention that."

Megan dismissed the critique with a wave of her hand.

"So, let me guess, and you are standing there wondering, 'Why is she telling me this?'"

"Absolutely. But then it got worse. She asked if I had ever seen him."

"Mr. Darcy? I mean Colin Firth? You're kidding." Malachi couldn't stop laughing.

"I kid you not."

"So what yuh tell her?"

"What do you think I said? I told her, 'All the time... I see Colin all the time. In fact he sat next to me in first class on the flight over here.'"

"You said that? Nah, yuh joking."

"I am most certainly not joking, as you put it. Believe me, she was not amused. But really, Malachi, what did she expect? A stupid question deserves a stupid answer."

"My English teacher once said there's no such thing as a stupid question."

"Lucky for you she or he wasn't teaching math."

They laughed.

"Anyway, can you believe I forgot my wallet in my room, so I'm just running up to get it and come back."

"Oh why do that? Here's a bill. I don't know if that covers it?" She slipped the hundred dollar bill in his pajama pocket.

"Megan I can't take your money. Five, ten minutes tops. I'll be back. Promise."

"Here's what, Malachi. Tonight, I'll trust you enough to take this drink from you, and you trust me enough not to have a hidden agenda by giving you this money. Deal?"

Megan took the cola from Malachi's hand and sipped it while maintaining eye contact. With her free hand she patted his pajama pocket where she'd placed the bill.

"And if you try to pay me back, I'll never speak to you again."

Malachi reached into his pocket with his free hand, but he didn't pull out the note.

"You drive a tough bargain, Ms. Dancing Diplomat. Something tells me whatever you decide to do with your life, you'll be great at it."

"Now you're making me blush."

Malachi took a deep breath. He'd taken money from a woman who wasn't his mother. The world hadn't ended, and somehow his pride was intact. He had to admit, the lady had skills.

"I'll go get my hotdogs. Should I ask them if they have any tofu dogs?" he enquired with a slight smirk on his face.

"You have jokes. But I'm fine. I had dinner, and I rarely eat after six."

"Why am I not surprised?" There was something about the expression on his face when he said it, and the way he looked her square in the eye that caused something inside her to stir.

OK Megan, it's just a line. Don't let this guy reel you in.

With that, he disappeared inside.

"Me think that he would never done chat you up." The tall, athletically-built Jamaican, who Megan remembered as Stanley, was saying to her.

"Oh Stanley. Didn't see you approaching, actually."

"So it must be—the element of surprise. You must never see it coming. Never."

"Ah," Megan replied and wondered if all West Indian men had a shortlist of trite pick-up lines.

"Anyway, me just come to colleck the dance you did promise me the other night when we did talk at your room door."

She smiled. He smiled back. She finished her drink, tossed it in a nearby trash bag and walked with him back inside to the middle of the dance floor.

"That was quick," Malachi muttered to himself when he spotted Megan and Freshman Blue Moon slow dancing to Teddy Pendergrass's "Turn Off The Lights." Malachi leaned against the hotdog bar. The man and three women behind the counter were busy cutting buns and refilling condiments. The guy, a senior whose name Malachi couldn't remember, was stirring a big stainless steel pot containing a fresh batch of wieners, having run out. Malachi was fortunate to get the last two.

There were at least thirteen couples on the dance floor, and about twenty patrons standing at the sidelines, watching, drinking, and chatting with friends. Some of the couples held each other so tightly that Malachi was reminded of high school grad all over again, only this time there were no chaperones and everyone was legal. The 1999 cover version of Lauryn Hill and Bob Marley's "Turn Your Lights Down Low" took up from where Teddy let off. Candace, a fellow Trini first year, asked Malachi to dance. He talked his way out of it and chatted with her for the next five minutes.

Malachi glanced down at his watch. It was one o'clock. He hadn't planned to stay that long. He whispered to Candace that he was leaving. She gave him a sad face with a pouty mouth and practically skipped back over to her waiting girlfriends. He finished his second hotdog and washed it down with a cup of watered down fruit punch from the bar. He looked around for Megan, but she was no longer on the dance floor.

"This one is for all the Jamaicans in the house," Deejay Gadget announced.

The intro to Buju Banton's "Untold Stories" elicited shouts from the youthful crowd. Without the Deejay having to say it, Malachi knew that the dancehall segment of the party was about to take over.

As he cleared the exit, he spotted Megan talking to a senior whose name he didn't know.

Malachi wondered for a moment whether he shouldn't at least say goodbye. That's when he felt the tap on his shoulder. It was Passion.

"You breaking the rules, Freshman. You can't leave Jama night empty-handed."

He was about to give her one of his clever comebacks when a hand grabbed her from behind.

"You a lef with dis ya fool, Ally?" Jerome slurred and spilled the concoction in his cup on the brick-tiled path.

"Let me go, eediot! We're over; I've moved on, as you can see!" She turned her head and shot Malachi a flirtatious look. Desperate kept his hand firmly on her arm.

Passion looked down at where Desperate's hand clutched hers. "You not letting me go? Maybe you need to cool off." She flung her cup and the contents in Desperate's face. In a split second, Desperate raised the back of his hand, and Malachi jumped in and intercepted the slap with his hand.

"Don't touch me. Never touch me!"

Desperate threw his fist, and it landed smack in Malachi's eye.

The word spread through the crowd that there was a fight outside. A number of patrons rushed toward the exit, hoping to catch a glimpse of the action.

It took three guys to restrain Desperate. Passion, now in tears, was being consoled by her blockmates. She stopped in between sobs to hurl expletives at Desperate.

Freshman Peeping Tom from Malachi's block had come to Malachi's side in what was meant to be a show of block solidarity. Malachi felt a burning on his face, but both his hands were now deep in his pockets. Megan was saying something to him, but he couldn't process what she was saying as his gaze was still trained on Desperate who, although much calmer, was pleading with his restrainers to release him so he could talk to his woman.

"Malachi, are you listening to me?" Megan demanded.

"Yes."

"Do you have antiseptic for that cut?"

"What cut?" He touched his eye and saw the blood on his fingers. Only then did he notice the specks of blood on his pajamas.

Walter, a senior he had barely seen twice since he arrived, announced to the gathering that he was third year med. The announcement produced an effect akin to Moses' rod. In seconds, Walter had front row access to Malachi's face.

"Let me take a look at that eye," he said, a bit louder than necessary. "Looks a lot worse than it is." He turned his back to Malachi to address the spectators.

"It'll be sore for a few days, but he doesn't need stitches," Walter announced.

"Do you have anything to clean it up?" Walter was talking to him again.

"Yes," Megan replied on his behalf. "Don't worry, I've got this," she told Walter with an aplomb that raised eyebrows amongst the spectators.

CHAPTER SEVEN

Hopeton sat in the third row of the packed lecture theatre. He'd earned a reputation throughout high school for hogging front row seats—a strategy that he felt had gained him leverage academically. But Toothpick, a lanky, third-year med student on Sutton, had advised him against it.

"Trust me, Tonto. You don't want to sit there," Toothpick had assured him the day before.

"The front row is for losers who like punishment," he'd said, before slapping his dominos on the table.

"You'll get spit missiles from Collins, Tuesday afternoon halitosis from Freakley, and how do you really expect to survive the constant rain of questions from big belly Burton? Sit in the front at your own risk, bro."

Hopeton couldn't stop thanking Toothpick for the "heads up." He had arrived at a quarter after seven on Monday morning and headed straight for the third row. The last thing he wanted was to be branded "Teacher's Pet" again—that would have been the most benign of the many names he'd been called over the years. Sure, he kowtowed a bit, but what was so criminal about getting along with one's teachers, he wanted to know. After all, Hopeton told himself, he was just an average *Hope*.

Hopeton chuckled to himself. He was just trying to get on with it like the rest of the guys—or girls for that matter, and boy were there quite a few of them, he noted. And all kinds too: tall, short, fat, skinny, dark, brown-skinned. How was a man expected to concentrate with all that estrogen in the room?

"Do you have any gum?" The tall darkie with the Miss Jamaica figure was asking him even now.

"No, sorry; I don't drink."

"Gum. I said gum, not rum. Why would I ask you for rum, you freak?" Her face contorted, and she inched closer to her girlfriend on the right.

He wasn't even in the front row and already the questions were coming, he mused.

The din in the room subsided suddenly as the lecturers took their seats on the dais at the front. A balding middle-aged man, whom Hopeton recognized as the dean from his Faculty of Medical Sciences handbook, approached the lectern and cleared his throat.

He clasped his hands behind his back and leaned forward toward the mike.

"Good morning. I am Professor Avery Livingston, your dean."

"Dr. Livingston, I presume?" came a whisper from a male voice in the row behind. A few sniggers followed.

"Welcome to the University of Jamaica and welcome specifically to the region's premier institution for the training of health care professionals."

A chubby girl in the front row began to clap. Her immediate neighbors followed. It didn't catch on.

"Stupid eager beavers," the voice from behind, said, as chuckles erupted from around the room.

Professor Livingston waited for silence to return.

"If you haven't yet asked yourself, 'Why am I here?' We will see to it that you do—very soon."

"Why does that sound like a threat?" The backseat commentator wanted to know. This time, the voice was shushed.

Professor Livingston continued.

"You got in here by your own merit, we assume. We assume." He went up on the balls of his feet. "But your friendly neighborhood lecturers will let you know if you can stay."

Light ripples filled the room.

"At the end of the day, however, it is up to you. Your ability to successfully navigate this journey and achieve your goal of becoming a doctor would depend, not only on the caliber of your mind and intellect, but perhaps more importantly, on the seriousness of your commitment to the rigor that lies ahead. For those who are successful at this leg of the journey, you will be rewarded with a higher level of rigor and so it goes. 'Why do we make it so hard?' I hear students ask, sometimes with tears in their eyes. Simple. People's lives are at stake: yours, mine. Yes, you have achieved a milestone by getting into this program. Some of you are island scholars, valedictorians. You've been led to believe you're special, but you're not ready yet. Don't forget this. If any of you are discovered to be playing doctor before your time, you will be out of here faster than you can say, 'bus stop, drivah,'" he said, code switching from Standard English to patois.

"If any of you are found cheating in any form, the same applies. If any of you are found to be taking illegal drugs, you will be expelled, possibly even jailed. Familiarize yourself with your FMS handbook. You will see that attendance and punctuality are not optional for this program.

"Those of you who are standing in the back, there are seats up front. Come quickly."

Seven students made their way down the aisle to vacant seats.

"What happened to your face, young man?" Dr. Livingston practically spoke into the mike.

All eyes turned to stare at the student whom he had addressed. It was Malachi Williamson.

"I uh. I tried to intervene in an altercation and was injured in the process. Sir."

"When did this happen?"

"Last night, sir."

"Have a seat. See me after class."

"Ladies and gentlemen, the doctor is very often the first line of defense. Not your police officer, not even your priest—your doctor.

"For the record..." The inflection in his voice crescendoed. "I take bruises and injuries very seriously, as do my colleagues. In a way, we are responsible for you while you are here. I implore each of you to remember that." He glanced at Malachi when he said it.

The rest of the lecture was spent introducing the various pre-clinical year-one lecturers and their subject areas: anatomy, physiology, biochemistry, pharmacology, and microbiology. One by one, each lecturer gave what was supposed to be a pep talk, although to Hopeton it sounded like different versions of the riot act.

When they broke for lunch, Hopeton scanned the room for Malachi, but his roommate was gone. He wasn't too concerned when he had awakened this morning and had not seen Malachi in the next bed. They were all adults, albeit barely. He just assumed that the Trini got lucky last night and had found alternative accommodations.

Now he realized that his assumptions might have been off. Hopeton wondered exactly how much trouble his roommate was in.

****

The dean's office was as sterile as the operating theatres Malachi had seen on TV.

The dean, Malachi figured, had either just moved in or had taken minimalism to an extreme. There was the basic furniture: a well-crafted, oak-stained desk; an ergonomically designed high back chair; a desktop computer; a chrome coat rack; and two four-drawer filing cabinets positioned side by side. One side of the wall was almost covered with empty wooden cubby holes in the same cherry oak finish as the dean's desk. There were two padded visitor seats at the opposite end of his desk. A television and DVD player lay enclosed within a glass-cased hutch. The mint green walls were bereft of certificates, photos, charts—anything that would hint of his interest, profession, or even family.

The secretary had instructed Malachi to wait in the dean's office. He was there for three minutes when the dean walked in. Malachi stood.

"Sit."

Professor Livingston unlocked his desk drawer and pulled out what appeared to be a sheet of letterhead stationery. He removed a gold, ballpoint pen from his coat pocket, twisted it, and began writing on the sheet. In less than a minute he stopped, twisted the pen again, pulled out a matching envelope from the same drawer, and stuffed the letter in the envelope. He scribbled on the envelope.

"Give this to the receptionist at the University Hospital," he said. "Today," he added, after a pause. "She would know what to do with it."

"Yes, Professor." Malachi took the letter from the dean's outstretched hand. He wondered why the Professor didn't ask him his name.

"You need sutures. I don't expect you to know that, but that letter will see to it that you are attended to… Was this a domestic affair?"

"No, sir. I—I went to a party on hall, someone got a little drunk and attempted to manhandle a female student. I tried to stop him, and I guess my eye got in the way." Malachi said it with humor in his voice. Professor Livingston remained stoic.

Professor Livingston took a deep breath and reclined in his chair. "Life, Mr. Williamson, is about choices, isn't it?"

"Yes, sir, how did you—" That's when Malachi remembered that his student ID was dangling from his shirt pocket.

"You are, Mr. Williamson, where the air is rare. For every student you saw in that classroom this morning, there are at least five others desperately clawing at our doors waiting, hoping, and praying that they will get to take one of those places. Perhaps yours." He rested his darkened elbows on either side of the padded handles of his leather chair and joined his fingertips in the steeple position.

"Each choice that you make, young man, will either move you closer to your desired goal or cause you to veer farther off course. The choice is, of course, yours. We are merely here to fa-

cilitate the discovery. Let this be the last time that you are summoned to this office for non-academic matters. Is that clear?"

"Yes, sir. Thank you, sir."

The Professor nodded and Malachi arose from his seat.

CHAPTER EIGHT

When he got back to his room at six thirty, Malachi was relieved to discover that he had the room to himself. It had been an exhausting day, eclipsed only by a far-too-eventful night. The cut above his eye had taken three sutures. The resident who had done it had been very efficient.

She'd joked a little about what the other guy must look like. Malachi had feigned a weak smile. What hurt the most was not his eye but the fact that he didn't even get a punch in. Desperate, he felt, more than deserved it. Imagine trying to hit a woman.

Malachi had visited the hospital during his lunch break. By the time he was all stitched up, it was time for the afternoon sessions. No breakfast, followed by no lunch, which probably explained the light-headed sensation he was now experiencing.

He knew that if he kept it up, he would be well on his way to becoming a poster boy for the starving student.

After his last class, Malachi had dashed over to the canteen. As expected, lunch was long over and the cooks were rolling out the dinner menus. All that was left were sandwiches. He picked up a turkey sandwich and a carton of orange juice. That would have to do for the day.

Malachi knew it was just a matter of time before he had no choice but to visit student services to get those meal vouchers his dad had been nagging him about, but he would do so when he was good and ready, and not a nanosecond before.

When "push comes to shove" was the Trini expression he had explained to Hopeton during orientation. "Basically, it means when things get from bad to worse," Malachi had said. His roommate had written it down on his index card "in case the seniors ask."

The room was empty. Malachi peeled off his clothes, stuffed it in his laundry bag, and pulled it out again. He forgot that he'd told himself to go easy on the detergent. The jeans had definitely passed the sniff test, but he had his doubts about his shirt.

Better safe than sorry, he thought, and stuffed it back in the laundry bag. He put the shower on cold. The slap of water on his bare skin caused his face to sting a little, even though it was now dressed and covered.

"No stitches needed huh?" he said aloud, remembering Walter's announcement. After the Dean's warning about *playing doctor,* he thought it best to exclude that little detail from the account. Alas, the goal of hall loyalty had finally been achieved.

His thought shifted to Megan. He had to admit that he was more than a little bemused when he woke up in her bed. Well, technically it wasn't her bed, but her roommate's, who obviously was not there at the time and whose name Malachi forgot to inquire about.

Megan's first-aid kit had been well stocked with gauze, antiseptic solutions, Epsom salts, smelling salt, and various types of bandages. She had told him that she used the stuff to nurse her feet after a hard rehearsal or a recital.

She had offered him herbal tea. He barely recalled her mumbling something about putting a little brandy in it to take the shock off. Too embarrassed to argue, and preoccupied with the sight of his swelling eye in her bathroom mirror, he took the tea and gulped it down practically scalding his mouth. That was the last thing he remembered. The next thing he knew he was waking up in her room dressed in his pajama bottoms and Superman vest. The pajama top was nowhere in sight, neither was Megan. That was seven thirty.

"Honey, I'm home!" Hopeton's voice reverberated on the wall of the shower. It was a stupid little call his roommate had taken to when he came through the door the evening after their first day as roommates. Malachi didn't find it funny then, and it wasn't growing on him.

"In the shower, Hopeton. Out in a sec."

He stepped out of the shower and tucked in the towel at his waist. Hopeton was at his desk huddled over his texts.

"Look how 'im mess up your eye! You should sue. Me hear 'im father have money."

"Really don't want to waste time talking about it, Hopeton. Not when I have work to do. You finish the assignments?"

"Can't believe it, yow! Is only day one you know and we have two assignments for tomorrow. Me jus' a come from the library and guess what? The text Dr. Sunju chat 'bout—gone!"

"Did you check the Reference Section? They had a couple of copies well when I checked this evening."

"You were in the library?"

"Yeah, how else would I get the info for the assignment?"

"Oh alright, alright, Malachi. You mind if we discuss the question? I mean, I don't want to copy your answer on anything. Is jus' that I was thinking, 'I'm in med, you're in med...'"

"Hopeton, Bro, relax man. I get you. We'll have our first group study session tonight. Let me just throw on some clothes, zeen?"

Malachi and Hopeton sat and discussed the anatomy assignment. By nine o'clock they were sure that they had covered the area adequately and the study session was over. Malachi told himself he'd take a half an hour break to stretch his legs then he'd come back to do some advanced reading for the next day's biochem lecture.

****

He turned left at the end of his block and bounced up the steps two at a time to Megan's room. Two first years who had witnessed the fracas the night before intercepted him.

"I cyah understand. Why is he still pon the hall? That's what I want to know. Look ah what he did to your nice face," the Bajan girl with the braces, Cathy, said, her arms akimbo.

"I hear his father is a big boy in Jamaican politics, so you know how it does go," her Trini friend, Tricia, chimed in. "By the way, Explorer, if you're looking for Catwoman, she's not in her room."

"Catwoman?" Malachi was lost.

"Megan Le Blanc," Cathy said, enunciating the surname with a coarse retching sound at the end.

"Is I give she the name Catwoman, because she chummy chummy with them black cats around here. Most of us can't stand the mingy monsters. They always digging up in we garbage, messing up the place," Tricia explained with a scowl.

"But I feel like your British nurse friend miss her calling. She should be studying to be a vet. We saw her feeding the cats milk every morning since she moved on hall. You could believe that? And not the powdered kind like wha wunna Trinidadians does use."

"Wha what?" Tricia exclaimed her face contorting. "Nah boy! Yuh hit the English language for six there yuh know, Bajan! Explorer, yuh ever hear that one?"

"Nope. It's a first for me," Malachi replied. The wide grin on his face reflected his own amusement, which, truthfully, was more over his fellow Trini's reaction than her Barbadian friend's creole.

"Wha. Wunna," a smiling Cathy repeated, a little slower this time. "It means not the kind all yuh. You Trinidadians use. I see her pouring it out from a milk carton."

"Explorer, you know how much that stuff cost back home? Hmm! She does pet them too, you know. Yeees, I see she petting and talking to them nice nice like is she pompek she talking to. Real TV thing, yuh know. Yuck man!" Tricia said and shuddered in disgust.

Malachi chuckled. "OK, well do you ladies know if her room-mate is there? I can leave a message."

Tricia and Cathy looked at each other and erupted in laughter. Cathy slid to the ground while Tricia doubled over, her hand clutching the nearby railing for support.

"Oh you must be mean Thumbelina?" Cathy guffawed as she wiped her eyes with the back of her hand.

"Thumbelina? Strange name."

"Doh feel no how. You had to be an Enid Blyton fan to truly appreciate that one, Explorer," Tricia added in response to Malachi's knitted brow.

With that, the two tittered as they made their way to Tricia's room, leaving Malachi to wonder what exactly had just happened.

****

"Malachi, what a surpri—yikes… that must have hurt," Abby said, with an ample dose of concern in her tone.

"You should see the other guy."

"I did."

"Oh. So you know." He forced a smile.

"It really doesn't look that bad. Don't worry your good looks are still intact."

"Hmm. So you think I'm good looking, then?" Malachi smirked.

Abby rolled up her eyes and opened her door wider, stepping aside. "Come on in, Mr. Conceited. I was just about to fix myself a late snack: peanut butter and jelly sandwiches. Want one? Consider this your official welcome to B34."

CHAPTER NINE

Some people are born with a knack for taking blah and turning it into wow. Abigail Shaw, Malachi concluded, was one of them.

He'd seen Abby's room when she'd just moved in. The before and after shot had the kind of page-turning magic that made consumer glossies fly off the shelf. The first thing Malachi noticed was the bookcase. It was the one piece of furniture that definitely hadn't come with the room. The four-shelf walnut stained bookcase with antique detailing at the corners, single-handedly elevated the room from student grunge to student chic. He knew that students brought TVs, sound systems, refrigerators, and aquariums with them when they came to live on hall. He'd seen them on display, especially from the rooms of seniors who were fond of leaving their balcony doors open. He couldn't say for sure, but he suspected that bookcases were not among the top five furniture items hauled from home.

Taking center stage on the top shelf, were the thick, fleshy leaves of an aloe plant as it blossomed and framed its hand-painted clay planter like a funky hairdo. To its left were three books resting one on top the other: a Study Bible, a concordance, and a brown, hard-cover notebook. To its right was a tangerine and yellow pencil holder in the shape of a mini watering can. The next two shelves of the bookcase were lined with medical texts, some of which Malachi recognized from his required reading list. The two lower shelves were home to an impressive assortment of books on clinical psychology and counseling.

Abby's balcony doors were still open. One side of her sheer lemon curtains wafted lazily in the sleepy evening breeze. The other side of the curtain was harnessed in the middle by a delicate, brown satin ribbon. The background to the mosaic patterns on Abby's sheet bore the same shade of chocolate brown as the ribbon on her curtain. Her bed was practically covered with an eclectic blend of throw cushions and pillows, which managed to give the room a whiff of rococo without evicting good taste. A beige carpet radiated from the area around her bed covering three-quarters of the room's floor space.

"Please remove your shoes. That's my one rule," she instructed.

Malachi obediently removed his sandals and placed them in the corner near the door.

"I hate having to clean the rug every time someone steps in something…" She made a face to illustrate. Malachi nodded. She turned her back to him and returned to the task of spreading peanut butter on sliced bread.

"Sit anywhere you want: the bed, the floor, the chair. The rug is clean. I had it shampooed after last semester, but you might want to take up one or two of those cushions for comfort, if you wanna sit there."

He chose the bed. Abby turned and handed him two peanut butter and jelly sandwiches on a white plastic plate with a pink paper napkin tucked under it.

She opened her mini fridge. "What would you like to drink? I have orange, grapefruit juice, coconut water—"

"Coconut water would be nice."

She poured coconut water into two medium-sized tumblers and handed one to Malachi. She then returned to slicing bread and spreading more filling.

"You know you just missed your friend."

"Who's that?"

"Caleb."

"Caleb was here?"

"Yep. He studied on my balcony for about two—no, make that three hours. He said things are a bit noisy on his hall."

"And you were cool with that?"

"Sure, he's great company."

Malachi noted she said *great*.

Abby finished her sandwich making. She pulled two pillows off of her bed, tossed them on her rug, and squatted next to them.

"Besides, social psychologists have done numerous studies as to why some people perform better in groups. I'm kind of wired like that myself which is why I use my balcony a lot to study. I managed to put in some hours myself." She sipped her drink. "It was quite constructive," she added.

"I bet it was," Malachi said, a glint of amusement in his eye.

"Hey, it's not like that. Get your mind out of the gutter." She took up one of the pillows beside her and tossed it at Malachi.

"Oh, you want a pillow fight, do you? Well, I think I have a clear advantage here." He patted the stack of pillows that surrounded him. Abby threw her head back and raised her hand to beg off.

An amiable silence fell between them as they ate their sandwiches.

"So you saw Desperate," Malachi finally said.

"Yep. He was quite drunk as it turned out. Still, it doesn't give him an excuse."

"You know he would have hit her if I didn't step in."

Abby didn't respond.

"Hello? Did you hear me?"

"Yeah. Look, I spoke to Alesha about this thing with her and Jerome months ago, but they are both playing games with each other, and it's obvious they've reached a stage where people are getting hurt."

"You spoke to Alesha? I thought you guys were enemies or something."

"A while aback...It's a long story. Let's just say I don't consider her an enemy, but I'm not sure she feels the same."

"OK."

"Well, all I can say is I hope she gets help. That guy is bad news," Malachi said as he chewed on his sandwich. "You know what's amazing?" He paused to sip his coconut water. "You would think that an educated woman like her won't even entertain an abuser like that. It's not like she's financially beholden to him or anything. We're undergrads for crying out loud."

Abby swallowed hard and looked up at Malachi. "So, you think that only poor, financially-dependent women are victims of domestic violence?"

"Well, all the cases I've heard of seem to fit that profile."

"Malachi, violence against woman is no respecter of class, financial status, or education level for that matter."

"Did you read that in one of those psyc books you have over there?" He inclined his head toward her book shelf. "Nice bookshelf by the way."

"Thanks. It was my nana's. Listen, smarty pants, I'm a trained peer counselor, I'd have you know? I've seen and heard some stuff and, yes, I do read a lot on these subjects."

"So are you just a dilettante or do you plan to specialize in psychiatry?"

"Oh, I'm sorry, Mister I-ate-the-dictionary-for-breakfast-this-morning, dile—who?"

Malachi crossed his hands over his heart. "My apologies. Let me break it down for you. Is it just a hobby or are you—"

"Planning on becoming a psychiatrist?" Abby finished. "I got that part. Truth? I haven't really figured it all out yet," she said with a sniff. "I know my dad would just love for me to specialize in neurosurgery like him."

"Know how that could be: those family expectations. But what do you really like?"

"Haven't got a clue," she said with a shrug. "And you?"

"Same clueless club," he replied with a chuckle.

Malachi finished the first sandwich and was already on to the second. Peanut butter and jelly never tasted so good.

"So you're a backslider, huh?"

He stopped chewing and stared down at her. "How long did it take you to bring that up? All of…" He glanced at his watch. "Five minutes?"

"I'm curious. I just don't get what would make you turn your back on Jesus. I'm sorry, I need to know."

Malachi sighed and stared beyond the curtains. "Let's just say I started to…question things. You know when you've been in church all your life, sometimes you start wondering if out there is as bad as everybody keeps saying it is. I'm sure you've had those moments."

"Actually, I haven't. Unlike you, I didn't grow up in church. I've only been saved for like a year and three months.

"You are lying."

"No, really. I got saved at a Christian camp someone invited me to in July last year and I started first year med in September. It's quite a story. Do you want the short or the long version?"

"Any version you're comfortable with."

Abby took another sip of her coconut water and crossed her legs.

CHAPTER TEN

She had just turned fourteen when her parents found out that she was bulimic.

"No one suspected me because I didn't quite fit the profile. I was in my early teens, not early twenties and thirties like most bulimics, and I was African American. Well, Jamaican American. You know what I mean."

She told him that she was an A student at a Jewish private prep school in Long Island. One of two blacks in her class and among ten in the entire school.

Dr. Stokely Shaw, her dad, was Head of Neurosurgery at the Long Island Jewish Hospital, and her mom was Head Physiotherapist at the same hospital. They had met at a medical conference in Chicago. He was a first-year resident at Brooklyn

County Hospital, and she was a sophomore who was working at the conference to get some extra cash.

"They started to date and within six months they'd moved in together. Then mom got pregnant with me. That changed everything. Mom told me that Dad's parents were old fashioned. You got a girl pregnant, you had to get married."

"Some people would call that doing the honorable thing," Malachi said.

"I suppose. But what if they're not meant for each other? Where's the honor in that?"

Abby told Malachi that her parents fought over everything: money, where to spend Thanksgiving, whose turn it was to take out the trash.

"When I was old enough to figure out what the arguments were about, I thought that it was my fault that they were so unhappy. I started to eat. I mean really eat, but that only made things worse. Then they started fighting about my eating habits. Mom blamed Dad for being too strict with me. He had me on a healthy food diet. It was awful. He blamed her for being too lenient. It was a mess, and I felt stuck in the middle of it."

"That's when you started purging?"

"I started to lose the weight that I had gained, but when we moved to Long Island and they enrolled me in private school, I was so desperate to fit in. All…well, maybe not all…but most of the white girls were skinny, and I thought I would help speed up the weight-loss process a bit by purging. Depressing huh?"

"Must have been rough for you."

"It was. The more they fought, the more I ate. One night…" She sipped her coconut water.

"One night, I heard him hit her. Imagine that? My dad, the big doctor, hitting my mom. I was so upset, I didn't speak to him for two weeks."

"That's how you know it doesn't just happen in poor families."

"Yep. I don't think he ever did it again, but that's when I took it up a notch."

"OK."

She found a stray thread on her pillow and rolled it into a ball. "I started cutting myself."

Malachi's poker face gave her the courage to continue.

"At first, I confined it to my thighs because I'd long stopped wearing shorts anyway. But then I started on my arms. I think, in a way, I wanted to get caught. That's what my therapist said anyway."

"Therapist?"

"Yeah, that came after, though. Anyway, to make this really long story short, I got busted. My teacher saw my arm, she called in my parents. My dad was a mess. He kept saying, 'I can't believe I missed this; I can't believe I missed this.'

"My mom blamed herself. She said she was the one who wanted me to go to prep school instead of public school. Our whole family went into therapy."

"Is that when you moved out here?" Malachi's voice was solicitous and gentle.

"I think that was primarily job related. Dad got this big offer to take the top post at the University Hospital. I guess the timing couldn't have been better since they both thought that the change of pace might do me good. 'A more affirming environment,' was how Dr. Patesar, my shrink, described it. Anyway, I continued therapy and was doing better. Even my parents were making an effort and being civil to each other. Then boom!—another bomb dropped on the family."

"Do you want another sandwich? I'm having one." Abby interrupted her story to ask.

"Why not?" Malachi tried to sound casual when what he really wanted to say was: "I thought you'd never ask."

Abby got up and busied herself making more sandwiches. Although the suspense was killing him, Malachi thought it best not to press her until she was good and ready to relate what happened next.

She handed him the sandwich with another napkin, restocked her own plate, and resumed the squatting position.

"It turned out that my dad had had an affair with some Jamaican woman and got her pregnant. I have a four-year-old half-sister, Tiffany. She's a real cutie pie."

Malachi didn't speak.

"Mom was devastated as you could imagine. She threatened to go back to the States and take me with her. They fought some more over that, and I guess I had a setback. It wasn't as bad as before, but it was what it was." She shifted in her seat, and her face suddenly lit up.

"You see, Malachi, that's how I know how powerful Jesus really is."

"OK."

"I mean, here I was in therapy, trying to regain control and sort through all the stuff that was going on around me, when out of the blue I get invited to this camp. My parents reluctantly released me. I heard the Gospel explained in a way that I'd never heard before. My folks were never religious, and Jesus wasn't exactly the most popular topic at my old school.

"I said 'yes' to the invitation to give my life to Christ and, Malachi, all I can tell you is that something inside me broke. I left camp knowing that it didn't matter what life threw at me; I was like, 'bring it on.' For the first time in my life, I allowed myself to hope; I mean, really hope that life would get better for me."

"So that was it for therapy?"

"No. I still go to the group outpatient sessions, though not as frequently. That's the other part that's so amazing. Before long, they were asking me to help others who had similar problems. My whole life had taken on new meaning. My parents were skeptical at first, and I couldn't blame them given my history, but when they saw my grades going through the roof and the positive reports from my counselors and my teachers, they knew that I'd turned a corner."

"Wow, Abby. One would never know by just looking at you that you've been through all that."

"Trust me that's the short version." She paused and looked at the curtain as it gave a light flutter.

"There's one more thing I should tell you. Alesha and I met at Immaculate Conception High School. Some of the students gave me a hard time when I first started school here in Jamaica. They teased me about my accent, about being American, stupid stuff like that. Back then, Alesha was the only person to really stand up for me. We became best friends in record time; we were inseparable, actually. I confided about what I'd been through, what I was still going through, and she was there for me as best she could. We'd planned to come on campus together, sign up for the same hall. When I got saved, naturally, I tried to share my faith with her, but I guess my zeal got the better of me.

"She and Jerome were already an item, and I saw signs that the relationship wasn't altogether...healthy. I hit her hard with the fornication, you're-going-to-hell-on-the-A-train, kind a thing, and she just switched me off."

"You think you shouldn't have told her all that?" Malachi asked, as he swallowed the last morsel of sandwich.

"I don't know, I think I was a bit self-righteous back then. If I had to do it again, I might have taken a different approach. You know, less fire and brimstone, and more love. I think that's what Paul meant when he said he's become all things to all men so that he might win some."

"I hear you."

Abby got up and closed the balcony door. Malachi took that as his cue to leave. He stood up.

"It's getting late. Thank you for the sandwiches and..." He lifted the empty glass. She took the utensils from him.

"My pleasure. Hey, wait a sec." She walked over to her bookcase and pulled a sheet of paper from a manila folder tucked between two med books and handed it to Malachi.

"What's this?"

"It's a—It's a letter to take to student services for meal vouchers. All the peer counselors and hall committee members are asked to distribute them to students...Basically...uh...as we see fit."

Malachi stared at the letter in his hand for five seconds, and then transferred his gaze to Abby. "Wow. I can't believe it. You know, you just killed a perfectly good evening?" He crumbled the letter with one hand, yanked the door open, and slammed it shut behind him.

Abby's body jerked as the door rattled. She stood in the same spot staring at the brown oil paint on the door.

"Stupid, stupid Abby," she said aloud and smacked her forehead with the palm of her hand. Abby turned and leaned against the door.

"I should have let it go. Why didn't I let it go, Lord?" she whispered as she used her palms to rub up and down her arms. It was a habit she'd adopted when she wanted to self-soothe, and it would have worked had she not been interrupted by the vibrations that accompanied the sudden knock on her door.

Without checking the peephole, she opened the door.

Malachi stood with his hands taut in his cargo pants pock-ets—an expression of angst on his face. "You think you're so smart and discerning. Saint Abby has it all figured out. I bet you fantasize about having your own radio talk show, 'Ask Dr. Abby.' Well, why are we waiting? Let's practice, nah. Maybe you can start by telling me—"

Sonya, one of Abby's blockmates, walked past Malachi as he stood in front of Abby's doorway. She slowed her stride and cut him a warning look as she passed. He lowered his voice and relaxed his posture.

"Tell me." He shook his head and bit his lower lip. "Why… Why, Doctor Abigail Shaw, did God allow my beautiful mother to kill herself? Hmm. Where are my answers, Abby?"

CHAPTER ELEVEN

The stainless steel electric kettle on Abby's desk spewed its steamy contents in one determined blast. Malachi watched on as the kettle reverberated, almost imperceptibly, on its base. He somehow understood the object's struggle to compose itself, to channel its energy so that, at the end of the day, it could be of some use. Anyone who'd ever handled one of these kettles knew not to be fooled by the placid exterior—that this was the most dangerous phase of the water-heating process, and that the object was better left alone until the automatic safety switch tripped.

She knew the drill. Abby allowed a few seconds to elapse even after the red light flicked off signaling the all-clear to pour the water. She didn't bother ask him if he wanted a cup. She simply handed him the bone white tea cup and saucer and padded over to her fridge to retrieve the cream and sugar.

"One or two," she asked, holding the silver sugar bowl in her hand. "Three," he responded and deepened his dimple.

Abby cradled the handle of her teacup between her fingers. She took a sip of her tea and crossed her legs at the ankles as if she had all the time in the world. She looked over at her guest from her favorite spot in the middle of her bed. He was still standing.

Malachi was conscious of the fact that he was standing on Abby's rug with his shoes on. He suspected she must have noticed, but she didn't look perturbed. Right about now, he didn't feel like following her rules.

"I don't like when people judge me—like they know me. We just met. We had some interesting conversations, but you don't know me."

"You're right. I don't."

"So what was the letter about? You suddenly got it in your head that I'm poor and needy?"

Abby sipped her tea. She took her time replacing the teacup on the saucer.

"I'm sorry the letter offended you, Malachi. I thought you might be interested in…support. Lots of students are. Perhaps I got it wrong this time."

Malachi looked up at the ceiling.

"You didn't get it wrong. I do…" He cleared his throat, "need support. I just didn't think I wore that fact on my sleeve."

"You don't. I mean that. You don't."

"Cool."

The pause stretched toward a minute.

"So, like I said, my mom killed herself." He said it nonchalantly.

Abby remained silent.

"No note or anything. I guess one day she just decided that I wasn't enough of a reason to live. Dad and me. Yep." He placed the cup and saucer on Abby's desk and leaned against the desk. He folded his arms and crossed his lower legs as if bracing himself for Abby's response.

She'd been trained well enough not to allow her emotions to dominate her face. Abby had also learned about attending and reflecting during her basic counseling training. She was supposed to be paraphrasing just about now, but in this situation the techniques felt contrived somehow, and she wanted to be real with him. She felt he needed her to be real.

"Um, Dr. Abby, hello? How yuh doing this wuk, girl? This is where you are supposed to say, 'So your mom killed herself' and I am supposed to break down, freak out, and spill my guts until there is no more guts to be spilt."

Abby cocked her head and smiled across at him.

"Well, first of all, I wish you would stop calling me Dr. Abby. I'm not trying to be something I'm not. Secondly, I'm not your counselor. This whole…" —she made a frantic hand gesture— "is way beyond my skill level. The most I can be to you is a friend—nothing more, nothing less. Hope that's OK with you, 'cause that's all I've got."

Her words were strong, but they were sincere. Malachi knew he had a choice: rebuff Abby's invitation or…open up. The latter was beyond difficult, but he figured he'd already taken the first step by coming back into her space when he could easily have kept walking.

"Do you want the long version or the short one?" He tightened the fold on his arms and lifted the corners of his mouth in a satisfying smug for throwing her own words back at her.

"Any version you're comfortable with," she replied without batting an eye and tossed a few pillows on the floor.

CHAPTER TWELVE

Malachi always knew that his mom was different.

"Different and beautiful," he said with a smile. "She was very pretty. Dark, smooth skin. Slim, athletic build, although I never saw her lift a dumbbell in my life. Natural, model-like features. Beauty and brains as Dad used to say. She didn't really look like the teacher type, yuh know?"

Abby wanted to ask what that type looked like but decided that it really wasn't that important.

Over the years, he would hear stories of how his mom would publicly interrogate and sometimes berate Mr. St. John, his former primary school principal, at PTA meetings. She questioned Mr. St. John about what he was doing about the leaky toilets, the promised computer lab, the pigeon droppings at the entrance of the Infant Department. She had no tolerance for administrators or teachers who were comfortably inept or absent from their duties without just cause. The other parents loved her; the teachers couldn't stand her.

"By the time I got to Form Two at secondary school, Dad started to insist on attending PTA meetings alone. I heard him telling someone over the phone that Lavern's poor judgment was an embarrassment. That she was putting me at a disadvantage with her harsh criticism of the principal and teachers. He said it was ironic that she was a teacher herself."

But Malachi never felt disadvantaged. As far as he was concerned that show of "poor judgment" helped him pass his eleven plus exam for one of the top high schools in the country, despite his below-par primary school. Thanks to his mom, the Form One French teacher at the new school was replaced midterm because, according to Lavern, "she was no good." It was his mom who'd told the math teacher, Mr. Butcher, during a packed PTA meeting that he had pervy tendencies.

That, according to his dad, was the final straw. After that, Mr. Williamson was politely asked to instruct Mrs. Williamson to sensor her remarks at the PTA meetings. Mr. Williamson knew that that was like trying to instruct the Niagara Falls to try trickling for a change.

Malachi often wondered how many people remembered his mother's comments two years later when two plain clothes police officers from the Special Branch unit escorted Mr. Butcher out of the school yard. That Friday was Butcher's last day at the school—any school.

"I knew what it was to have fun and enjoy the finer things in life because of my mother."

Malachi told Abby that his mother was the one who introduced him to fine dining, designer brands, or "the good stuff" as she called it. Her shopping sprees were legendary, and the result was often the same: ridiculously high credit card bills and heated arguments between his parents about money.

"Your mom was bipolar?"

Malachi, who was lying on the floor with just a pillow under his head, pushed up on his elbows. "OK, I'm officially impressed. You know, I never heard that word uttered in our house. I had to do my own research to figure it all out. You tagged it in two seconds."

When his parents argued, Malachi told Abby, he would often hear his dad reprove his mom about her judgment, or lack thereof. It was the reason that for all her shopping sprees, especially the ones to Margarita, New York, and Miami, his dad never allowed Malachi to go with her.

"How did she function on the job?" Abby wanted to know.

"She was a brilliant teacher. In fact, that's how she and my dad met."

Lavern Hospedales was a bright, young English teacher fresh out of university. She was accepted to teach at her alma mater, a convent in Port of Spain. Teaching was her passion and her facile manner made her easily a favorite among the girls. One day the convent hosted a career open day and a dapper, young social worker named Malachi Williamson was sent to man the booth on social work.

"Dad said he believed it was love at first sight. It's the most romantic thing I ever heard him say in his life."

Malachi said his mom knew a different side of his dad—a fun-loving side that visited museums and historical sites. In their early years of marriage, they even went island hopping every chance they got.

"I don't know what happened to that person, but the father I remembered growing up was seriously tight-fisted. Do you know he cut up my mom's credit cards? She was a mess after that. Didn't talk to him…or me, pretty much for days."

"He probably felt he didn't have a choice. The manic episode could be pretty brutal to the family's finances, from what I've read."

Malachi shrugged.

"She hated doctors." He searched Abby's face for a reaction.

"Well, maybe *hate* might be too strong a word. Let's say she didn't have much faith in them."

Malachi told Abby that a doctor had told her mother that she probably couldn't have children. Something about polycystic ovaries and slim chances of getting pregnant.

"I remember her saying to me, 'He was wrong, Malachi. The silly doctor was wrong. You are living proof."

Malachi slumped down on the rug again, his fingers entwined behind his head.

He pushed up on his elbows again. "Why don't you get a couch? I bet this would go much faster if I were laying on a nice, comfy couch. Your parents have money; ask them for a couch," he said, and scratched his dimpled cheek.

"You have jokes. That's good," Abby said with a nod, and left it at that.

When it was time to choose subjects at the end of Form Three, Malachi told Abby that he came home excited one day. He'd enjoyed his introduction to the pure sciences and was pretty sure that he had a natural interest in medicine. His chat with the doctor who visited his school for Career Day, sealed it for him.

"You know some parents would be excited about the prospect of their child wanting to become a doctor. Not mom. She was in a dark mood that day. She was still in her night gown when I got home—same way I left her that morning. I thought the news would perk her up, you know. She just sighed and said 'I guess you could do worse.'"

"Wow," Abby said without inflection. She knew she wasn't supposed to say stuff like that, but her mouth outran her brain on that one.

"I guess a doctor also told her that she was bipolar," he continued. "She must have figured that if the other guy was wrong about her not being able to have children, the head doctor must be wrong, too. I think she was on lithium at one point."

"She was on lithium?"

"At some point, yes. I think she'd stop taking it, though. I suspect she got fed up of having to depend on a mood stabilizer to keep her centered. I don't know. She never really talked about it. Sometimes I wonder if she ever accepted that she was...you know."

He suddenly sniffed out a laugh.

"Want to hear something funny?"

"OK."

"She used to accuse dad of having a mistress."

"Why is that funny?"

"It's funny because she said the mistress was the church! She said he loved the church more than her."

"Was she into church too?"

"Yeah. They were both big on church. Church, ministry, missions—the works. She got saved first when they were courting I think. She invited him to church, and he gave his life as well. They raised me in the Lord, I'd have you know: Sunday school, Bible Study, prayer meeting—the whole shebang."

"OK."

Malachi stared at the ceiling. "I think things got weird for my mom," he said. "You know, it's hard to always figure out with the mentally ill what is the illness talking and what is...well, God. I think some of the brethren branded her. Nobody seemed quite sure how to help. I mean, what do we do here? Do we cast out a demon? Do we tell her to take her meds? Do we agree with her that she's healed? It just became difficult for her to function, and I think, in some small way, Dad was relieved that she had stopped going."

"What? No. I mean, isn't that a bit… judgmental? I don't know your dad or anything, but that doesn't sound fair at all."

"Maybe it isn't, I don't know…I guess I just wish somebody knew what to do. You know? Maybe it would have been different."

"I so hear you." Her voice was almost a whisper as she reflected on what he'd shared so far.

Malachi sat up.

"She…Things got real bad, real fast. I think she was trying to get pregnant again. I overheard that conversation too…What can I say? My dad talks really loudly over the stupid phone. She used to tell me that I needed a brother or sister—that I shouldn't be alone in the world. I told her I didn't mind…that."

Malachi bowed his head. His arms dangled loosely from their perched position on his knees.

"I told her that I had her… that she was enough." His voice had cracked in mid-sentence. He cleared his throat.

Abby pulled at a lock of her hair and began to twiddle it around her finger.

"Mom had to take early retirement because she started doing erratic things at school like crying for hours in the staff room. She would go to the chapel on the school compound and try to light all the candles. She would kneel and pray the rosary and, of course, we weren't even Catholic. I mean they always knew Mrs. Williamson was a little… quirky, I suppose, but it was cute and endearing… until it wasn't anymore. Parents began to complain—pressure the school to act. The girls were scared I guess."

He stopped to nibble at his thumb nail.

"The worst part was when she didn't come home. It didn't happen often I think, but it happened. Dad was a mess.

"I would…cry. I cried so much back then. After the funeral, people told Dad they were worried about me because they didn't see me bawl my eyes out. I hate when people judge you like that. I mean by the time she…you know…I felt like I was all cried out—like somebody just took me and wrung out the living daylights out a me, like a jeans that you have to wear later and you want it to dry fast, and you don't have a dryer, so you have to put it in front the fan."

It was Abby's turn to bite her nails.

"Do you know that she…at the end of my first year in Sixth Form. I'd just finished my final exam in Lower Six. Everyone was surprised that I did so well in Upper Six—given the circumstances. But I had to do well, Abby. It was school or nothing, and nothing wasn't going to cut it for me."

"Did you see anyone?"

"Counselor-wise?"

She nodded.

"Course. The school provided one. I saw someone at church. But I told them what they wanted to hear; I wasn't ready to talk. I guess I was still very upset with her."

"With your mom?"

"Both of them. Dad…He basically shut down. I mean, big deacon, could preach his head off. He's real good, by the way. But he had precious little to say at home to his own son. I mean, we were both hurting. What's so wrong with hurting together— showing that you're human, instead of behaving like it didn't all just happen to us—like our world didn't just crash and burn before our very eyes. I hated that. Man I hated that!" He'd raise his voice again.

Abby waited as his breathing rate reverted to normal again.

"How?" She cleared her throat. "Excuse me. How did she…?"

"Yuh rushing me, Abby. I—I don't know how you're doing this thing, nah. Man!"

"I'm sorry!" Abby said, affronted.

"Abby, jeeze. I'm just kicksing. You're a pro. Relax. Trust me, I'm telling you more than all the counselors I saw back then put together."

Abby exhaled. She tossed a pillow at him.

"Would you just go on, please. Thank yew," she said, imitating a more nasal version of her accent.

He'd known something was wrong when his dad had showed up at his school just after lunch with Mr. Quashie of all people. Malachi explained to Abby that the Quashies lived next to the Williamsons. Mr. Quashie was a portly man in his sixties. He drove a taxi which over time nobody in the neighborhood would patronize simply because they felt Mr. Quashie didn't know how to speak to people. When Mr. Cummings had mentioned that Mrs. Riley's daughter was getting married,

Mr. Quashie was reported to have asked if it was one of those Internet relationships.

"Come now, Cummings, who Mister that get a good look at that girl would marry she, eh? Leh we speak the truth," was how he'd summed up the situation. Of course, it got back to the Rileys.

And when Boysie, who owns the neighborhood mini mart, bought the corner house for his youngest son, Ravi, Mr. Quashie was the one who'd told Boysie to his face, "Well yeah. Yuh have to wash the money somehow."

It was meant to be a joke.

"Dem kinda joke eh funny, Willie boy," Boysie had told his dad one Saturday morning when Mr. Williamson was buying a hand of green fig to make fish broth.

Malachi had had his own experience with Mr. Quashie. It was raining, and he was sheltering under the eaves outside the roti shop near the Tunapuna taxi stand. The taxi stand was empty at the time. Someone in a white Bluebird had pulled up in front of the roti shop and was blaring his horn with determination. When Malachi looked, he saw that it was Mr. Quashie, motioning for him to run to the car. Malachi did as told. That day, Mr. Quashie had seemed overjoyed to have the young student as a passenger. He'd chit chatted about how hard taxi work had become with all the private cars undercutting the legitimate taxis, and the school children who were only looking for new cars with shiny rims and hard pong.

"That's Trini slang for loud music from a seriously sweet sound system," he explained.

"Figured as much."

Malachi told Abby that Mr. Quashie lamented the fact that even his own neighbors would hold their heads straight when he would drive by.

"Ah know they see meh, yuh know, but they pretending not to see meh," the elderly man had said, the faint smell of moth balls in the air. "But young Williamson, I eh begging nobody. Yuh doh want to travel with meh, yuh doh want to travel with meh. No biggie."

The topic switched to school, and Mr. Quashie told Malachi said that he'd heard through the grapevine that he'd done brilliantly at his Fifth Form exams. Malachi confirmed that he had.

"So, what yuh want to be when yuh get big?"

"A doctor," he'd replied without hesitation.

It had been his only choice for some years now, and despite his mother's indifference, his heart was fixed. Mr. Quashie had nodded and stolen a glance at his front seat passenger before returning his gaze to the road. The answer had pleased him.

"Yesssss man. Dat is what I like to hear. I is a big man and yuh make meh want to release meh eye water. Beat them books hard, young black man. Yuh hear what ah telling yuh? Become a doctor and help out yuh poor mother, boy. Because yuh know she need plenty, plenty help. Nice man."

When Abby caught herself she was covering her mouth. Her brain was short-circuiting again.

Malachi said he never told his dad about what Mr. Quashie had said that day. Instead, he quietly joined the list of neighbors who would rather walk their soles thin before they hop in Mr. Quashie's taxi.

So when Mr. Quashie pulled up at his school with his dad in the front seat, he knew, as the local saying goes, "water was more than flour" with his mom.

Malachi recalled that she'd come home in the wee hours of the morning. He was up late doing last minute cramming for an exam later that morning, so he'd heard when she'd got in. There was no argument with his dad—at least none that he'd heard.

Her moods were changing faster now. She'd been more troubled and restless than usual for days. That morning, before Malachi left for school, she'd been up cooking eggs. She'd made him sit and have breakfast. She'd kissed him and wished him good success in his exams when he'd told her that he had to go. Then, she'd called him back, and kissed him again.

His mom had looked normal enough to him that day—except for what he'd known of the time she'd got in. Her insomnia was also beginning to show up as puffiness under her eyes.

"Next thing I knew, I was sitting in the back seat of Quashie's car. Dad didn't even tell me where we were going or why he'd come for me. But I'm not stupid. I figured we were either going straight home or to the hospital. Either way, my gut told me it was about mom."

It was a ten minute drive to the Port of Spain General Hospital, give or take two minutes, depending on traffic conditions.

Malachi didn't ask his dad any questions when he saw him. He simply got into the back seat of Mr. Quashie's car and stared at his dad's face in the side mirror. Malachi Junior figured when his dad was ready, he'd talk.

"Dad looked sad and tired. Very tired."

There was a distinct smell of vomit in the car, despite the fact that the car glass was all the way down.

"For the first few minutes, nobody spoke. I still remember the howling of the breeze as it blew through the window. It felt like it was louder than even the sound of the traffic. Thought that kind of howling only happened in movies."

Mr. Quashie had kept glancing across at Mr. Williamson who was still staring out his window. Every now and then Mr. Quashie cleared his throat and mumbled something. When he'd reached the part of the Queen's Park Savannah that would lead to the General Hospital, the lights had changed to red. Mr. Quashie had looked over again at his front seat passenger and had shaken his head. Malachi figured that's when he knew he had to be a neighbor indeed.

"Young Williamson. Today boy. Like today is when yuh become a man. Yuh hear meh, son? Yuh mother, like she take some pills, boy, and she not looking good at all. Yuh father...well, yuh see he condition. Yuh is a small man, but a small man is still a man. Call on Jesus, boy, and He will hear yuh. Yuh mother had tell meh that years ago when meh sugar was sky high and yuh same father here had was to rush meh to the hospital. They was threatening to cut off meh foot. Ah take she advice and it work for me. Look ah still have meh two foot good as ever. What ah go say, boy? Sorry it didn't work out for she."

With that, Malachi Senior released the most heart-wrenching wail that Malachi had ever heard from a grown man.

CHAPTER THIRTEEN

"Thalia, that was good. No, I mean it." Megan bent slightly and rested her hand on the shoulder of the fifteen year old. "It's obvious that you've been working very hard, but we're not quite there yet."

Megan took Thalia's hand and led her to the center of the rehearsal hall. All eyes followed.

"Where is my Prince?"

"Here I am, here I am," the sixteen-year-old dancer practically sang, before leaping across the studio in traveling jete and landing just shy of Megan and Thalia. Parents on the sidelines applauded.

"So, you think you have skills, do you?" Megan asked, a flicker of a smile on her face.

"I know I have skills," Devon countered, his smile now obliterated and his chin hoist in what Megan recognized as a posture of defensiveness.

"And you do. You also have confidence, which is good." She reached out and took his hand in her left hand and Thalia's in her right. Her voice lowered as she spoke to the two dancers in front of her.

"I need you guys to work together as a team, help each other. Right now." She tightened the squeeze on Devon's hand. "Your pas de deux at the end with the Sugar Plum Fairy leaves much to be desired.

"It's obvious you have skills, Devon, but you need some of Thalia's consistency and discipline." Devon shook his head.

"Thalia." Megan swung her arm. "You have so much potential, but I wish you would believe in yourself. If you had half of Devon's confidence it would make a tremendous difference. Remember you are Clara, the principal dancer in this show. My dear Thalia, you are..." In one seamless move, Megan lifted her chin and rose en pointe with both arms in an arch above her head. "The Ballerina."

Thalia beamed.

An older woman with salt and pepper hair pulled back in a tight bun, began clapping to summon the cast center stage.

"Where are my mice? Where are my mice?" The lady with the hair called in a voice that seemed to devour the room. Two dozen squealing and tittering children—mostly girls in various colored tights and leotards—scurried to the center of the hall and formed a semi-circle around Megan, the leads, and the older instructor.

From his spot just left of where the parents were seated, Malachi crouched with his back against the waist-high wooden panel that encased the inside wall of the auditorium. The panel, he thought, gave the state-of-the art theatre a touch of retro elegance.

He couldn't hear what they were saying in the huddle. The lady with the salt and pepper hair was speaking now—something she said made everybody laugh. A moment later the noise level soared as children scampered across the auditorium to where their parents were waiting.

"Don't forget to do your turn out exercises at home between rehearsals," Megan shouted above the din.

It was obvious she was in her element here. Malachi had never really given much thought to ballet or any other kind of dance for that matter. His only encounter with ballet came at age eleven, in the school break after he found out that he'd passed his eleven plus exam for the secondary school that he had elected as his first choice. He told his mom that his friend Darren's parents were taking him on a trip to Europe to celebrate his first-choice placement.

"They are going to take him to England, France, Germany, and Italy." Malachi was practically breathless as he related it all to his mom, who, as he recalled, was washing dishes by the kitchen sink. "Can you and Dad take me there too? Pleeease Mom!" he had pleaded.

Two weeks later, his mother had woken him up from sleep to tell him that she had bought tickets to see Sleeping Beauty as performed by a visiting French Ballet Company at Queen's Hall—the island's oldest venue for all things artsy.

"We may not be able to take you to France right now, Malachi, but it looks like France has come to us! Isn't God good?" She'd practically leapt with joy.

The details of the ballet were a bit fuzzy now, but Malachi recalled that it was a very elaborate performance—the only one he'd ever seen live, not counting the fleeting images he had picked up while channel surfing at his Aunt Barbara's house. He remembered sitting next to his mom feigning absolute boredom, but being secretly awed by the male leads that were single-handedly lifting ballerinas as if they were petals in a flower girl's pomander. But as fascinating as it all seemed, Malachi knew back then, as he did now, that he'd rather die before he allowed any of his friends to see him skipping around in a pair of tights. The young dude he saw in action a moment ago, he thought, was a better man than he.

"Hey, you came, "Megan said as she walked toward him. She looked slightly flushed, and she had a wide grin on her face.

"Of course, you didn't leave me much of a choice. Your note said 'Pick me up from the theater at eight p.m. Thanks, Megan.'"

"And here you are." She practically beamed.

"Here I am," Malachi said, and bit back the smile that was sending his dimples into overdrive. They stood for a few seconds staring at each other.

"Give me five minutes to change into my trackers," she finally said after clearing her throat.

"Only five?"

"Oh yes, we ballerinas invented the term quick change. When that curtain goes up, you better be in place." With that, she skipped toward the side door that led to the dressing rooms.

****

At night, the university lit up like a small, bustling town. Students zip about from hall to hall, entering and leaving the campus, making trips to and from the library, the grocery, nearby eating establishments, and recreational spots.

A pizza delivery man puttered past on a motorbike. No helmet. The familiar smell wafted over reminding Malachi of the big step he had taken earlier that day. He'd awoken early that morning and had gone across to the student services department before his first class to sign up for meal vouchers. The Jamaican woman who had attended to him at the counter had been neither sentimental nor brusque about the whole thing. She moved like it was just another transaction, as if he were paying fees or collecting a bursary check. There had been nothing patronizing in her tone when she was taking his contact details, nor when she was briefing him on the rules for using the vouchers. Malachi was grateful for that.

He had Abby to thank for nudging him to chuck his pride and go for the vouchers. After storming out of her room the night before, he'd returned, and ended up spending an extra half an hour telling Abby about his family's many adventures with his bipolar mother. In a sense, the talk, which was more like a monologue now that he thought about it, had been cathartic. He had never shared quite so much about his mother's illness. Not even with Caleb.

"If you're thinking about auditioning for *The Nutcracker*, the answer is yes. We can do with some more male dancers," Megan said, breaking the silence.

Malachi's smile was quick. "Sorry, I went into a bit of a zone there. I was thinking about how this place really comes alive in the night, don't you think?"

"I've noticed that. My best friend, Sylvia, who happens to be white, attends the University of Sunderland, and she has been complaining bitterly about how everything seems to shut down after six, except for the pubs of course."

"So how did you and Sylvia become friends?"

"We attended the same boarding school, and I guess we were both hopeless misfits that found each other. She, because she was from Newcastle and the girls used to make fun of her Geordie accent, and I because I was biracial, I guess, and a bit of an introvert back then, I must confess. I still am to some extent."

Malachi thought of the Catwoman moniker and decided against telling her.

"So do you and Sylvia keep in touch?"

"We call each other fairly regularly on our cell phones."

"Isn't that like… expensive?"

"I don't know…I never thought of it, actually. Dad gets the bill. If it's ridiculous, I'd imagine he would tell me. He likes to complain about bills. Says it makes him appear more down-to-earth in some quarters. He's always saying that he doesn't want Paul and me to behave like the nouveau riche; he wants us to appreciate that money doesn't grow on trees."

"You and your brother are close."

"Oh, we're as thick as thieves, the pair of us. He calls me every two days or so. Actually, he's the reason I asked you to escort me home tonight."

"Really?"

"Yes. When I told him about my rehearsal schedule, he went into typical big brother mode asking a zillion questions about how and when I got back to hall. When I told him that I walked and described how busy and well-lit the campus was, he cursed and told me that he would not hesitate to fly over and clobber me in the head like he did when we were little if I didn't get a worthy male to escort me home."

"Well, I guess I should be truly honored to be considered a worthy male, Ms. Le Blanc." Malachi bowed slightly.

She curtseyed. "You should be…Besides, I figured anyone who would intercept a slap and subsequently take a punch like you did the other night is more than worthy. Should be knighted, really. In fact, I'll be sure to call her Majesty with the request. Given my deep connections with all things British—as you'd recall from the Colin Firth episode—it should be a breeze. Fear not, Bob's your Uncle." She shrugged.

"Bob's my Uncle? Megan, where do you get these things?" Malachi laughed until he felt his eyes water. He had to admit that her droll brand of humor was one of the things that he found most attractive about her.

"I was wondering when you were going to bring that up...the incident I mean," Malachi said, suddenly conscious of his injury. "Actually I didn't get an opportunity to thank you for your first aid. You were gone by the time I woke up. Sure you don't want to join me in Med Sci? I hear the island is short of nurses you know."

"Who says I would want to be a nurse? Doctor or nothing!"

Malachi lifted his palm. "Excuse me."

"You're excused," she said with a hoist of her chin.

She looks so gorgeous when she does that.

They passed Turner Hall Cafeteria. Malachi saw the place in darkness, the doors tightly shut.

Drats, I should have bought that sandwich before I left to pick her up.

A comfortable silence fell between them.

Malachi looked ahead at the poui trees that lined the final stretch that led to Sutton Hall. The trees on both sides of the road intersected to form a natural arbor which provided a break from the merciless midday sun, especially for Suttonites who were returning to hall for lunch. In the dry season, from January to May, the blossoms transformed the street into a yellow and pink canopy that made the world seem perfect. Those who'd seen it, described it as nothing short of breathtaking.

The night was a different story. The same picture-perfect image that rejuvenated the soul after a long day of classes, appeared eerie when the sun dipped, despite the sporadic people and vehicular traffic, and intervals of lights poking out of the shrubbery to illuminate the footpath. Even the vibrations of leaves as they swayed to the strum of chords from the evening breeze, struggled in their efforts to charm.

Malachi's eyes scanned his surroundings. He was glad that Megan's brother had insisted on her being escorted back to hall after rehearsals, and he was still intrigued with the realization that she'd chosen him.

"So you're involved in a major production?"

"Oh yes, *The Nutcracker*; it's so exciting. For the majority of the cast, it's their big introduction to classical ballet."

"Is that another secret reason for choosing to study in Jamaica?"

"Oh heavens no; it's a bit of luck, I suppose. I went to get more information about everything dance and I saw the rehearsal in progress. Afterwards, Madame Francois, the older lady you saw in there, asked me some questions about my experience, and when she heard that that I was part of a prestigious dance school back home, she asked me to show her some moves."

"And you dazzled her?"

"And the eleven-odd parents there that day apparently. All I did were some arabesques en pointe, a few pirouettes, pose turns, and fouettes. That's all."

Malachi sniffed out a laugh. "You know very well I didn't understand a thing you just said, but…" The smile that cradled his cheeks just moments before, fell. "I sure like the way you said it."

Their eyes met and held for what seemed like eternity.

Was it her imagination or did the timbre in his voice dip a decibel with the compliment? Megan wasn't sure. She was, nevertheless, grateful for the darkness so that Malachi couldn't see how her color had changed.

Get a grip Megan. She chided herself.

She was the first to look away. "Well, um, OK. Madame Francois told me that the university asked her to do an adaptation of *The Nutcracker* this winter. Sorry. December. The cast had begun rehearsing since August, and she asked if I would like to join. She said she needed someone with my experience to help her train the leads, and some of the other older students, in the classical ballet bits—take everyone in turn out exercises, that sort of thing.

"And you said 'of course.'"

"Absolutely. This is a rare opportunity for someone at my level. That was the Friday. By Monday, I suppose word got around because the class had doubled. Many of the parents, who, I was told, were used to coming just before the end, were there from the very beginning and stayed for the entire rehearsal. I'm actually thinking of asking my dad to start up a ballet charity here."

"Why?"

"Because I noticed that many of the children, especially the younger ones that are not attached to a ballet school, don't have the basic tights and leotards, and Madame Francois warned me not to be too particular about the rehearsal dress code because many of them genuinely can't afford it."

"I guess that proves my theory that ballet is a rich kid thing," Malachi said, not fully conscious that a layer of irritation had suffused his tone.

"Well, remember what I said about ballet and the black thing? It's changing. That's why the cast is so diverse. Madame Francois could have picked her cast exclusively from the island's ballet schools, but she didn't. Things must change. She gets that. The rich kid thing, as you call it, is changing too."

"Not fast enough apparently." Malachi didn't quite know what about a ballet charity offended his sensibilities, but it did. Or perhaps it was because her father, who sounded so stodgy and pretentious, would be the one doling out the handouts.

"But what about IR Megan—you know that little degree you signed up for?"

"Under control. I don't intend to mess up there. You see when I first told my parents that I wanted to do ballet, they said 'yes,' but if it starts to interfere with my grades it was 'bye bye ballet'. Well that was a challenge that I took quite seriously, and I've always performed brilliantly in my studies. It's the way I'm built. I study hard in the day so that I can dance in the evening. I already told Madame Francois that my Saturdays are for catching up on assignments, and my Sundays are for dinner with my parents and personal time, which for me means more ballet."

Malachi and Megan walked up the steps at Sutton and along the S-shaped pathway that connected the blocks. They passed the communal reading room. It was half empty, but it reminded Malachi that after he saw Megan safely to her door, he was in debt to his books for at least two hours of study time.

They arrived at Megan's door. She turned the key and stepped inside. Megan looked around to see Malachi still standing at the door.

"Hey, I have something for you. Come on in," she said, and unzipped her trackers.

CHAPTER FOURTEEN

Malachi scooped out the last bit of yogurt from the little cup and pulled back the lid on a second. In less than two minutes he'd finished the second.

Megan had told him to help himself to whatever was in the fridge, but there wasn't much real food: bottles of water, yogurt, milk, cheese, and about a week's supply of fruit. He choose an apple and decided to cut a decent size bundle of grapes. He wrapped it in a napkin and tucked it between the pajama top that Megan had folded and left on the black and white ottoman he was standing next to.

Was that stealing? Of course not; she told me to help myself. Why am I hiding it then?

He reached over and removed the bundle of grapes from between the pajama top and placed it on the napkin which he adjusted to protect the ottoman from possible stains.

He'd seen the room before, but when he got up that morning after the Jama Night incident, he was already running late for his first class and there simply wasn't time to appreciate his surroundings. Here was his chance to take it all in. The design and layout of the room reflected careful thought and discriminating taste. Megan had maximized her space by pushing the two single beds together with only an infinitesimal space between them.

I wonder how her roommate feels about that?

The sheets on the single beds had two distinct patterns, one was black with a black and white polka dot pillow slip. The other sheet was white with a diagonally-striped pillow slip and a cluster of diagonal stripes near the center of the bed. A chrome and glass entertainment center, complete with television, DVD player, a sound system, and two built-in shelves which contained books, stood to the right of the beds. It was angled in such a way that you couldn't see the TV screen from the bed.

Malachi noted that it was the second room he'd visited in the past few days with significant edits to the original furnishings. In Megan's room, the entertainment center, fridge, wall-mounted mirrors and ottoman, were the big ticket items that he knew the standard accommodation fees did not cover.

Half of the room was empty space. Two floor-to-ceiling mirrors were placed side by side covering half of the wall facing south of her beds. Malachi imagined that they were installed especially for her. He had no idea that those kinds of requests were facilitated.

Megan's desk and chair were missing. Malachi figured they could be behind her closed balcony doors. Her chest of drawers and wardrobe were pushed against the wall to the left of the beds.

Malachi walked over to the large, framed black and white photo of Mahatma Gandhi that stood to the right of the mirrored portion of her wall. A line of framed black and white photos of ballet dancers in various positions radiated out from the right of the Gandhi photo.

Megan reentered the room from the bathroom wearing a white robe. She was drying her hair with a big, white towel.

"The girls' rooms have side tables. Where are yours?"

"Didn't want them; didn't need them," she said, as she made her way to the chest of drawers. Malachi saw her open her top drawer and pull something out. She turned around and saw him watching her.

"I'd like to put on some extra clothes. Do you mind?"

Malachi returned his gaze to the black and white photos. He resisted the temptation to glance into the mirrors.

"Who's your roommate, Megan?"

"Thumbelina."

"That's a real person?"

"Well, it's the name I gave the nosy girl who asked me about my roommate. You can look now."

The robe was off. Megan had somehow changed into an olive-colored tank top and gray three-quarter drawstring sweatpants that bunched up just above her knees. She took a seat in the center of the left bed and tucked her legs under her.

"So, there's no roommate? But all the first years have one. How did you manage that?"

"The same way I managed to have the studio mirrors installed," she said, and waved her hand blithely toward the wall-mounted mirrors. "I wanted a barre as well, but, alas, the warden grew a spine and said no."

"But you have two beds; why not just one?"

"The warden. Again. He insisted I keep both to perpetuate the charade of having a roommate. He didn't quite put it like that, of course, but what he said was tantamount to it. Malachi, you'd be surprised what you get away with when your parents make a little donation here and there."

"My dad calls that bribery," he said, without an ounce of guile in his voice.

She shrugged and decided to save the challenge for another time.

"How come the TV is angled like that? You can't really see anything from here, nor from your—beds for that matter." The laughter in his eyes, rang through as he said *beds*.

"Oh we have jokes, do we?" She took up her nearest pillow and tossed it at him.

"Hey, you should have tossed your own pillow. I don't think Thumba would appreciate you messing with her—."

She fired the second pillow before he could finish.

"You have strong arms to go with those legs. Nice."

"The TV is angled like that so that I can view my dance videos. I don't watch TV really." She got up from her bed and walked over to her stereo. She slipped in a CD and in two second the room was filled with some kind of classical piece that Malachi didn't recognize.

Everything about her oozed money and privilege.

She lowered the volume.

"Who is this?" he asked.

"This is Tchaikovsky's score. For *The Nutcracker*," she added, in response to his blank expression.

He watched her sit up straight on her bed, close her eyes and imbibe the music. Her black hair framed her face at the front and fell loosely onto the towel draped across her shoulders. She looked peaceful, contented.

That's the look I will have one day when I'm rich and can buy my way to Timbuktu.

"What is turned out? You said you would explain turned out to me."

Megan stood up on her bed and jumped down. She grabbed her ballet shoes from beside the bed and slipped them on. She then sat on the floor and did a split. She leaned over at the torso and used her hand to inch down lower and lower until she could practically kiss the floor. She then sat up and opened her legs so that both knees on either side were touching the floor even as her back was straight.

"This is the frog position. Dancers do these exercises to improve their turn out. This is when you turn your legs from the hips so that your knees face the side rather than the front."

"That helps your legs to lift higher."

"Very good, Doctor." Megan got up from the floor and walked over to the ottoman where Malachi was now seated. The scent of Jasmine aroused his senses. He dared not move.

"When you are well turned out as a dancer you can do interesting things like this." In one sweep she lifted her leg, turned and bent at the torso so that the raised leg was extended over Malachi's head. Her arms extended in a soft arch and her head slightly up.

"Arabesque penchee," she said as she balanced en pointe.

Malachi stood up suddenly and held Megan's extended leg by her calf. She drew a quick breath as he slowly ran his hand along the length of her calf stopping by her knee.

Slowly, Megan lowered her leg until it was firmly planted on the floor again. Her face felt moist, and for all the leg strength she had worked so hard to develop over the years, today, at that very moment, her legs felt like mush.

Without shifting his gaze, Malachi stepped forward, closed the gap between them and kissed her. Megan responded in kind, and in seconds, their kiss deepened. Megan slipped her hands under Malachi's gray T-shirt and began to pull up. Malachi pulled away.

"Hold on, wait a minute. Listen, Megan, there's something I need to tell you," he said as he struggled to control his breathing.

"What is it?" Her fractured breaths matched his.

"I don't want to disappoint. I wouldn't want to shatter your expectations, but the truth is. I'm…I've never actually done this before."

"Done what?"

"This."

Understanding washed over her. "Malachi Williamson, are you telling me that you're a virgin?" she said, her tone incredulous.

"Don't be so surprised. I know we're a rare species, but I'm pretty sure there are lots more of us out there, Ms. Le Blanc."

"Oh gosh, no. I didn't mean to lau—. OK, let's try this again." She took a quick breath and looked him in the eye. "Malachi, tell me, what do you want to happen tonight? It's all up to you."

CHAPTER FIFTEEN

The face on his watch said quarter past six in the evening.

I guess Caleb is still on Trini time.

Malachi looked at the half a hot dog on his plate and thought of Megan and the night of the Pajama party. Instinctively, his hand went up to his eye. The cut that needed sutures was now hardly visible. He was grateful that it looked as if it wouldn't leave a scar.

It was a month since the party. In some ways though it felt like yesterday. The images, smells, and sounds were still fresh in his head. Thanks to Megan's brandy-spiked tea remedy, he had awoken the next morning in her bed. It had been strange at the time—shocking even—when he'd opened his eyes that morning and saw Mahatma Gandhi staring back at him.

Now Megan's bed was the most familiar place in the world.

He had never experimented with drugs before, but he knew people who had, and their account of that first high sounded eerily similar to how he'd felt when he'd slept with Megan for the first time. It was sweet and exhilarating all at once—beyond his wildest expectations. But he also remembered the cocktail of guilt, regret, and loss he felt the next morning when he realized that he had given away his virginity, and that the beautiful woman lying next to him was not his wife.

That first journey back to his room on his block had been the worst. Even the canary yellow parkinsonia that framed his block's entrance on either side, appeared to him as if they were bowing their spidery sprouts lower than usual. It was as if, somehow, they knew what he'd done, and were now pained to make eye contact.

But Malachi had to admit he was still getting used to having a sex life. For the first few days he'd got up at ridiculous hours so he could sneak back across to his room, hoping to escape the raised eyebrows and knowing smiles of Megan's block sisters.

That was before Python, who he thought had specific interest on the senior block, but was now seen regularly on Megan's block, approached Malachi at four one morning just as the Freshman was closing the door to Megan's room to return to his own.

""Yow! You don't have no condom? Me ah beg you two."

Malachi was dumbstruck.

"You never hear me? Condoms. Yes? No?" Python looked as if he was in a hurry.

"Uh nah. Don't use—I mean…I don't have any con—."

"Alright but I hope that you use something my yout'. Some of the girls they freaky and some of them…Hm. Watch yuhself." He smirked and slipped back into his love nest.

Oh, how the mighty has fallen, Malachi had thought of himself.

Malachi was about to get up and leave when he saw Caleb strolling toward him with a "don't kill me" look on his face.

"Sorry man. I had to go grab some books from the library before they all get taken out. Them Jamaicans in my program competitive boy." He took a seat opposite Malachi.

"Listen eh breds, yuh do this to me again and next time, I will blank you. You need to respect people's time. This is stupidness, man."

"You're right. Ah real sorry. Old habits; I wasn't thinking." Caleb rocked back in his chair and scratched the stubble on his face.

"Malachi Williamson Junior, my best friend since kindergarten, wow! I am in trouble with a capital T!"

"What's up, man? Failed an exam or something?"

"Nothing like that boss, nothing like that." Caleb rubbed his head.

That's when Malachi noticed how unkempt his friend looked. He needed a shave and his T-shirt had a stain on the right sleeve.

"I broke up with Brandy."

"Doh make smoke! You did what? Why man?"

"One word, boy: Abby. I think I'm in love with her man."

"I seem to recall you expressing similar sentiments about Brandy."

"Yeah, but Brandy. Man, Brandy is over here." He gestured with his hand a few inches above the table. "Now Abby." He whistled softly. "Abby is over here." He stretched his arm way above his head.

"OK."

"It's like silver and gold. There's just no comparison."

"So let me get this straight: You dumped Brandy to be with Abby. Ah ha. How did Brandy take that? And Abby. Is the feeling mutual?"

Malachi asked the latter even though he was pretty sure he knew the answer. Recently when he popped in on Abby she always managed to bring up Caleb: something funny he said, a passage of Scripture he had shared with her. She even showed Malachi a bouquet of wild flowers that Caleb had picked which she had displayed in a drinking glass on her desk. Malachi had recognized the flowers as the ones that grew between the ficus hedge that formed a natural fencing around one of the dorms on Turner.

"Yuh boy ent dotish yuh know. I wouldn't have said anything to Brandy if I wasn't a hundred percent sure how Abby felt about me."

"OK."

"As far as Brandy goes, she said she wasn't completely surprised. Said she had sensed a pulling away. She wished me well and even agreed with me that it was probably best since the long distance thing can be a bit tricky to sustain.

"Brandy. Your Brandy said that?"

"Yeah, I couldn't believe it either; I was so relieved. I thought she would get all hysterical and try to cling. You know how these girls can be. But it was all good. And Abby knows all about Brandy in case you're wondering. I told her everything."

"What do you mean everything?"

Caleb shifted in his seat and diverted his eyes to the cafeteria's door.

"Man, I messed up big time. I didn't tell you before because I guess I was too embarrassed."

"Embarrassed about what, man?"

"Brandy and I had sex."

"What! When did this happen?"

"Right after my final exams. We were getting pretty hot and heavy with the make out sessions, you know how that goes—law of diminishing returns. Anyway, after exams, I felt like I needed a brain cooler, and so I suggested to Brandy that we hit the beach. She was game and it kind a happened there."

"Dude! Tell me you didn't do it in the church bus?"

"Yuh mad a what? I won't disrespect my father like that. Anyway, I was pretty messed up after the whole thing. Man, it's funny how it all feels so good when it's happening and the minute it's over— " He slumped back in his chair.

"The guilt takes over," Malachi offered.

"Exactly. Well, I couldn't deal with it. I told my dad."

Malachi was silent. Words failed him. He'd always been a little envious of the relationship between Caleb and his dad. They seem to be getting closer and closer, even as he and his dad got more estranged.

"I had to. I was so convicted! I even stopped talking to Brandy—that was the worst. Chantel, her best friend, braced me after church one Sunday demanding to know what I did to her friend. But I really wasn't even thinking about her. What was going through my mind was how I was sure to join that special department in hell with all the pastors' kids who had careened off the straight and narrow and made their parents' ministry that much harder."

"What did my pastor say, man?"

"Well, I could see how disappointed he was. He's always droning on about how he and Mom were virgins on their wedding night, and what a beautiful gift it was that they gave each other."

"But you wanted yours before Christmas," Malachi said and guffawed.

"It ain't even funny, man."

"Sorry. You're right. I'm sorry, man. Continue."

"Anyway, Dad counseled me and prayed with me. He helped me to get back on track. It was cool. He helped me to come to terms with it."

Malachi shook his head and rubbed his nose.

"What?"

"Come on, Caleb. Don't be such a drama queen. It's not like someone died or you lost a limb. It was just sex for crying out loud. Some men actually like it, duh?"

"There's no such thing as 'just sex.' I'm convinced of that now more than ever. The Word tells us that our bodies are the temple of the Holy Ghost. Are you that far gone that you've forgotten all that stuff?"

Malachi didn't respond. He rocked back in his chair and clasped his hands behind his head.

"Sorry man. That just came out. Didn't mean to judge you like that," Caleb said, with chagrin in his voice.

"It's cool."

"No, it's not cool, and I'm tired of saying it is. Look Malachi, what happened? You and I used to be tight. Best friends. We went to the same schools. We were baptized around the same time. We were both in ministry together—I in Sunday school and music ministry, you headed up the After School Ministry. Do you have any idea how many lives we've touched for the glory of God? Now, it's like you don't care for the things of God anymore. And it really pains me to see it. Remember we used to joke about how we'd ask God to put our mansions next to each other when we get to heaven so we could lime? Listen." Caleb leaned forward. "I know that when your mom di—"

The chair scraped crudely on the tiles as Malachi got up suddenly.

"Can't talk about this now. I have to go pick up Megan around now, and I have an anatomy lab tomorrow to read up on, so…"

"Megan huh." Caleb folded his arms. "Hope you know what you're doing."

"Everything's under control. Kiss Abby for me."

"Actually we're holding back on that. We thought it best to delay the physical for as long as poss—."

"Hey! Too much information. It was just an expression. I really don't need to know your business, man. C'mon, what are we, twelve? Just. You know… be careful with that one. That's all I'm saying. She's—She's the genuine article."

"I know."

****

The trees fussed and fretted as the cool October breeze stirred its leaves. The days were getting cooler—a sign that December was approaching. Although Jamaica, like all the islands, was spared the bite of a winter, there was no doubt that its proximity to the United States rendered the tropical isle a bit nippier than its windward and leeward counterparts.

Malachi zipped up his Sutton Hall blazer as he walked briskly past the library with Megan at his side. He thought about Caleb and the fact that though they had been best friends practically all their lives, he'd held back about losing his virginity to Brandy. That's just as well since Malachi knew he had no intentions of telling Caleb about himself and Megan, although he was pretty sure that Caleb had figured out by now that he and Megan were well beyond hand holding. He wasn't stupid.

"Slow down, Malachi. What's the hurry?" Megan asked as she quickened her steps to catch up with him.

"Sorry. I guess I'm hoping that walking faster will help me warm up a bit."

"Warm up? Don't be silly. Malachi, there's absolutely nothing to warm up to. This is fantastic weather. Please don't tell me you're cold?"

"OK, I won't."

"I don't mean it like that. Really, it's just that cold takes on an entirely different meaning where I come from. Have you ever been to Europe in winter or even fall for that matter?" Megan cocked her head when Malachi didn't answer.

"To tell you the truth, I really haven't been anywhere, Megan. I guess I'm one of the barbarians your father talks about."

"You're in a dour mood this evening. Did you have a bad day at class or something?"

"No. Sorry, I have a lot on my mind. I have all this reading to catch up on plus labs to write up and prepare for, that kind of stuff. Besides, I really want to get back soon since I completely forgot I promised Abby that I would drop in on her cell group meeting tonight. She'd been behind me about it for weeks."

The mention of Abby's name raised the hackles on Megan's pores. She knew it was probably totally senseless of her but she couldn't help but be less than enthused about Malachi's friendship with the American. It could be her propensity to go on about God and her faith, especially with Malachi, though to be fair, she'd seemed just as eager to drone on about her religion to anything that moved. But it's more than that that bugged her, Megan was forced to admit. It was also the way Malachi seemed to let her in, while she, his girlfriend and lover, continued to knock.

"They really pile it on, don't they?" Megan broke the silence. "Talking about school, I was doing a bit of research for an assignment recently, and I thought life would be so much easier if we had reliable wireless Internet access in our rooms. Sylvie told me she stays in her room and gets all the journals and articles she needs for assignments online. I, on the other hand, have to practically claw my way with the masses at the library just to get my hands on the required reading. This system—this whole place in fact—is so backward I can hardly stand it at times."

Malachi shoved his hands in his blazer pockets. He knew that Megan was telling the truth and that he too had lamented about the inconsistencies in access to the online medical library, but somehow coming from her, it felt superior—like Third-World bashing. He just didn't like it.

Let it go Malachi. Let it go.

"I need to call Daddy as soon as we get back to hall. I can't wait for you to meet my parents. I think a nice intimate dinner would be great. I just know they're going to love you."

Malachi coughed.

"Dad absolutely has to give me a check to set up that ballet charity I've been going on about. More children have joined the cast recently, and it's heartbreaking the clothes they come to rehearsal in. Some of them have holes the size of plums in their stockings—if it can even be called stockings. My ballet teacher would cringe if she saw it; she was such a stickler for things like that that she would refuse to even let us near the barre if our practice clothes weren't up to par."

Malachi stopped walking.

"So Daddy is going to throw some money at the poor little black kids and that's supposed to make it all better? How clueless can you be, Megan? Do you really think buying leotards and tutus or whatever you guys call the stupid thing is going to make a difference? Help them deal with the realities of not having enough food to eat when the day comes, or having to dodge bullets on their way to school? Wake up, Princess Megan; this is the real world. You know—I really think you might be hanging around that Nutcracker set too much."

Megan felt her face flush. She was suddenly aware of the cold that her companion was complaining about. It was a cold night indeed.

"Let me tell you something, Mr. Williamson. I might not be in touch with all the realities that those children face, but at least I care enough to do something. I'm not volunteering my time and know-how day after day for fame or to assuage some sense of guilt I feel for being born privileged. I'm doing this because it makes me feel alive and happy to know that in some—some tiny way—I can be an extra on the stage of their lives, their success. That's right, I said success, because despite the odds, most of them have what it takes to make it."

The tears that pooled in her eyes as she spoke defied her instructions to hold their position, and were now sliding down her cheek. She brushed impatiently at them.

"The truth." She paused to regain control of her voice. "The truth is that I get far more out of my encounters with those children than I put in. So don't you dare stand there and make me out to be some snotty little rich girl. I expect that, I can deal with that, from the girls on hall but not from you, Malachi. Not. From. You."

With that she spun around and walked off in the other direction.

Malachi ran up to her and reached for her hand. She yanked it away. He reached for it again. This time he held on.

"I'm an idiot," he said. The contrition in his voice matched what she saw on his face. "You're absolutely right. I should know better, and I do. I'm an idiot, and I'm sorry. I'm sorry, Megan. I didn't mean to hurt you." He slid his arms around her waist and drew her into a hug.

Her body wasn't ready to acquiesce. She stood there tense and unyielding. Her hands fisted around his back. She still tasted the saltiness of her own tears, but as the seconds rolled on, she allowed herself to exhale and meld into his embrace.

CHAPTER SIXTEEN

Abby asked Jason to read aloud the passage from Matthew 16:13-19 where Jesus entered Caesarea Philippi and asked his disciples: Who do men say that I, the Son of Man, am?

Jason's baritone voice filled the room as he read the passage in Matthew.

"Thanks Jason," Abby said, when he had finished the reading. "Now as I told you guys, this is not a sermon. I'm not here to preach. This is more like a Bible Study with a facilitator. I know that's new to some of you, but that's the way we do it in these parts."

"Gotcha Sheriff," Caleb said, saluting. The group chuckled.

"Well, thank you, Deputy," Abby saluted back and rewarded him with a smile.

"I'm so psyched to see all of you here tonight," she continued. "For some, it's been a long time coming."

With a smile on her face, Abby glanced over to where Malachi and Megan sat. Megan cleared her throat softly.

"Ladies, we're actually even tonight—four men and four women. A special 'yeah' for the guys. Anyway, like I said, I'm not going to be the one doing all the talking, OK? Hope that's OK with everyone?"

There were tepid noises of consent from the group.

"Great. So let's jump right in then. Well from what Jason just read it seems like Jesus was quite interested in what people's position was on Him. Any thoughts, Renata?"

Renata was a second year economics major and a regular at Abby's meetings. "Sure Abby. I think by asking the question, Jesus was trying to tell us that it is important to have an opinion or perspective as to who He is."

"I hear you loud and clear. Anybody else?"

"What stood out for me was verse fourteen—that people had so many views as to who Jesus was…is. I'm sorry. I mean, come on," Tracy, a first year English major counted on her fingers. "John the Baptist, Elijah, Jeremiah, one of the prophets. It's just like today."

"Great observation, Tracy. Let's think about that a bit. Our day—Twenty-first century. Who are people saying Jesus is today? Anyone? Malachi."

Malachi shifted on his seat cushion.

Nice Abby. Since when anyone is Malachi.

Malachi plunged in: "Today, I know that some people believe he's just a prophet. Some say He is God; some say He's not. Some don't see Him as significant at all. Some say He's one of many gods."

"Me like the part in verse fifteen when Jesus did ask Simon Peter 'Who do you say I am?'" Eric, a third year med student, said.

"Why is that your pick, Eric?" Renata wanted to know.

"Well, Simon Peter did just find out wha' everybody else did a say and is like me can just hear Jesus a say 'OK, yeah, alright, but wha' YOU a say breddren?'"

"I'm just fascinated that you're imagining this conversation in patois, Eric," Abby said.

The group laughed.

"Patois right through, sista. Yeah. So Jesus a say 'me waan fi know whe you think?'" Eric continued. "Is a personal ting, you see."

"Exactly!" Megan blurted and made everyone jump.

"Go on," Abby prodded.

"Actually, I didn't plan to contribute, but I think Eric is right. From the little I understood—I agree—it is a personal thing, and I can't understand why there has to be a homogenous position."

"OK. I see where you are coming from, but is not that I did really mean. Sorry, I forget your name…"

"Megan."

"Megan. When me did say is a personal thing, me did mean that Jesus wasn't only interested in the myriad of opinions and perspectives. I think that by soliciting Peter's perspective 'im narrowed down the unit of concern to the individual. Wha me a try say is that Him a tell we that we can't hide in the collective view. Your individual perspective of Him is the real crux of the matter."

"That's definitely what I got from it," Renata chimed in.

"'Unit of concern.' I love that Eric," Tracy added, her eyes bright with admiration.

"I think we're ganging up on Megan, that's what I think," Jason with the baritone voice, said.

"Hey nobody's ganging up on anyone here, Jason. We're talking. That's all," Abby said with a hint of irritation in her voice.

"Abby, do you want to know my favorite part?" Caleb enquired with an inflection that failed to hide his affection.

Malachi bowed his head.

Could this get any worse?

"Of course, Caleb," Abby responded, the smile on her face crept into her voice.

"When Simon Peter said, 'You are the Christ, the Son of the living God.' Jesus responded in verse seventeen by saying 'Blessed are you Simon Bar-Jonas, for flesh and blood has not revealed this to you, but my Father who is in heaven.'

"Abby, this tells me that there was a right answer to the question Jesus asked, and Peter nailed it. Jesus affirmed Peter's answer. He didn't just rubber stamp the whole barrel of responses which would have basically communicated that I am whoever you say I am. No. Jesus didn't leave us confused or wondering if there was merit in the myriad of opinions that were bandied about in those days. So I personally really like the fact that Jesus ended the debate. At least he did it for me."

"Amen," Tracy said, and continued to nod her head.

"But what about Socrates?" Megan blurted.

Malachi inhaled deeply and fixed his gaze on the water stain on Abby's ceiling. Hers was over her bookshelf.

"Explain, Megan," Abby said. Malachi had to give Abby full marks for appearing unruffled.

"You see I was kind of on board when Jesus was asking all the questions and all these answers were pouring in. It reminded me of Socrates. He was also very fond of asking questions and—"

"Hold it, Megan." The interruption came from Caleb. "Are you comparing Jesus with Socrates?" Caleb's finger pointed up, his forehead furrowed. The last time Malachi saw that face was when Caleb was teaching Sunday school back home and Quincy Subero openly challenged the virgin birth.

"All I'm saying, Caleb, is that Socrates too was a student of human life and its conditions. Jesus reminded me of him when he asked the questions. Socrates was fond of questions. And I— well I can relate to him because I too have questions—lots of them in fact—about God and who he, or she, for that matter, really is."

"Definitely a he," Caleb interjected.

"Some cultures actually think it's a she," Renata said. "Shak- tism, as it's called, is very popular in some eastern cultures."

Megan went up an octave. "The point I was making about Socrates is that it is said that he never lectured his listeners. He just questioned them. I think that's rather profound, don't you?" Her eyes pleaded for an ally among the faces in the room.

"But didn't he off himself at the end?" The question came from Jason.

"I beg your pardon?" Megan inclined her head slightly, her gaze fixed on Jason.

"Socrates. Sorry, philosophy major, you're on my turf here. Socrates drank some kind of hemlock cocktail and killed himself if I remember correctly. So why then Megan should anyone take advice from him?"

The room fell silent. Megan turned and shot Malachi an incredulous look. She then lifted herself from her cushion seat on the floor, uttered a terse "good night" and strode out of Abby's room.

"Sorry, Abby," Malachi gestured with a twitch of a smile. He too pushed up from his seat, bid the group good night and left the room.

Jason threw his hands in the air and looked toward Abby, baffled.

"But he did. No joke." He lifted his right hand as if under oath. "How was I to know she had a thing for Socrates?"

****

Malachi leaned against the outside of Abby's door and sighed deeply.

I shouldn't have invited her. I shouldn't have invited her.

Megan was nowhere in sight. He knew if he ran he could probably catch up with her, but what would he say? It was one of those things that he had absolutely no control over. And what was the big deal anyway? If anyone should have been offended about the Socrates killing himself comment it should have been him.

He heard a voice that sounded like Abby's on the other end of the door. He couldn't quite make out what she was saying, but her speech pattern sounded slower, more deliberate—it's the way she sounds when she was in counselor mode. Malachi thought of the anatomy lab that he had to finish up for tomorrow's class and the group study session he was supposed to join at ten with Hopeton, Franka, and Alison. The girls were med students from the Freshers' block who had muscled their way into their two-man study group two weeks ago. But he didn't mind. They were both relentless when it came to getting it right, especially Franka. She'd make the dean's List for sure. He had all that on his plate tonight. Now this.

His head throbbed. He closed his eyes and massaged his temples.

"Trouble in paradise, Freshman?" Malachi's eyes remained closed for five more seconds, as he tried to diffuse the new round of irritation that had been triggered by recognition of the voice.

"You know if ever a hall name was right on target, it's got to be yours," Malachi shot back at Desperate. The comment caused the smirk on Desperate's face to transform into a scowl.

"Careful Freshman, you won't want that nice stitching to be messed up now, would you. Bleed all over the floor again like the night I had to teach you a lesson for crawling up in me business."

"You know I'm glad you brought that up. I wondered about that night. Tell me something, does it make you feel big and powerful when you hit women? Hm? Because that just seems kind of low and—how should I put it?—desperate, to me." With that Malachi pushed off from Abby's door and began to walk down the corridor, away from the senior.

"Ever thought some girls might like it rough?" He practically shouted to Malachi's retreating back. "Take your girlfriend, Megan."

Malachi stopped and turned.

"Hey man, for your sake don't go there," Malachi warned.

"Oh, I'm so scared," Desperate scoffed. "Well pretty boy, you started it asking me about me and me woman. You know what's sad about you? I mean real pathetic? It seems to me like you really don't know when you jus' out of your league."

Malachi clenched his jaw and swallowed. He knew he should turn and keep walking, but curiosity kept him grounded.

"That's supposed to make sense to me?"

"Naw. I would never expect such things. You see it clear to me, meh breddren, you don't realize when you outmatched. Really, you mean you never truly ask yourself 'now I wonder what could a classy, obviously well-to-do woman like Megan, with good breeding see in me?' You think she in it for the long haul? Pathetic. That's what it is. Bet you never even see what her home in Cherry Gardens look like. Take it from me, it real nice. I was telling Mrs. Le Blanc that just weekend gone when they had me over for cocktails. What? She never tell you? Hey, maybe she forgot. But don't take my word for it, ask your girl." He made air quotes, "And I would use that term loosely if I were you."

By this time, Desperate's raised voice had drawn the attention of a few of the girls on the block.

"Malachi, hey." The calming voice was Abby's. Malachi was so caught up in Desperate's spew that he didn't even realize that her door had opened, and that she'd joined the growing gaggle of spectators who'd vacated their rooms.

"Come in here for a second. I want to talk to you." Abby tugged at his arm which was still firmly lodged in his jeans pocket. That having failed, she positioned herself in the closing gap between Malachi and Desperate.

"Yeah! Listen to your otha woman. Oops." He put his hand over his mouth. "Guess me buss yuh secret." He shrugged and gestured with outstretched hands as his eyes swept the eleven odd onlookers who already assembled and the others who were still coming out of their rooms.

Buoyed by the audience, Desperate continued. "But don't get nuh ideas there either. She's loaded too. I must say you're a lucky dog. One lucky dog." Desperate feigned amusement. He stretched his arms toward Malachi.

"Look at you: A man to be admired. Reminds me of that song 'Torn Between Two Lovers.' Can't decide between the little angel over here. God knows Mary Poppins here never pay me any mind."

"Jerome, stop it, you're drunk!" Abby shouted, a firm but nervous edge in her voice.

"Actually, Fanciful, I'm quite sober. Only two beers tonight. Like I was saying, lover boy here cyaan seem to decide between the angel in his dreams and the devil in his bed. Well player, it looks like you better stick with the devil." His eyes found Caleb's and shot him a mischievous grin.

"Cause word on the blocks is that you can't afford the wager for this fine angel."

It's hard to say exactly who made the first move. Some eye witnesses said that it started when Abby slapped Desperate's hand away as he brushed her cheek. Others swore it all unravelled when Caleb, in his Turner Hall jacket, shoved Desperate against the wall. But things definitely took a turn for the worse when Malachi jumped in and tried to peel Caleb off of Desperate. Caleb had swung around with a punch that was likely to connect with Malachi's face. Malachi ducked and Caleb's fist struck the wall. He doubled over bellowing in pain.

Then two Sutton hall freshmen, coming out of nowhere, and thinking it was some sort of inter-hall turf war, started punching Caleb until the female onlookers who were scrambling out of harm's way, shouted to them that they were punching the wrong guy. By then, Desperate had shrugged off the scrawny senior that attempted to restrain him and had lunged at his primary target. Malachi, the smaller of the two, landed on top of Desperate and to everybody's amazement started raining blows on his attacker. It took three men to peel Malachi off of Desperate who by then had slumped to the ground and laid motionless on the floor.

"Jerome. Jerome, honey?" Passion, who appeared out of nowhere, was now bent over the senior patting his face. Her locks fell freely over Desperate's face, torso, and the terrazzo floor. "He's not breathing!" Passion's panic-stricken voice pierced through the noisy corridors. Her head began to travel back and forth between Desperate's chest and his face. Seconds into her frantic search for signs of life, she lifted her face to the crowd and yelled: "Anybody knows CPR? All you stupid med students, don't just stand there, do something!"

CHAPTER SEVENTEEN

Until now, Malachi had always regarded time as a friendly ally—a facilitating partner in the pursuit of his ambitions.

He'd respected it, revered it even. And he'd paid his dues, hadn't he? Studied when he could've been out pursuing any number of youthful pastimes: partying, hanging with friends, watching TV, experimenting with drugs, or fulfilling any one of a number of well-documented teenaged vices. But today was different. Today, time was a well-constructed torture chamber, and the dean had conspired with the infernal ticking of his desk clock, to be his tormentor.

He'd been sitting in the dean's office for the last twenty minutes trying not to think about the morass that was now facing him. It had been eight days and seven nights since the famous second incident. Some zealous journalism student had leaked the story, if it could even be called a story, to the press.

A reporter, eager to find out more about what the paper had dubbed a campus love triangle, had snuck onto his hall and had found him. And he'd been easy to find. After all, where exactly do you go as a foreign student when you've been suspended. The hall, understanding his plight as a foreigner, had not been quick to kick him off. But med school had been different. In record time he was suspended, pending investigation.

Malachi Williamson Senior had been disappointed. That was the word he had used. As far as Malachi Junior saw it, his dad had been much more concerned about how he was going to explain Caleb's broken right hand to his father, who was, after all, his boss. Then there had been the police, the ambulance, the endless questions. The waiting. Mr. Williamson had told his son that God had been merciful to him: What if he'd beaten the boy to death? What if those thugs, as his father had called them, had beaten Caleb within an inch of his life? What if it had triggered an inter-hall incident, as had happened before?

As he sat in the dean's office with nothing but his thoughts as a companion, he replayed the last conversation he had with his dad.

"What if that guy had really hurt me or killed me, Dad? I told you what had happened before." That was his response to his father's string of 'what ifs'.

"Yes, that would have been bad," Malachi Senior had agreed. "Especially because you would have gone to a Christless eternity given your backslidden state. I would have been inconsolable."

"That's all you care about, isn't it? My future, my life's dream of becoming a doctor is hanging by a thread, and that's all you care about—whether I go to heaven or hell. Unbelievable!"

"Son, what will it profit a man if he gains the whole world, and loses his own soul? Or what will a man give in exchange for his soul?" his old man had rebutted with the Mark 8:36 and 37 Scripture.

"Think God's impressed with your passes, Son? Your ones, your As, distinctions, your medical degree when you get it. Plan to wave it like a passport and tell him 'Just step aside and let me pass please because I'm highly qualified to poke around in people'? He's the one who gave you the brains, boy. Without Him, we are nothing! So of course, I'm going to be on your case about your soul. I can't understand why, for crying out loud, when some people get a little education, they suddenly feel they brighter than God!"

He'd never hung up on his dad in his life, but as angry and tempted as he was, he couldn't bring himself to hang up on him, especially when he was quoting Scripture and in full-throttle preach mode.

"I need a lawyer, Dad," Malachi Junior had said calmly as he tried to steer the conversation back to what he considered to be the substantive matter. "Everyone is saying that I deserve a second chance. Even the media isn't painting me as the villain. They said I was provoked."

"I don't have lawyer money, Son, but I will call the school and try to talk to the dean."

"Geez. Thanks a million, Dad. Maybe you can scan and email him my baby pictures too."

The conversation had ended there. He was left holding the phone listening to the dial tone. His dad, it appeared, had had no qualms hanging up on him.

****

The door opened suddenly and Professor Livingston bolted into the room.

"You students have me busy this week. Between the cheaters, the drunks, and the fighters, I could hardly get in a good game of golf anymore." He didn't smile, neither did Malachi.

The professor walked over to his chair, plopped down, and started to swivel. Despite his complaint, his face appeared fresh, his mien unperturbed.

He took a key from his pants pocket, opened a drawer from under his desk, and pulled out a manila file. He flipped through some of the pages. Malachi recognized his certificates and references. He also noticed some scribbling on a sheet of paper. Professor Livingston unclipped the gold pen from his shirt pocket, twisted it, and placed a tick next to some of the scribbles. He kept the file open on his desk and leaned back in his chair, eyes trained on Malachi. Again he swiveled.

"Remember what I said to you the last time you were in here?" Malachi nodded.

"Sorry, is that an answer, young man?"

"I remember, sir. You said life is about choices."

"Aha. And didn't I say something about some moving you further to your goals and some away from them?"

"That's correct, sir."

"Well no doubt your recent actions have moved you away from your goal, won't you say?"

"It would seem so, sir." His response was barely audible.

"Mr. Williamson. There is nothing about your academic performance in the past, or present for that matter, that would lead me to believe that I'm sitting across the table from genius. It's not that it's bad, it's just that it is not particularly—um—remarkable. On this alone, I really wouldn't feel like I was doing the world a great disservice if I drop you from this program. I'm being honest. In fact based on the fact that you've come before me not once but twice now on account of altercations, I'd say you seem to be better suited to another field. Say, boxing perhaps?"

Malachi looked down at his sneakers.

"It's nothing to be ashamed of. Lots of young men your age have seen old movies like *Rocky* and harbor fantasies of slugging meat in the freezer." Professor Livingston stopped swiveling. He leaned forward, resting his elbows on the desk.

"The thing is, Mr. Williamson, when med students entertain that kind of fetish, we have to be concerned. As stewards of this faculty, we have to be very concerned indeed. Firstly, there's this pesky oath we take to do no harm. Secondly, we have cadavers to protect. Can't have our students going all Rocky on our cadavers now, can we?"

Malachi opened his mouth to respond, but Professor Livingston's raised hand, stopped him.

He looked at the file again and began twiddling the pen in his hand.

"It seems that you have a bit of a fan club."

"Sir?"

"Oh yes. Within the last week I've been bombarded with calls. Some of the calls were from some very high profile people whom I've never even met. Yes, they sought to posit an argument as to why I should recommend to the disciplinary board that you should not be booted out of this establishment—the very one that you have disgraced by your actions. They feel that I should not send you packing on the first flight back to Trinidad."

Malachi's heart began to race.

"The thing is." Professor Livingston rocked back on his chair again. The swivel started up again. "Most of those calls, from people who I suppose just wanted to help you, had just the opposite effect to the one I'm sure was intended. I'm going to say for the record that I'm not a man who can be browbeaten by the Who's Who in Jamaica or anywhere else for that matter. I'd like to think that's one of the reasons I got this job. I weigh facts, Mr. Williamson," he said, pounding his fist on the open file. "Facts. Do you realize that you could have killed that young man?"

"I would not have uh…Well you know, if I knew he had an enlarged heart."

"The fact that he had cardiomegaly is beside the point. The first rule of being a doctor, or aspiring to be one, is to do no harm. Are you aware of that?"

"Yes, sir."

Professor Livingston took a breath. "I also received a call from one of our long-standing contributors to the university's endowment fund. That was the money call. This man, who has very deep pockets, all but threatened to withdraw his support for the medical school, if you are not dismissed."

The professor's face was animated. His eyes were dilated and eyebrows hitched. In contrast, his voice was almost a whisper. "This university is heavily dependent on persons like that to fund its research projects. Did you know that?"

"No, sir." Malachi no longer had the will to hide the defeat in his voice.

"There are powerful people in this society, Mr. Williamson, who would love to see the back of you." He was pointing now.

The dean paused for what felt like an eternity.

"Nevertheless…" He swiveled some more. "We've decided to keep you. From all reports, your actions, though reckless, appeared to have been provoked. We also considered the fact that by using your head and administering CPR to the young man until the first responders arrived, you might have actually saved his life. I noted also with interest that your roommate, uh." He flipped a few pages of the file.

"Mr. George, was one of those who took the time to write a letter basically talking about what a great roommate and study partner you had been. For whatever it was worth, as he put it. Spelling was all over the place, but it was sincere, I suppose.

"In spite of this, I tell you the truth. The vote of the disciplinary committee held two days ago, could have gone either way had it not been for a very well-timed phone call from your father."

"My dad called you?"

"Yes. Your father obviously did his research and found out when the disciplinary committee was meeting. He called a few minutes into the meeting and told the secretary that he was not putting down the phone until he had the chance to say his piece. Well, after holding on for nearly ten minutes, we put him through on speaker. When he was finished, we sat in silence for close to a minute. He was very convincing, your father.

"You see, I happen to know a thing or two about good fathers, so I can tell the real deal when I hear one."

"Yes." It was all Malachi could managed as he struggled to rein in his emotions.

"You will be on probation for the next six months. During this time I personally will be monitoring your progress very closely, Mr. Williamson. If you give me any reason to regret our decision to keep you on at this institution, it will be corrected forthwith. You hear me? Forthwith! I mean if it's just the white gear you like, I assume you know you have plenty of options. You can be a nurse, a lab tech, a taxidermist for all I care. Doctors don't have any special patent on the color white you know? Chicks dig pharmacists too, I happen to know. I have many pharmacist friends who have to practically beat off the ladies with—."

"It's much deeper than that, sir."

"It better be for your sake." The professor leaned forward, closed the file on his desk, and tucked it away in the secret place below his desk.

"I would expect you to catch up with your assignments on your own time. Don't expect your lecturers to cut you any slack. That's it. You may leave. It seems like the gods have smiled on you."

"God, sir. Just one that counts," he said to his professor.

"Well."

Professor Livingston glanced at his watch. "And that's all the time I have for you, young man. Now if you would excuse me, I need to go look for some alternative funding."

"Thank you, sir," Malachi managed to get in before closing the door behind him.

CHAPTER EIGHTEEN

"No, no, no, stop. Please stop. What was that? What was that?" Megan stood at the sidelines of the rehearsal hall. Her hands on her hips.

"Thalia, you look unsure. Which, of course, is the very opposite of confident. I don't understand why your steps are so tentative today, as if you're trying to figure out what to do next. And I'm especially not feeling the connection between you and the prince, who, I must add for the record, has greatly improved. But the connection—the magic: it's mysteriously vanished. Poof!"

The expression made some of the children, who comprise the mouse army, titter. Megan turned and gestured to the cast for silence with a wave of her hand.

"OK, we'll have an early break today, not that you deserve one. So make the best of it: hydrate and use the loo, because once we've resumed, we're going straight to the end."

Megan turned to the lead whose eyes were already filling up. She hooked her arm into hers and led her to the other end of the hall.

"Thalia! It's obvious that something is terribly off, and not just today. I've noticed it for a few days now. Your expressions, which we've worked on from day one, are simply not there. You're actually regressing."

Thalia crossed her arms and hugged herself as she listened to the instructor whose technique she greatly admired.

"You know I'm not very good at sugar coating. It's perhaps my greatest flaw. But I must tell you the truth. Clara's role is critical. She makes or breaks the show. Right now, when I watch you dance, there is no delight on your face. There's none when Drosselmeyer gives you the doll, no sense of awe when you find yourself in this magical land that you didn't even know existed. And, most disappointingly, the enchantment with the prince, which I felt you had clinched, is now gone."

Thalia's grip on herself tightened. Her eyes averted Megan's and looked instead at the parents and cast members, many of whom were trying not to stare in their direction.

Megan's voice rose an octave and her face flushed as she continued. "And on the technical side, moves which were effortless before have now become labored and awkward. Do you not recall my telling you about keeping your thumbs in for the pirouettes? But you're giving me this." She demonstrated. "What is that? Hmm?"

Thalia's gaze shifted to the floor.

"My goodness, Thalia, we're but two months away from the big day. You see those parents over there? They are coming day after day because they are expecting this event to be the talking point of the season. The Who's Who of Jamaica are going to be here in this very auditorium. Their little princes and princesses are going to be photographed and reviewed in *The Gleaner* and the *Jamaica Observer*. You think they're going to stand by and let you ruin the show? Of course not! In fact, I'll be straight with you, many of them are already putting pressure on Madame Francois to make the tough decisions of letting your understudy take the lead."

"No, Miss Megan, please! I can do better, I promise. Is just that..."

"It's just what, Thalia?"

"Is me boyfriend, Ms. Megan." Her voice was almost a whisper.

Megan suddenly felt sick to her stomach. "Oh Thalia, please. Please don't tell me you're pregnant?"

"What? No. Yuh mad? I mean, sorry, Miss Megan. I didn't mean to be disrespectful. Is just that my mother would murder me if me ever bring home a belly to her right now. I would never do that to my mother."

"Well, I'm sorry. You said boyfriend and I thought. Well."

"No, miss. Besides, I love Jesus too much to end up in fornication," she said earnestly, Megan noted.

"OK."

"Well is just that my boyfriend Terry say he's fed up of me practicing long, long with this production. And on top of that some idiot from round here gone and tell him how me and Devon always look all lovey dovey at one another when we dance, and him say it look like I want to be with Devon.

"Devon you know? I mean him strong, but him skinny." Thalia looked across the room to where Devon stood doing his warm-up exercises, her facial muscles bunched into a scowl.

She continued. "Terry did call me last week and ask how I could disrespect him like that. He say it's him or Devon, and if I stay in the show, then it mean that I chose Devon over him."

The tears that were threatening began to fall down her cheek. Megan hugged her.

"Thalia, listen. I'm glad you shared that with me. And I understand you're probably feeling a bit manky right now."

"Miss?"

"Out of sorts, upset, sad, heartbroken even. Believe me I understand. But this is where you need to be a big girl. Firstly, I'm not sure if at fifteen having a steady boyfriend is best for you, especially as you are trying to be um—chaste. Secondly, ballet is kind of like a sport, isn't it? Just like football, cricket, tennis or gymnastics. And how does one become proficient at any sport?"

"Practice."

"Lots of practice. Now what you do when you dance in major productions like this is that you…well you do a lot of pretending, don't you?"

"I guess."

"Of course you do." Megan made an exaggerated swoop with her hand. "None of this is real: the music, the elaborate costumes, the set. In real life, Thalia, there are no Sugar Plum Fairies. There's no Mouse King. And toys just don't come to life and dance, now do they?"

Thalia giggled at the absurdity of it all.

"You forgot the prince, Miss Megan. There's no prince."

"Oh yes. Sadly, Thalia, there's no prince. Though many a man would like to believe that they come quite close," Megan added with a smile and wondered at that moment how she would rank Malachi on her imaginary prince-o-meter.

"So that whole dance number with Devon, Thalia, is pretend. Nevertheless, we have to do it well. It must be convincing, because it is part of what we dancers call artistic integrity. It's a concept that, if you are in the arts, you must pay homage to. Understand?"

"Yes, I think so, Miss Megan."

"Now if your friend, uh."

"Terry."

"Yes, Terry. If he cannot understand that simple concept then I seriously question whether he is your equal."

"Miss?"

"Yes, Thalia. I'm left to question whether he's truly worthy of you. You see, my dear, some boys take a bit long to grow up, and when you come across one such boy—well—it's often best to leave him alone until he matures. Do you follow?"

Thalia perked up. "Yes, Miss Megan, I think I do. It's like—It's like ackee.

"Ackee? You mean the fruit—like the one you have for brekkie?"

"Ee hee, Miss Megan! You know if you cook ackee before it ripe fully, it can kill you."

"Oh my goodness, Thalia, that's absolutely brilliant. I couldn't have come up with a better analogy."

****

"I see you had a little chat with our girl. Looked intense." Madame Francois's tone was smothered with concern. "Are things back on track, you think, or do we have to get Tamika ready for the lead? Her mother, whom I don't know if I mentioned before, is a well-known magistrate in Jamaica."

"Yes, it was mentioned."

"Well, she whispered to me just now while you and Thalia were talking that Tamika has been stepping up her practice at home." Madame Francois's eyes were practically bulging, yet her hands were serenely clasped in front of her as she awaited Megan's response.

She looked particularly elegant today, Megan thought. Her high cheek bones and flawless, ebony complexion added tangibility to what Megan suspected would be an ageless beauty. Today she outfitted herself in a black leotard with a light gray, slightly sheer knee-length ballet skirt that flattered her taut fifty-some-thing-year-old body. Hers was a household name in Jamaica. Her accolades, Megan quickly learned, have been many. From the first day she peeped in on *The Nutcracker* rehearsal, Megan knew that this daughter of the soil was no stranger to world-class performances. She could hold her own anywhere. Megan was learning a lot from working alongside her, witnessing the way she balances the need for patience with the imperative of pressure, with so young a cast. Excellence was her signature, and Megan knew in her heart that, right now, things were not living up to her expectations.

"That's good to know," Megan finally responded. "All I can say at this stage is that you have my word, Madame Francois, that I will support you with whatever you feel is necessary to get the best performance from all concerned." Madame Francois nodded her approval. "But let's not give up on Thalia just yet," Megan added. "She's a fighter, from what I see. And fighters don't quit easily."

"Hope you're right," Madame Francois said before clapping her hands to summon attention.

"Warm-up exercises everyone! Take your places and one, two, three, four and one, two, three. One, two, three...

By the way, Megan." She lowered her voice while keeping per-fect timing with her hands. "There's someone waiting to have a quick word with you. You go ahead, I have this session covered."

Megan's heart began to beat a little faster. She had told Malachi after the fight, not to bother to pick her up from rehearsal. In fact she'd told him that it was best that they kept a bit of distance until the whole thing blew over. She hadn't slept on hall since the incident. The student who'd leaked the story also told the press that she was a diplomat's daughter. That detail, though veiled in terms of identifying her or the specific embassy, had appeared in the newspaper adding another layer of intrigue to what most had realized by now was a virtual non-story. Nevertheless, her parents had insisted she pack a bag and spend the next few days at home in Cherry Gardens. She had felt badly about leaving Malachi to face matters by himself. The disappointment was etched on his face when she'd told him she was spending the next couple of days by her parents.

It might not have been much of a story, based on the fact that only one newspaper followed it up, and the talk shows left it alone, but it did cause her parents some embarrassment. One fallout was the cancellation of the meet-the-parents dinner that Megan had organized for next weekend, though she had not had a chance to tell Malachi that it was off. Her mother had been the bearer of the news, which was always the case when her father was too angry to speak.

But for Megan, the deepest wound was made by the insinuation that she was somehow involved with a man who, at best, was ambivalent in his feeling toward her. The story also painted her as a stuck-up little rich princess, who because of her father's diplomatic status, enjoyed no end of privilege and fawning that was not extended to other students, like "a wing to herself"—a slightly exaggerated, but not entirely false, description of her room on hall.

Megan was grateful that the cast, if they had seen the story and guessed that it referred to her, had treated her no differently. She'd avoided Malachi long enough. It was time to face him.

"Hey, Megan."

It wasn't Malachi; it was Abby.

"Hello Abby," she said, in her most formal tone. "To what do I owe the honor?"

Megan thought it was a rare occasion that she'd seen Abby so unhinged. Her eyes looked tired as if she hadn't slept for days. She appeared thinner, not by much, but definitely thinner. And her hair, which is normally immaculately groomed, was fraying at the ends.

"I was hoping to catch up with you back on hall, but I haven't seen you since…" She didn't complete the sentence. "Actually, Megan, I just wanted you to hear this from me. For the record, I am not, nor have I ever been interested in Malachi—romantically that is."

"Oh?"

"You seem surprised? You didn't honestly believe the nonsense you read in the paper? I mean, I know he visits me now and then, and we talk about stuff, but that's mainly because we're in the same program."

"So what you're saying is that it's a med-student thing. Your interest?"

"Yes. No. I mean, all I'm saying is that we're just friends. That's it. People see things—things that are innocent and jump to their own conclusions. It's a blood sport around here, in case you haven't noticed. I can't help that. This thing has sent my life into a tailspin. I had to answer a zillion questions from my dad. My mom is freaking out and saying she thinks we should all go back to the United States. Caleb is not speaking to me, because he thinks I'm holding some secret torch for Malachi, which I'm not! What I don't get is how could he even—"

"Abby, you might not be holding a torch for Malachi, but something is going on," Megan said, interrupting, her own voice near derision. "You feel I haven't noticed? Malachi tells you things—he lets you in in a way that he hasn't with me. Do you know when I found out how his mother had died? I found out about a week before the showdown outside your door. The funny thing is he didn't even realize that he never told me. It came out in casual conversation. I had chided him just a few minutes earlier for not calling his dad for two weeks and he joked that Dr. Abby—which is what he calls you, by the way."

"I know."

"Of course you do." The words were doused in sarcasm. "Anyway, he said that you told him that maybe some of the anger and resentment that he feels toward his dad could be coming from the fact that a part of him blames his dad for not insisting that his mom took her lithium; that maybe if she did and her condition had stabilized, she would not have killed herself. I was washing my hair when he said that, and it was a good thing, so he probably thought the tears that were flowing down my cheek was water from my hair and the shampoo. This time Abby I was crying—crying over the fact that my boyfriend—the man whom I love—didn't trust me enough to tell me straight out that his mother was bipolar, and that she'd killed herself."

Abby looked at the pain etched on Megan's face, and it stung that she could be perceived to be the cause of it. She had to admit, she did have a special relationship with Malachi, but it was entirely platonic. She was sure of it. The rest of the world, apparently, was not convinced.

"Would you rather that Malachi and I stop speaking? Is that what you want, Megan?"

"Of course not; that would be pointless. I guess, I just want… I just want him to trust me and want me as much as I want him."

Abby studied Megan as she looked afar off. Her voice had become small, almost to a whisper as she confessed her innermost thoughts to the woman that Abby now knew she considered her rival. It was one of the rare occasions when Abby was speechless.

"Abby, despite what you may think of me I'm smart enough to know that what I need from Malachi has nothing to do with you." Megan stood with one arm crossed across her chest massaging her shoulder.

"I'm glad you realize that, but you're wrong about one thing."

Megan looked at her quizzically.

"You couldn't be that smart, Megan, if you have no idea that that man is falling for you as well."

****

"Bye Miss Megan. See you tomorrow." Thalia waved enthusiastically. "And thanks for everything," she added in lowered tones.

"Anytime. Where's your brolly?"

"My what?"

"Your umbrella. It's pouring outside. I can't have my lead dancer getting sick."

"Nuh worry, Miss Megan. Madame Francois offered to drop me home. Bye."

"OK. Practice, practice in front of the mirror!" Megan practically shouted as the last group of cast members scampered out the door. The session after the break was apparently greatly improved, Megan noted. Her tête-à-tête with Abby caused her to miss most of it. Thalia was certainly in a better frame of mind. Megan hoped that their little chat bore fruit. She felt slightly sickened at the self-accusation that here she was doling out relationship advice when her own relationship was in limbo. She hoped that whatever Thalia and Madame Francois talked about on their ride home would seal the deal for Thalia.

Madame Francois popped her head back in the door.

"Megan, I was about to ask how you were getting back to hall, but I see your escort is here."

"Oh, the driver is outside. He's actually on time today. Tell him I'll be a minute."

"No, not the driver, your young man, and he seemed to have come through the rain." With that Madame Francois disappeared behind the side exit that's used for rehearsal. Seconds later, Malachi appeared. Soaked.

"What are you doing here? I told you my dad arranged for a driver to pick me up this week. You didn't have—."

"I know what you told me. I wanted to see you. Talk to you. The stupid rain just got in the way."

"Oliver will be here any minute now," Megan said, suddenly self-conscious in a way that she wasn't before. She brushed imaginary lint off of her practice tutus.

"Well then, I hope the AC in his car is cracking, because what I have to say can't wait."

CHAPTER NINETEEN

Everything about Oliver Chateau screamed that he was not a man to be trifled with. He'd been given instructions to pick up Ms. Le Blanc and bring her safely home. Now he was being asked to deviate from the plan.

"Ms. Le Blanc, look here. The rain a fall bucket a drop, and I wouldn't mind if you did wet and soak up the car, but me never know this youth, and if him wet up and smell up Mrs. Le Blanc Lexus, is my head on the noose. Is cream dem seats ya color you know."

Oliver looked across with naked disdain at the young man who was making his own private stream as he trotted from the bathroom situated east of the rehearsal hall to where he and Ms. Le Blanc stood. Toe to toe, the boy was admittedly a tad taller, but he could more than take him down if it came to that, he reasoned. Back in his day, he'd handle much tougher-looking opponents, and he had the scars to show for it, including the one on his right temple.

"Actually, Oliver, the seats are beige. Furthermore, if my friend catches pneumonia and dies on account of your negligence, do you think your tenure with my family would be more secure?"

Oliver stared at Malachi and tsked.

"Is your funeral, ma'am. Let the record reflect my objectivity."

"So noted," Megan said, and shot Malachi a warning look against sniggering at Oliver's word choice.

****

The Lexus smelled floral and feminine. The interior was in fact beige leather. Megan scooted over to the far end of the back seat. Malachi slipped in quickly and closed the door. The blast from the AC sent a shiver through his body. He thought of asking Oliver to take it off or lower it, but he wasn't up for the confrontation.

He figured he would've had enough time to say what he had come to say right there in the Creative Arts rehearsal hall, but he'd miscalculated how much time he needed. He'd darted to the bathroom to wring out as much of the excess water as possible from his clothes, but by the time he reemerged, the driver had showed up. It was just as well since Brother Stanley, the middle-aged caretaker with the waist-length dreadlock who rumor had it, was said to be Madame Francois's gentleman friend, was already taking off the main lights and had begun rattling his keys more violently than usual—a sign that he was not prepared to entertain any petitions tonight about staying back late.

Malachi had only got the tail end of Megan's conversation with the driver, but he'd gathered that whatever difference of opinion they'd had had been sorted, and he was now being given a ride, albeit reluctantly, back to hall.

Megan, he observed, was practically up against the door on her side. Her body was angled away from him and she was staring out the window. In less than five minutes, they would be back on hall, Malachi knew he had to move quickly.

"The disciplinary committee decided to give me a second chance. I'm staying in the program."

"That's great. I'm really happy for you, Malachi." Her voice, he noted, was flat: devoid of spirit.

"When I found out, you're the first person I wanted to see to share the good news with."

She smiled weakly. He caught a glimpse of Oliver's eyes staring at him in the rear view mirror.

Nosy bugger.

"My dad, could you believe. My dad called and said something to the committee that made a difference."

"There you go. That's dads for you."

"Speaking of dads, I was wondering if yours might have made any calls in my favor. Apparently, I got a few from influential people."

Megan shifted in her seat. "That, from the little I know, is strictly against his code of conduct as a diplomat. I don't imagine he would do anything like that for you… or anyone for that matter," she added quickly, and stole a glance toward Oliver's rear-view mirror.

"I guess the dinner with your parents is off," he said, with a smack of his lips.

"The timing is…" She shrugged.

"Right. Well, I didn't hear from you, so I didn't want to assume. We never really got a chance to talk much after… Anyway, Megan, let me get to the point since we're almost there. I came here tonight to tell you that I know I've messed up. I didn't stop to think of how my actions would've affected you or your family. Or my dad for that matter."

Oliver switched on the car stereo and turned the knob until it found IrieFM. Whether it was an act of empathy or spite, Malachi would never know. The Lauryn Hill and Bob Marley "Turn Your Lights Down Low" wafted through the car's speakers.

"I have a lot of work ahead of me to catch up on," Malachi continued. "And I need to focus on that so I'll be spending my time between the library and the Med Sci Faculty. I just wanted you to know that… you're in my thoughts."

Did he say, "You're in my thoughts." Is that the best you can do, Malachi?

Oliver cleared his throat and sniffed. Malachi stared with annoyance at the back of the man's head. Oliver had some type of psoriasis, he noted.

Malachi moved across to the middle of the seat and leaned closer to Megan. She could smell the curious mix of rain mingled with his scent and that of his favorite cologne, the one she liked.

"I was actually hoping to convince you to spend the night with me. We need to talk and I—I need you, Megan. I want to be close to you tonight." His voice was a low whisper.

"I, uh. I don't know," she said and glanced in the mirror again. Oliver's eyes were on the road. "Right now I'm a bit confused about things. About us."

"Well, I need you to know that on my part, there's no confusion. Absolutely none." He cupped her face with his wet hands and kissed her right there in the backseat of her mother's Lexus.

Malachi broke the kiss and traced her jawline back and forth with his thumb.

"I guess I can stay on hall tonight," she said, demurely, as she whipped out her cell phone.

****

"Hello?"

"It's me."

Great. Dad.

"You're sleeping already. It's just after ten thirty. I thought you might have been with your group studying or trying to catch up on all the reading you told me you had. It seems like your body clock is changing. No longer a night owl, huh?"

There it was again, the unmistakable pang of guilt. It was getting less and less intense though, Malachi noted, but it was still there gnawing at him every time he had to lie to cover his tracks with his dad. The rap on the door to answer the phone had jerked him out of a deep and satisfying post-sex sleep. Hardly the kind of detail one shares with one's deacon dad.

"I decided to hit the sack early tonight. Big day."

"So I realize. I got your voicemail message when I got home from church. I was really happy to get that news, Son. Much prayer, much prayer has gone up for you over this situation. God is good."

"All the time, Dad." He practically yawned out the expected flummery. This was not the night to disappoint.

"Have you talked to Caleb as yet?" His dad wanted to know.

"I tried to get him couple of times, but he seems to be laying low. I'll try again, I promise."

"Well pastor told me that his hand is on the mend. No surgery necessary, thank God. He might have to do some exams orally, though, if he can't become ambidextrous in time for them."

Malachi yawned again. He shivered slightly as a nippy night breeze, remnants of the rain that had now settled to a drizzle, blew on him. Only then did he become conscious that he'd left Megan's room with nothing but a worn pair of jeans. No T-Shirt.

"Well, I guess I should leave you to get your rest."

"Dad, before you go I just want to say thanks for whatever you said to the disciplinary committee. It made a difference. The dean said he could tell a good dad when he hears one."

"Well. I did what I had to do."

"Thanks anyway."

"Yeah, well you know what I expect of you going forward, so hunker down and keep your focus."

"Uh huh."

"Junior uh…before you go I need to say something to you. Something important."

"I'm listening, Dad."

"You and I have never had much of a talk about sex and—."

"Whoa, Dad! Where did that come from? Are you for real? I'm like nineteen years old. I think it's a little late for the birds and the bees chat, don't you think?"

"Junior, I know you're having sex, and I want you to be… well, careful for one."

"Why do you think I'm having sex, as you put it?"

"Son, I wasn't born yesterday. I had my days of university life, remember? Besides, every time I call for you they transfer me to the girls block. And whenever your roommate transfers me he makes a point of reminding me to ask for Megan in F4."

Malachi closed his eyes and ran his hand across his head.

Busted.

"Are you there?"

"I'm here, Dad."

"So who is this Megan? Is she your girlfriend now?"

"Something like that."

"I take it she's not saved."

Malachi took a deep breath. "She's not a believer. No."

"Son, I know you're backslidden. I guess I've known that for a while. I know I should have confronted you on it more directly before now but…I suppose what I'm saying is that it's hard—it's just hard to accept that the child who you raised to know the Lord, the one you took to church every Sunday, made sure he was involved in ministry, that he knew the Word—that one day he would suddenly wake up, smell himself, and decide that he doesn't want it anymore. Quite frankly, it hurts. Makes me feel like a failure as a man of God."

Malachi knew that this was his cue—his turn to say something that would placate what he perceived was his father's bruised ego.

But he didn't speak. He simply allowed the silence between them to swell.

"So you have nothing to say?"

"What's there to say, Dad? I'm not where you want me to be. That's accurate. I won't lie."

Malachi heard his father release a sigh into the phone. He closed his eyes. It's been a while since he consciously petitioned God for anything, but just then he silently prayed that this conversation would somehow end.

"So is it serious with this Megan girl? I mean, are you two… you know?"

I guess I prayed amiss, Malachi thought, recalling the passage in James.

"Dad, I'm not sure what you're asking, but whatever it is, it's very intrusive."

"Oh, I'm sorry. So I must only intrude when your neck is on the line or when you need to be rescued? Is that what you're saying, Junior?"

"I'm saying that this conversation—interrogation—might be the better word—into my personal life is crossing the line, Dad," he added, hoping, as he always did, that the word would somehow cushion his repartee.

"I see. Well, excuse me, but I think I've earned the right to cross some lines with you Junior, given the fact that I pay your tuition and probably just saved your skin from being kicked out of med school."

There was the money line. I was wondering what took you so long.

"Dad, obviously you have something to say. So please go ahead, you have my attention."

"Well. I want to tell you that HIV is no respecter of persons. That's what I want to say to you."

Malachi couldn't believe what he'd heard. Although he tried to will himself not to, a snicker escaped.

"Sorry. Did I say something funny?"

"Dad, for crying out loud, I'm a med student. Don't you think I'm au courant with all the facts about AIDS? Let me put you at ease. If I want to have sex, and I'm not saying that I am, I would ensure that I do so with an HIV negative person. That's like sex 101, Dad. I'm not one of those crazy people who can't control themselves. I'm more responsible than that. You didn't raise an idiot. So you can sleep easy about that, OK pops?"

Silence banged from the other end.

"Dad?"

"I'm here. I had this dream about you, Junior. It was kind of disturbing."

Merciful Father, not the dream!

"In the dream, you were in a classroom, like a lab or something, and the lecturer was calling your name over and over 'Malachi Williamson' and everyone turned around and was looking at you and some were shouting: 'Malachi it's you he's calling' and you, you just sat there looking so smug and sure of yourself and telling everyone that it's not you he's calling, and I was standing there too shouting the loudest. I was shouting, 'Son, the man is calling your name, Son,' and you were ignoring me; ignoring everyone. It's like you didn't even know your own name. The name your mom and I gave you. What do you think that means?"

Malachi held the receiver to his chest and sighed deeply. He placed it back against his ear.

"Dad, honestly, if I knew the answer to that question, I'd be a very rich man."

CHAPTER TWENTY

Beat season was officially here.

There was still no sign that flowering poui trees were getting ready to dot the campus landscape with their cheerful shades of yellow and pink. The seniors had painted a vivid picture during orientation. "They bloom like clockwork," one senior had told the group of first years, a reference to the legend. Malachi suspected that it was all part of an elaborate hoax meant to ensure that the freshers prepared themselves well for exams.

For most students, November was the month of do or die. Malachi had been in strict work mode since the day after he found out that he'd been given a reprieve—a second chance by the Faculty of Medical Sciences. His days had been filled with the kind of routine that had produced results for him in the past.

Sleep was now officially a concept. He was surviving on an average of four to five hours per night. He knew people who were content with less, but that had never worked for him.

Megan, apparently, was just as caught up in school work. They spent one more night together after the one when he'd convinced her to ditch the driver and stay with him on hall. She had told him the next morning as they lay sated in each other's arms that she would have to cut back drastically on her extra-curricular activities, which in her case meant dance. The wake-up call was triggered when she saw the C on her most recent assignment. It was the first one she recalled ever receiving in all her years at school. She knew what she needed to do for her academic survival, she'd told Malachi, but like so many things in her life, doing the right thing, was easier said than done.

So they agreed to beat the books in their respective rooms at nights and meet over lunch when they could during the day, but even that had whittled down to three times over the past two weeks, not counting the time she surprised him with a "just because" kiss, as she termed it, before apologizing and running off to the library.

"Well you heard of eat and run? Well I guess that was kiss and run," Anya, his Jamaican classmate, who had witnessed the gesture, had said.

"That's just us," Malachi had replied with a smile that didn't quite reach his eyes. He knew he was in no position to be too demanding of Megan. After all, he too was struggling to find the balance.

Thanks to Anya, and her penchant for fastidious note taking, he was able to obtain most of what he'd missed during the time he was suspended. Hopeton had been surprisingly cagey about sharing his notes—a fact that, despite his efforts to brush it off—bothered Malachi. After all, hadn't he spent hours tutoring Hopeton when he was having trouble with his anatomy assignments? And what of the letter Hopeton, on his own accord, had taken the time to write in his favor? Now that they were inching closer to exams, Malachi had to face the reality that the prevailing mantra appeared to be "every man for himself."

Fortunately, he'd always been amiable and even a tad chatty with some of the lab assistants in his faculty, so when he'd approached them about make-up labs for those he'd missed, some had volunteered, giving up their lunch breaks to facilitate him. One such lunchtime, when he was busy making notes for one of his labs, Professor Livingston had walked in in search of one of the lecturers. He'd nodded at Malachi when their eyes had met. Malachi had nodded back.

He was going to make it after all, Malachi told himself. His academics were almost back on track. If only he could get his relationships with Caleb and Abby to do the same and line up.

****

Abby sprang to her feet the moment she heard the knock on the door.

"Coming," she sang as she skipped over the clutter of books that had begun piling up on her bedroom floor. It was the knock she'd been waiting, praying would come. She was sure of it. Alas, her prayers had been answered.

"Hey Abs."

"Malachi," she said with a hint of surprise. Her voice was cheerful enough, Malachi noted, but it was hard to miss the slump in her shoulders—a visible sign of her disappointment.

"Well, good to see you, too. Please try to control your enthusiasm," he said, matching her disappointment with his own.

"Sorry, Mal. Thought it was Caleb. The knock sounded like his. Come in, excuse the mess."

Malachi walked in, took off his shoes, and headed straight for Abby's desk and leaned against it.

"Don't you want to sit? I just made tea. I can make you a cup if you like."

He refused with a shake of the head. Malachi folded his arms across his chest and stared at Abby as she sat up on her bed, her back against the wall, sipping tea. It was only seven and she was dressed in a gray T-shirt and gray-and-white striped cotton slacks. The top sheet on the bed was turned down. He wondered if she'd been napping.

"What's going on, Abs? I came here couple of times, left notes. I really thought we had more of a friendship than that."

Abby didn't respond.

"Well, was I wrong?"

Abby unfolded her legs and crossed it again in the opposite direction. She stretched over and put the tea cup on the floor at the foot of her bed. She sat up again, folded her arms, unfolded them, and began massaging her temples, her eyes tightly shut.

"Malachi, right now I have my own drama to deal with, so hear me good when I say 'I. Can't. Deal. With. Yours!'" And to his surprise, Abby started sobbing. In fact her sobs were so loud that Agatha, a blockmate who was passing in front of Abby's open door, pushed it and came rushing in.

"Oh sorry, I didn't know you had—"

"It's OK, Gathy," Abby managed between sobs. She buried her hand under a mound of pillows and found her box of tissue. She pulled out a few sheets and blew her nose.

"I'm OK, really. I'm just having a really bad day. Actually, it's been a pretty bad month come to think of it." More tears flowed.

At fifty, Agatha often asked herself what she was doing back in school amongst all these youngsters who were as grown as her own children, but it was on days like these that she saw the benefits of being the eldest student on the block.

"Come on, baby girl, you know you gotta suck it up," she said, her motherly Bahamian voice already producing the desired result.

"Whatever it is, you know your God is able!" Agatha took a seat next to Abby and draped her arm around the girl's shoulder. "You know that's what you're always telling us. He's still able, not so?"

"He sure is, Gathy." Abby sniffed out her confirmation.

"I mean." Agatha pulled out a tissue and handed it to Abby. "Is He on vacation in the beautiful Bahamas? I won't blame Him if He is."

Abby couldn't help chortle at the question. She dabbed again at her nose.

"Maybe, I should leave," Malachi said softly, reminding the women that he was still in the room.

"No, please Malachi, stay. I really need to talk to you."

"Well, that's my cue. Mission accomplished." Agatha bounced up from Abby's bed and headed for the door.

"Thanks a mil, Gathy," Abby called out as Agatha hoisted her hand in a wave.

The room fell silent.

"Sorry about the meltdown," Abby started.

"No need to apologize. Really, Abby, I'm the one who should be apologizing. I'm sorry. I sincerely regret that your good name got dragged into that whole mess. You didn't deserve it. I wish there's something I could do to erase the whole thing; make it like it never happened."

"Yeah, well. You and me alike. The thing is, Malachi, it really wasn't your fault. Jerome was being stupid. He made some stupid statements and left everyone cleaning up the mess. By the way, I heard he's OK—physically. I know he got kicked off hall, finally. I think the petition did him in. I don't know what his status is as a student at this point."

"He got kicked off hall?"

"Yep. There was a petition started by the girls on my block who saw the whole thing. It didn't take much to convince the warden that he would have a major situation on his hands if he didn't act."

"Well. I'd be lying if I said I'm sorry to see him go."

"I hear you."

"So. No word from Caleb?"

"I saw him at the hospital, and I visited him at his room when he came out, but his mom was there and neither of them seemed particularly thrilled to see me. She probably blames me for what happened. What a way to meet the mom, huh?" She blew her nose into fresh tissue.

"I passed by his room around lunchtime today and slipped a note under his door. That's why I thought…Never mind what I thought." She shrugged her shoulders.

"He's pretty much done the same to me," Malachi confessed. "One time I visited and I could hear him stirring inside. I knocked and called his name. He didn't open the door. I guess it's safe to say that I've lost my best friend."

"It hurts doesn't it?" Abby whispered, with a catch in her throat. "What hurts me the most is that he chose to believe Jerome. Jerome—a total stranger—over me. Us. Did you know that Caleb invited me home for Christmas to meet his family?"

"I didn't know that."

"I know it sounds crazy, but although we haven't known each other for very long, there was a genuine connection. We really clicked. I even started praying and fasting, asking God if he was the one. Silly, isn't it?"

"There's nothing silly about that."

"Malachi. I'm sorry for shutting you out. A lot was going on, and I didn't quite know how to deal with all of it."

"Abby, I understand, although I can't pretend that not hearing from you didn't add an unexpected layer of disappointment to the situation. You just ignored me like I was lint or something."

"I know, I know, but I was dealing with the fallout from Caleb and something else that's just as big—probably even bigger. I told my parents that I've decided to drop out of med school."

"What? Why? Were you failing exams or something?"

"No. Actually, I was doing pretty well, all things considered. But Malachi, the more I thought of it, the more I realized that I'm so much more interested in psychology than in the medicine side of it. That's what I want to do. I want to be a psychologist. I want the PhD, sure, but I don't really care for the MD."

"What can I say, I'm stunned. I mean I know you'd make a great psychologist, but are you sure about this move, Abby?"

"Yeah. To be honest, I've felt that leading since the end of my first year, but my dad was so excited when I made the dean's list, and I guess I just didn't have the heart to pull out. I mean don't get me wrong, it's scary starting over, filling out college applications. I want to do my program in the United States this time. So you see I've had a lot on my plate. Besides, I really think you and Megan needed some space to just be, you know."

Malachi walked over to where Abby sat on her bed surround-ed by her pillows and used tissue. He released his hands from his pockets and stretched them out in front of him palms facing upward toward Abby. She pulled herself up on her knees and placed her palms face down in his. He held them.

"Listen to me and listen good. You are my friend. I'm not go-ing to allow anyone—anyone, Abby, to make me feel dirty about our friendship. It's not about that; it's never been about that with us. People say men and women can't be friends; I don't believe that. You were the first one I ever really opened up to about my mom and how she died. I don't know why I did—why I chose you—but I did. For me, that was huge. Not even Dad and I have talked so much about it."

"Which is something you need to work on. I'm just saying," Abby interjected with a sniff.

"Yes, Dr. Abs," he said and rolled his eyes. "You see that's another thing. Do you know you're the only one I allow to call me Mal?"

"You call me Abs."

"Yeah, but you don't understand, I'm not supposed to let people call me Mal. Lavern's rules." He felt a slight sting in his eyes as he called his mom's name. "And I had to go easy on you. You know very well that you Americans are much better with monosyllabic names."

"Hey, buddy that's below the belt." Abby pulled away her hands and shoved him playfully.

"You see, Abs, that's why despite your disappointments and fears about starting afresh, I look at you and I have no doubt that you would make an excellent doctor of psychology someday. See, I refuse to let go of the doctor thing."

Abby laughed and allowed the happy tears that were threatening to fall down her cheeks.

"Know what I appreciate most about you, Abs, since I'm on a roll?" he continued, his dark eyes pierced into hers. "From day one I could tell that you cared for my soul. I know that sounds super corny, but don't think I haven't noticed that there's hardly a conversation when you haven't reminded me subtly or otherwise that life would be better if I get back to where I should be."

Abby cast her eyes at her sheets and smiled.

"You may be a baby Christian, Abigail Shaw, but when I see you I think of what Paul said to the Philippians. I believe that he who has begun a good work in you will perform it until the day of Jesus Christ. So finish up, Abs; don't do like me and abandon ship." Malachi swiped at the tear, which, despite his resolve had made its descent.

He cleared his throat and steadied his voice. "Shoot. Stupid sinus." He wiped his eyes with his T-shirt. "I must really need therapy. I got to stop doing this. Not my most manly moment is it?"

Abby squeezed his hands.

Seconds passed.

"I sometimes ask myself if I jumped out the boat because I'm afraid that if I stayed I might never see my mom again. What do you really think happens to people like her who take their own life?"

"I don't know, Mal. God is the only one who can judge that."

He nodded. "So I'm expecting you to finish, Abs. Don't let me down."

"Malachi Williamson Junior, you may have dropped out temporarily, but we're both finishing this race and that's that. Amen?"

He smiled and pulled her into a hug. "So be it, Abs. So be it."

As they embraced, neither of them noticed Caleb as he retreated quietly from Abby's partially-opened doorway.

CHAPTER TWENTY-ONE

Abby's watch read five o' clock.

Good, plenty of time to go back to hall and put in a few more hours of work. She'd been beating the books for the last three weeks, even as she struggled to come to a decision about her future in the med program. And even though she'd made a decision and had written to the dean on the matter, she was taking her father's advice to sit this semester's exams; after all, it was already paid for.

"Can I get you another cup of tea while you wait for your guest?" the petite young waitress with the white bodice, frilly collar, and Jamaican accent, asked.

"Oh yes, please. Fill me up," Abby replied with a smile.

"Actually, make that two," Megan said, as she eased off the straps crossed diagonally on her satchel before pulling out the chair and taking the seat opposite Abby.

"No problem, ma'am. I'll give you a few minutes to look at the menu. Just to let you know, the smoked salmon sandwich is on special today. That comes with a fresh garden salad topped with a lovely vinaigrette dressing."

"Sounds like just what the doctor ordered, doesn't it, Abby?"

"You're probably right," Abby replied with a chuckle. "But I think I'm gonna defy the doctor's orders today and go with a cheeseburger with the works. I haven't had one of those bad boys in ages. I need my cheesburger fix. It's the American blood in me, I guess," she said with a wink.

"I hear you ma'am," the waitress, said. "Should I place those orders, now?"

Abby looked at Megan.

"Fine with me."

"Excellent," the young woman remarked before taking up the menus. "I'll be back with your teas."

"OK, Abby, I'm truly impressed," Megan remarked as soon as the waitress was out of earshot. "Where did you find this place? I haven't tasted the food as yet, but the service is refreshing."

"I know! Trust me the food is all that. I kinda stumbled across this joint in my first year when I was shopping in the mall for sandals or something."

"Well if the food is good, this can easily become my new favorite spot. Sometimes you just desperately need to get off campus and join the real world for your sanity sake."

"I totally agree."

"So how's college applications, going?"

"I've narrowed it down to three. Columbia is still my first choice. They have an excellent program."

"Does it still look like you may have to start over as a freshman?"

"I've been making enquiries. It's been truly frustrating with the Internet being so irregular because of the upgrades, but I should get final word on that this week."

"Don't worry, God is in control. I know He'll work it out for you, Abby."

Abby sat back in her chair and folded her arms. A big goofy smile crept up on her face as she stared at Megan.

"What?"

The waitress approached and placed their tea on the table.

When she'd left the table, Abby continued. "You know what. I mean it's almost surreal. Here you are sitting there telling me about how God is in control. Really, Megan, I look at you and I have to pinch myself. Sometimes when I talk with you lately and the things you say, I'm genuinely at a loss for words, and you know that's a rare thing for me."

Megan grinned. "Abby, come on, don't be so dramatic. You're acting as if I were the spawn of Satan or something."

"But Megan, you don't get it, you didn't even believe there was a Satan a week and a half ago. Now…" Abby shook her head and released an audible sigh.

Megan looked at the black and white photos that lined the fuchsia walls of the patisserie, each encased in a black frame. She knew Abby was right. Her own conversion had taken her by surprise. She and Abby had started talking after Abby's unexpected visit to the Creative Arts rehearsal hall. At first, Megan later confessed to Abby, her motive wasn't exactly pure. She'd approached the budding friendship with a hidden agenda: get enough insight into Abby's personality to find out why Malachi was so enamored with her. The last thing Megan expected was to be the one to be drawn toward the chatty American. They'd talked about life, love, family, and school mainly. Abby had shared about her intention to quit med school to pursue psychology—a decision that was still not sitting well with her father. She'd even opened up about her disappointment over how things had gone down with Caleb.

When the subject switched to religion, she'd found Abby surprisingly insightful, although still too preachy for her taste. She'd reluctantly accepted Abby's invitation to attend another cell group meeting. Some of those who were there the last and only time she and Malachi had visited together had seemed genuinely surprised to see her back. But no one was more surprised than she when, at the end of the session and Abby had asked if there was anyone who'd wanted to make a decision for Christ, she'd felt the urge to slip her hand up.

"Earth to Megan, come in Megan," Abby was saying in response to the faraway look she was getting from Megan.

"Sorry about that, I'm just thinking about how quickly things can change. For all of us, actually."

The waitress approached the table again. She placed the respective orders in front of them.

"Enjoy," she said, before slipping away.

"Megan, I just got to come out and ask you. Have you told Malachi as yet?"

"I told him I needed to talk to him tonight. We've both been ridiculously busy with exams around the corner and assignments to complete. I saw him only once this week, actually."

Megan caught a whiff of the salmon sandwich and immediately bowed her head. She had a lot on her mind since the big decision. She'd basically picked at her last two meals, but her growling tummy was alerting her that her poor appetite was heading for a showdown with her hunger. Abby followed suit and bowed her head. She took the lead in offering a quick prayer that was loud enough for the both of them to hear.

"I was thinking, Abby, maybe I should wait until after exams. Malachi has so much on his plate. He's still on probation, you know. What do you think?"

"Megan, I can't tell you what to do here, but in my opinion, I think you should tell him sooner rather than later. And," Abby sipped her tea, "as I mentioned before, this decision you've made has far-reaching implications for your entire life, including your love life. It can't be business as usual, if you know what I mean.

You don't get a waiver on the rules just because you're a babe in Christ; it just doesn't work like that. Sorry, but I'd be lying to you if I told you differently. You've got to come to terms with the reality that you're a Christian now."

"And Malachi is not," Megan added, solemnly, as she tossed around the salad with her fork. "I know what that means, Abby. Believe me, I know exactly what that means."

****

Malachi felt a little silly as he squirted cologne on his collar. After all, he wasn't going anywhere special per se, but he was meeting up with Megan for a chat. At least that's what she'd said over the phone. She'd called from her home in Cherry Gardens early that morning sounding both relaxed and chipper at the same time—a feat that only true morning people could pull off.

"I'm glad you called; it's been a while," he'd told her in the closing seconds of their conversation.

"Too long," she'd practically cooed into the phone. He imagined her in a reclined position on her four poster bed; her right ankle resting on her left knee—a position that made her look relaxed. It bothered him a little that he'd never actually seen the antique bed she'd often raved about, not to mention the fact that Jerome of all people had been to her home, albeit a tag-along with his politician dad. Desperate had probably sipped cocktails from her crystal, and shared jokes with her parents. Malachi wondered how long it would be before he got the clarion call to meet the parents.

"Patience, Malachi. All in time," he told his reflection.

He'd decided on his cocoa brown designer polo with the cream collar—the piece he pulled out only for special occasions. He figured he would complement it with regular blue jeans. Malachi pondered over whether to put on his beige corduroy instead of jeans for their little meeting. He'd opted for the jeans, however, since somehow the corduroys made him feel like he was trying too hard to impress. He'd purchased the corduroys mainly for style, but except for the occasional trip to cold venues like the movies, he hadn't gotten much wear out of it back home. Even in Jamaica, they still made him a little warmer than was comfortable, but with the temperature acting all winter wonderland these days, he'd actually found more opportunities to wear it.

Megan had told him how "yummy" he'd looked when he'd donned the combo the only Friday night that he'd been able to take her to dinner and a movie. The simple gesture had been well-received, though it had cost him about a week's worth of meals.

Suddenly a thought came to him, What if she was planning to surprise him: pick him up with her driver and take them to meet the parents? He'd learned the hard way that she was fully capable of stunts like that under the guise of spontaneity. It was a discovery he'd made six weeks ago when she'd pulled up in her dad's Benz and lured him into the car with the assurance that they were only going for a spin. That spin had taken them to Tree Top, the most exclusive restaurant in New Kingston.

Malachi had complained bitterly for the first ten minutes about the lack of notice.

"If I'd given you notice then it wouldn't have been much of a surprise, now, would it?" she'd said in her defense.

"Better safe than sorry," Malachi said aloud, as he unzipped his jeans and reached for the corduroy.

CHAPTER TWENTY-TWO

The signs that exams were right around the corner were everywhere.

Coffee became an endangered species on the shelves of the campus commissary. The *Do Not Disturb* postings on dorm room doors had quadrupled and grown meaner. Even the cats were having a hard time securing their midnight snacks in peace, with the endless parade of student traffic. Still, the pink, yellow, and white flowers of the various poui trees were nowhere to be found. A second year botany major on hall had told the Freshman what he'd already suspected—that the seniors had been full of folly, that he would probably have to wait for the next dry season if he wanted to see some decent poui. The news had disappointed him. Why all the waiting? Why couldn't the poui trees behave more like the flamboyant Poinciana which seemed to have been blooming on demand throughout the campus.

The November breeze was cooler, more invigorating, according to some. So much so that many students dragged their desks, chairs, and lamps onto their balconies to get the nippy slap they needed to make them wrestle a little longer with sleep for precious study time.

It was a nice evening for a stroll, Malachi had to admit, although he'd been a bit disappointed when he met Megan outside the rehearsal hall and realized that the only place they were going was to the library. Malachi walked in silence across the mounds that provided a welcomed departure from the relatively flat landscape of the campus. Megan loved this part of campus because of the burn it gave to her leg muscles. They both knew they always had the option of walking along the tree-lined pathway but she enjoyed the exercise so much that he'd actually suggested that they take the mounds.

"Every time I pass here I'm reminded of how much I miss my home gym," Megan said, slightly winded. "I'm so out of shape it's horrid."

Malachi shook his head.

"What are you talking about? You are one of the fittest people I know, and notice I said people and not women. You're definitely fitter than me." Malachi was pleased that the sentence came out in one breath instead of the staccato words that he would've uttered when they first started climbing the mounds together. He took it as a sign that his own fitness level was improving.

He hadn't mentioned to Megan that just after the incident with Desperate, he'd taken to getting up on mornings and taking a jog around the campus. It helped him diffuse the stress of the situation, especially the waiting and not knowing part. He couldn't quite figure out why he hadn't mentioned it to her. He figured he just wanted to catch up quietly to her level of fitness, and even surpass it before she had time to process what had happened. It was a good plan—one that he might employ for other areas where he lagged.

"Malachi, let's slow down a bit. At the rate we're going, we'd reach the library before we get a chance to chat."

"OK." He slowed his pace.

"How is exam prep coming along for you?" She was asking.

"Great. I'm pushing hard. The group study thing seemed to have crashed. Hopeton is hoarding, but it doesn't matter, since I actually study better on my own coming closer to exams. How 'bout you?"

"I had some scary moments as I mentioned, but I think that's behind me. I think the time I spent off campus helped, somewhat."

"Good. And the production? Your lead looked excited tonight. She almost knocked you over with that hug."

"Thalia is amazing. She's certainly come into her own. She had us a bit nervous for a while there, but she's over that hurdle now it seems."

"Boyfriend trouble, you said."

"The worst kind, I'm afraid."

"I'm sure you're glad you don't have that kind of stress to contend with. At least not for the last two weeks." He bumped her shoulder and chuckled.

Megan turned her face and bit the inside of her lips.

"Was a joke, Megan, you know, ha ha."

"Yes. It wasn't lost on me, Malachi."

"Right," he said unconvinced.

It rained earlier in the day. The earthy smell of wet grass and flowering trees squirted their perfumes into the air.

"And Madame Francois is cool about you not being around as often as you were to take them through their paces? I mean, this is the home stretch for the big show."

"Yes. She's fine with it. Listen, Malachi there is something very important I must tell you. It's sort of difficult to say, and I'm pretty sure you're not going to like it."

Malachi stopped walking. His hands slipped out of his pocket and cupped his head with his fingers laced at the top. A pained expression pinched his face.

"Please, Megan. Please, please don't say what I think you're going to say?"

Megan turned to him; her mouth fell open.

"You know, what I'm going to say?"

"You're pregnant aren't you? Stop beating around the bush, just say it."

"Malachi Williamson, I am not pregnant for crying out loud!"

Malachi clutched his heart in exaggerated relief, and despite himself, started to laugh.

"I'm sorry, babes, you said I'm not going to like it and I thought—" He puffed out a breath.

"I know what you thought!" Her voice was now raised. "It's good to know that you see such things as the end of the world for you."

"What? Hey, come nah, babes, that's not fair. You know I love you, but neither of us is ready to be parents right now. A baby would have been really bad timing, that's all I'm saying. I'm a first-year med student. It's not like I'm graduating in three years and could look for a job. Let's at least be honest about that."

Megan didn't hear much after he said "I love you." She thought of bringing it to his attention since it was the first time he'd said it to her, but how could she dangle his confession of love on the same night that she was going to break up with him. That would be cruel.

"I want to break up with you." The words escaped from her lips and straddled the air between them like a foul odor in an enclosed room.

"Because I thought you were pregnant and wasn't happy?" He laughed, incredulously. "You for real, Megan?"

"It has nothing to do with that. It's me. Something has happened. I—I've given my life to the Lord, and it just can't be business as usual between us."

She'd borrowed Abby's words. Hers were having trouble organizing themselves into sentences.

"Sorry, I must be experiencing some hearing loss. What did you just say?"

Megan raised her chin and steadied her voice.

"I said, I'm a Christian now; I've given my life to the Lord."

Malachi chewed at his upper lip as he tried, in vain, to stop the cynical smirk from spreading across his face.

"I'm sorry. Didn't mean to...." He held his stomach. "I mean, is this even for real? When did all this happen?"

"It happened on the fifteenth of November at Abby's cell group meeting."

"At Abby's cell group what? You! The girl who practically ran out of one of these said cell groups—deeply offended, I might add—went back and..."

For some reason, he couldn't finish the sentence. Next option: shift gears.

"This happened on November fifteenth, you say. It's the twenty-ninth. What took you so long to tell me?"

"Well, we've both been extremely busy; in fact, we've hardly seen each other." She looked off into the trees and met his gaze again. "Honestly, Malachi, I guess I was also a little afraid to tell you. I needed to figure out what this meant for me, before I dealt with the us."

Malachi took his right hand out of his pocket and rubbed his head.

"Well, Megan, as I see it, this is a good thing." He said it with more pep in his voice than she expected. "Truth be told, I was never really comfortable with you being an atheist or agnostic or whatever you actually called yourself. I know you were never big on labels. Now, at least you understand that there is a God. I think that should move us closer together…Spiritually, I mean."

Megan couldn't believe what she was hearing. He was in denial. Either that, or he'd totally miscalculated the strength of her conviction.

"I don't think you've realized what has happened. Malachi, I didn't just get some epiphany about the existence of God; I've entered into a relationship with the Father through Jesus…His begotten Son." She prayed silently that she'd got the lingo right.

"I'm not the same Megan that scoffed at all things Christian, and I hate to put it so bluntly, but I'm not the same Megan who feels comfortable jumping into bed with you anytime either one of us gets that itch. You know what I mean?"

There it was. The statement, though brusque in delivery, that clearly stated where she, and by extension *they*, stood. This was no dalliance with spirituality; this was serious.

"Cool. You want to break up, no problem." He held his palms up in the air. "I guess Desperate was right on target about our chances of going the distance."

Even in the dark, he saw the color drain from her face.

"Desperate? What does that idiot have to do with us?" She felt her throat constrict.

"Well Megan, he basically said what I guess everyone but me knew, that we probably wouldn't have lasted beyond the first semester anyway because I was—how did he put it?—out of your league. The truth is, I foolishly thought I had a shot. After all, I figured a doctor is still a pretty respectable profession. Not even snobby diplomats could argue with that. But what can I say? I guess not everyone can wait five or seven long years to see who someone would become. That's just unreasonable, right?"

Megan closed her eyes and prayed for God himself to come down and quell her rage. She knew her unexpected conversion might be a bit of a shocker for him. Goodness—it even had taken her by surprise. But she wasn't quite prepared for anger—let alone anger laced with stupidity. There was no way she was letting those erroneous assumptions stand.

"If you're trying to hurt me, you're doing a brilliant job," she finally said, her lips trembling. "You know, ever since we met, Malachi, you've never missed an opportunity to point out the disparity in our economic circumstances. At first I saw it as a bit of insecurity on your part, but I've come to realize it's more than that—it's an obsession. That you honestly believe that becoming a rich doctor will give you an 'all access' pass to the playground of the wealthy snobs of this world, is just sad on so many levels."

She raised her index finger in the air. "For the record, your financial status has never been an issue for me, nor has it ever come up in conversation with my parents. I love you, not because of what you bring to the table, as you're fond of putting it, and frankly I don't care if your name doesn't have the same cachet as mine in somebody's ear. I've always been proud to be with you, simply because you have a good heart, and I saw that from day one. Now?" She lowered her voice to a whisper.

"Now, I see a man who needs to find himself, and more importantly I suppose, I see someone who desperately needs to find his place in God."

"Well, what can I say? I guess that's that. You and Abby have me all figured out," he said, in a voice that belied the tailspin that his system had suddenly been thrown into.

Was the air becoming thin? He needed to get away. Far away.

"Well Ms. LeBlanc. It was…It was real. You taught me a lot." He stretched out his hand in a gesture that was meant as a show of magnanimity.

With silent tears streaming down her face, Megan stared at Malachi's outstretched hand before turning to walk off in the direction of the library. She refused to start her journey as a Christian mired in hypocrisy. Without a backward glance, Megan hiked up the final mound that eventually descended toward the library.

CHAPTER TWENTY-THREE

"Where am I?" Malachi called out to the middle-aged man in the green and gold bathing trunks—the man with an uncanny resemblance to Professor Livingston.

"You're the hot shot med student. Figure it out," the Professor Livingston lookalike replied and continued to study the coiled structure.

"I'm in the body again, aren't I?" Malachi asked. The man ignored him. "Please, sir, I really need to know where I am," he pleaded.

"What's that? I can't hear you." The man in the trunks sang mockingly and flicked his ear with his thumb.

"That's some kind of a clue, isn't it? I'm in the ear!"

"Is that your final answer, Mr. Williamson?"

"Wait! But it doesn't make sense. If I'm in the inner ear then this should be the cochlea and shouldn't there be fluid—perilymph or is that endolymph." His mind was a bit foggy.

The mention of the word fluid triggered an immediate response. Fluid started to fill the cavity, and within minutes, Malachi was waist deep in it. His gaze shifted to the direction of the cochlear nerve where he saw another man beating up in the fluid. No it couldn't be. It looked like….

"Dad? Dad!" he yelled to the drowning man. "Grab the hair cells. The hair cells, Dad, in the organ of corti. Dad, grab the hair cells!"

"The organ of what?" His dad shouted back.

"Malachi help!" The sound did not come from the drowning man this time but from behind him. He turned only to see Megan in full ballerina regalia complete with tiara on her head, clinging to the mouth of the round window.

"Megan, wait! Hold on I've got to save my dad," he yelled to her.

"I can't wait, Malachi; I'm slipping. Help me, please. Don't let me die!"

"Save me, Son," his father's voice beckoned. Instinctively, he began to swim toward his father. He glanced back and saw Megan's head going under, her flailing arms still visible from the surface. He turned again to swim toward her and heard a whistle. He turned frantically to the direction of the whistle.

"There are rules," the man in the trunks was saying. "There are rules, Mr. Williamson. Rules, rules, rules!" Suddenly, he heard laughter. It was coming from Megan and his dad.

"Oh, you think this is funny? I'm killing myself to save you both, and you think it's funny?" His voice was almost hysterical. They laughed harder.

"It's not funny. It's not funny at all! It's not funny!" he chided.

"Malachi, wake up man!" A well-dressed Hopeton was standing over him, shaking him.

He couldn't believe it was happening again. The dream was over; he was awake now. He felt his face. It was damp with sweat. He felt the bed too, as if half expecting it to be soaked.

"Mal, man, you have to do something about these nightmares. Get a purge or something, man," Hopeton said.

"Not a bad idea," Malachi mumbled, his voice still heavy with sleep. "What time is it?"

"Time for me to go," Hopeton replied, glancing down at his watch.

Malachi sat up on his bed and ran his hand over his face. Hopeton was brushing his hair. He looked pretty dapper with his black jacket, matching trousers, white shirt and black tie.

"Look at you. Hot date tonight? You and Petrina having your own private post-exam brain cooler, huh?" Malachi's smile dropped as he caught a whiff of his cologne. He didn't really mind that Hopeton was wearing it, although he would have preferred if he'd asked first.

Hopeton stared at Malachi nonplussed.

"Mal, don't tell me you forget."

"Forgot what, Hope?"

"Today is the big day: *The Nutcracker*. Megan's ballet thing."

"Right," Malachi said. He sounded cool and unfazed, at least to his own ear. He dared not give Hopeton an indication of the knot that the mere mention of her name triggered.

"You still alright with me going on your tickets, right? I mean, this is VIP seating. You know, well, neither a we could pay for that. I mean, if you change your mind…" He didn't complete the sentence.

"Nah, Hopeton. Listen, I gave you the tickets. It's cool. I'm really not in the mood. Besides, what would I wear?"

"Yeah, true," Hopeton said, with a chuckle and sigh.

"Well, got to run. The limo outside, you see," Hopeton said and guffawed.

"Have a good time," Malachi called out as Hopeton opened the door.

"Will do. Couldn't have ask for a better brain cooler. Doh fret yuh head. I'll kiss Megan for you and tell her you have fever or something. People tend to believe doctors about stuff like that." He brushed at his jacket. "And med students, I suppose. Anyway, later man."

Malachi couldn't remember being so happy to see someone leave a room. If ever there was an award for saying the wrong thing, he felt Hopeton would snag it every time. But he owed him. Hopeton had stood up for him when he needed it most, and he didn't have to. Malachi had thanked him, of course, for the letter he'd written to the Dean. The tickets were a way of saying it tangibly.

He'd got back to his room about five after his final exam. The last thing Malachi remembered was kicking off his sneakers and slumping down on his bed. He'd completely forgotten about the production. He had given Hopeton two tickets. What he didn't tell him was that he had an extra ticket. The second one was originally meant for Abby. Megan had asked him how many extra tickets he'd wanted about a month ago, and he had told her two. A week ago he came into his room and saw the red envelope with the gold seal on it addressed to him. When he'd opened it he'd seen the three tickets to the show. He assumed that Megan had slipped it under the door, not even bothering to knock. He had been in his room all day, so if she'd wanted to hand it to him she could have done so. He had not seen her since the night she told him that they were over. It was a night he had been trying hard to forget. He'd willed himself to focus on exams. Everything else was a distraction.

And Abby. Malachi felt a double whammy with this betrayal. The more he thought of the conversation he had with Megan and her decision to end things based on her new-found faith, the more he suspected Abby's hand. And for the life of him, he couldn't understand why Abby, knowing what he'd been through in life, would deliberately put a spoke like that in his happiness. Unless…

Maybe she does like me and wants me for herself.

Immediately, as the thought was conceived, Malachi realized how utterly ridiculous it was. His relationship with Abby was the purest thing in his life, he had to admit. And even if she had the hots for him, a theory which he seriously doubted, she just wasn't the conniving type. It's not her style.

He had given Hopeton Abby's ticket out of spite. Besides, he reasoned that if she and Megan were so chummy now, Megan should supply her new best friend with tickets of her own. The local press had been abuzz with pieces about the upcoming production at the university. He even saw a newspaper interview with Madame Francois and her eager young charges during one of their final rehearsals. He thought Megan's picture would have been in the article. The piece and quotes by Madame Francois had credited her for her contribution, but there was no photo.

In the end, Malachi reasoned that his absence was the biggest statement he could make to the two about how he felt. It would hurt Megan especially not to see him there after all the nights he picked her up and escorted her safely to her door, not to mention how he patiently listened as she dilated about some technical aspect of *The Nutcracker* adaptation, which most of the time, went over his head. Yes indeed it would hurt, and quite frankly, he didn't mind one bit.

Certain kinds of pain must be shared.

****

"Explorer, yuh in there?"

The voice sounded like Tallboy, a first year Jamaican on his block.

"Yeah!"

"Phone call."

"Right. Meh soon come."

Malachi grabbed the room keys on the top of his chest of drawers and pushed his socked feet in his slippers. He slammed the door behind him and shuffled as fast as his feet would allow him toward the phone.

"Hello goodnight."

"Junior."

"Caleb?"

"Yeah."

"Wow, this is a surprise."

"Yeah, well. I know it's been a while."

"OK."

"Listen man, I'm calling because I found out something and thought you should know."

"What's that, man?"

"It's about your dad; he's in hospital."

"What? My dad's in the hospital? Why? When?"

"Listen, that's all I know. My dad told me, and he said your father apparently didn't want to tell you because you're writing exams."

"Are you serious, Caleb?"

"As serious as a heart attack, man. I told my dad no way that excuse would hold water. If it were me, I'd want to know."

"Thanks, man."

"Besides," he paused. "I checked the exam schedule posted in admin and I saw that first year med had their last exams today."

He knew Caleb meant well, but right now the last thing he needed was more shielding. If his father had concealed something this big from him, out of concern for his academic performance, he'd done enough. He knew that if the tables were turned, he would not have heard the end of his old man's berating.

"The hospital, boy. What could it be?" Malachi said into the receiver, as he speculated about the endless conditions that could warrant a hospital stay. "I'm thinking if it were something really serious like a heart attack, he would have called me, right? Or asked them to call me. He wouldn't keep something like that from me, would he? Are you sure you don't know anything more. I hope you're not holding back on me, Caleb. I mean it."

"All I know is that he fell and broke his wrist, but my dad said something about fever."

"Dengue fever? Are you sure he didn't say dengue fever?"

"I asked if it was that. Dad said they're not telling him much because he's not family."

Malachi's throat went dry. He knew he had to go home immediately. His dad had bought him a round trip, but they'd agreed that he'd use it at the end of the academic year rather than the semester breaks. That meant that he would have been spending his first Christmas in Jamaica—a fact that up to two weeks ago didn't look like such a bad prospect. But if he went home now, where would he find the money to go back up, especially if it turned out that his dad was much sicker than he was being told?

What am I thinking?

It suddenly dawned on Malachi that if it turned out that his dad was sicker than he was being told, getting back to Jamaica would be the least of his problems.

Caleb seemed to have read his thoughts.

"Listen, Malachi, I think you should go home. I know you told me you're planning to spend Christmas over here, but you need to go and find out what's going on."

"You don't have to tell me that, man. It's my dad." The words came out with an edge.

"Here's what I propose, and hear me out because I know you and your stupid pride. Let's go down to the airport in the morning and ask the airline to switch us, meaning you take my flight back home, and I'll come home when I get the next available flight."

"But we both came up here on round trips Caleb, I'll just use mine to go home."

"No."

"No? What do you mean, no?"

"I'm saying, keep your ticket to come back up next January. Listen, I have enough extra cash in my account to buy a ticket to go home."

"I don't know, Caleb. I don't think I can—"

"OK, well let me ask you a question. If it were me, and you were in a position to help, would you do this for me?"

"You know I would."

"There we go."

Malachi couldn't argue with the logic. He would do that for Caleb in a heartbeat, and as much as he hated anything that smelled of handouts, he knew that this was not the time for false pride, as his father would call it.

"What time tomorrow?" he asked his friend.

"The flight is at two thereabout. I think we should go down in the morning and explain the situation. I'll have a cab pick us up around ten thirty. Just be packed and ready, cool?"

"OK. Caleb."

"Yeah?"

"Thanks, man."

"It's going to be all right, Junior. Your dad's as tough as they come."

"Caleb I know the timing is kind of crappy, but I want to clear up whatever misconceptions you might have about me and Abby."

"Forget about it. Ancient history. Besides, I heard she's going back to the United States soon. Sometimes things just don't work out because they're not meant to, you know."

"Yeah," Malachi said and thought gloomily of Megan. "Ten thirty?"

"Ten thirty sharp. Don't worry, Junior; God has the final say."

Malachi dared not tell his estranged best friend that that's the fact that scared him the most.

CHAPTER TWENTY-FOUR

Despite his ambitions of becoming a doctor, Malachi couldn't boast of having a love for hospitals. He heard some of his classmates describe the rush they experience when they smell the hospital-grade disinfectant or felt the vibrations of a gurney as it's wheeled along the seamless resin floors. There was even one guy, Ricardo, a fellow Trini who confessed that he has a fetish for blood. Some of Malachi's classmates had laughed when he'd said it. Malachi failed to see the humor. He shuddered to think that some sicko like that could be attending to his father—anybody's father.

"Mr. Williamson is in bed eight I think," the bright-eyed nurse at the nurses' station said, more to herself, as she flipped through the white pages of the black hard-covered notebook to find his dad's name.

"There it is. Yes, bed eight."

"Nurse…?"

"Roberts."

"Yes, Nurse Roberts, is there anything you can tell me about my dad's condition? I'm a first year med student in Jamaica, by the way." He forced a smile that wasn't returned.

"You would have to speak to his doctor."

"Is he or she around? I don't know anything. I don't even know why my father's in the hospital. Please nurse, is there anything you can tell me?"

"Sorry. You'll have to wait for the doctor. It's outside of visiting hours, but if he's still awake, I will allow you a few minutes with your father."

Malachi checked his irritation. He might have been wet behind the ears but he already knew the golden rule about not getting on the wrong side of nurses.

"Sure. Thank you, Nurse."

When Malachi turned into the room where his father was assigned, he was conscious of the fact that his own heart was beating faster. His heat rate slowed ever so slightly when he saw his father lying on his side reading his Bible.

"Dad," he said softly. His father's head shot up like a deer who'd heard a rustling noise in the bushes. He turned at the voice. "Junior? What are you doing here, Son? Don't you have exams?"

"It's OK, I had my last exam yesterday. Dad it's OK, really. Relax." Malachi saw his dad's shoulders slump as he exhaled.

"But when did you get here? Who told you? I asked them not to bother you about this."

"How could my father being in hospital possibly be a bother? Hmm? Dad, please, I'm not a child anymore. I can handle way more than you think. But right now I'm still in the dark, and I hate it. Why are you here? What are they saying?"

"Lower your voice, Junior. You don't want them to kick you out."

"Sorry."

Malachi reached for the chair adjacent to the vacant bed next to his dad and sat in it. His father still held a slightly startled look on his face. He broke eye contact with his son and gave it instead to the white pages of the Bible which lay open at his side.

"Well, I guess this is the moment of truth."

Malachi didn't answer. He swallowed hard and told himself to ignore the lexicon of pathology that was zipping about in his brain.

"Well, I can't tell you to sit; you're already sitting," Malachi Senior said with a chuckle.

Malachi could almost hear his own heart pounding in his chest.

Slow down heart, for heaven's sake. Slow down.

He took a breath and looked impatiently at the wall on the other side of the room.

"Remember when I told you that I was fed up of the public service, and I wanted to do something different?" his dad began.

"Yes."

"Well, that wasn't entirely true. I loved my job very much. It was very demanding but fulfilling at the same time."

"OK."

"You know your mom was ill for quite some time."

"Yes, Dad. She was bipolar."

"Yes, well it's something that I had a hard time coming to terms with…the fact that your mom—my wife was…" He rubbed his chest gently.

Malachi Senior cleared his throat. "Just pour me a cup of water there, Son. The bottle's in my locker."

Malachi removed the bottled water from the metal side table locker and poured water into a sanitary cup. He handed it to his dad.

He seemed to finish it in one gulp.

"When I met your mom, I thought she was the most unique woman I ever met. She had beauty, brains, and she was very opinionated. She had strong views on everything. It was attractive. I found her very attractive. You basically know the story of how we met and hit it off. Pretty soon we were inseparable. A year later, we were man and wife."

"Dad, I'm sorry to hustle you, but I don't think I have enough time to hear the long version. I'm going to be asked to leave soon."

"OK. OK. I'll try to get to the point. It soon became clear to me that your mom wasn't just eccentric. She was mentally ill. Even though I knew it, I guess I was in denial for years.

"Things got really bad when she started going on these shopping sprees with our money. It got pretty bad, Junior, and it was one of the reasons I decided to retire early. Someone needed to be there for her and I decided there was no passing the buck. That someone was me."

"That's why you retired, to take care of Mom?"

"Yes."

"OK, but Dad what does that have to do with you being here."

Malachi Senior smiled. "You were never a patient kid."

"Dad."

"It's true, but it's a good thing most of the time. I always knew that you were going to be something special. You were never one to settle. We knew it from the questions you would ask even as a little boy. I remember one time your mom told you that our house, the one we live in, is for you when you grow up. I think you were nine years old at the time. I was helping her pack away dishes. Do you remember what you said?"

"What did I say, Dad?"

Malachi Senior was laughing now.

Apart from losing a few pounds, Malachi Junior thought that his dad didn't look too bad. Not bad at all.

"You said, 'Mom, if this house is for me when I grow up, where would you and Daddy live?'"

"I said that?"

"You sure did; you sure did." The dimples in his cheek deepened. With the evidence staring him in the face, Malachi Junior could not deny just how much he resembled his father.

"You know that was the day when I realized that if all I had to give you was an inheritance when I die, that wasn't going to cut it. It may sound stupid to you, but that statement changed my whole outlook on life: made me work even harder. I figure this kid was going places if at nine years old he had enough sense to reason out that when he grows up, his parents might still be alive so that he's going to need that house long before that unfortunate day comes when we die. How about that."

"Dad, what's this about? You're freaking me out now."

"Bear with me; this is harder than..." He signaled for more water.

"Son, when I decided to work for the church I did so to keep a closer eye on your mother. It worked for a little while, but I think she began to feel stifled. I think you were old enough to sense that."

"Yes. Most of the time she just complained that you were cheap. She told me a couple times that you were trying to control her with money. She said her friends told her that that was abuse."

"I had to, Son. If I didn't put the brakes on her spending, we would have been in the poor house, and you would have had to kiss med school goodbye."

"I guess you did what you felt was best. I must confess, I took her side on that. I, too, felt that you were tight-fisted where money was concerned; you still are, pretty much." He smiled down at his dad. What Caleb said about his wrist must have been correct. His wrist was really bandaged and his arm was in a sling.

Malachi Senior smiled back. "I guess I am…pretty much."

A nurse entered the room and approached the cubicle. She checked the IV line, cocked her head, and smiled at father and son.

"How is our model patient tonight? I understand you have a special visitor, Mr. Williamson."

"Yes, Sister. This is my son, Malachi Junior. First year med in Jamaica."

"Very nice. He got his father's good looks too. Well he's come a long way to see you, but I'm afraid I can only give you five more minutes. You can come back tomorrow during visiting hours."

"Thank you, Sister."

She smiled again and continued on her rounds.

"Money was a problem with me and your mom, but there was something else. Are you familiar with the term hypersexuality?"

"Yes. I've come across it when I was doing my research on bipolar. It's a symptom of mania."

"Your mother had that particular symptom."

"No she didn't. No, Dad, I'm sorry you're mistaken. If something like that was happening I would have known."

"Son, it's true. Your mom developed an addiction to sex. At first I enjoyed it, I mean, what husband wouldn't, until I realized—"

"Realized what? Realized what, Dad?"

"Realized that her sexual interest didn't stop with me."

He couldn't believe what he was hearing. His dad was accusing his mom of being...He couldn't even say it.

"At first I talked myself into thinking that it was all in my head: the late night phone calls, disappearing for a night here and there without an explanation."

"But she explained that. She was staying by Aunt Barbara's!"

"Not so loud, Junior. Calm down....She wasn't, I checked. Besides, you know she never had a great relationship with her sister. Why would she stay there so often?"

"I can't believe what you're telling me."

"I'm sorry, Son, but I couldn't bring myself to tell you this before; I didn't want you to think any less of your mother."

Malachi Junior threw back his head. He shut his eyes.

"It gets a bit worse I'm afraid," Malachi Senior said as he observed how his son's eyes settled at the site where the intravenous access entered his vein.

That was the moment when Malachi Junior knew. His dad didn't have to say it; he knew.

"Mom gave you AIDS? You expect me to sit here and accept that Mom gave you AIDS?"

"HIV," his dad corrected with a nod. And as if someone punched him in the diaphragm, Malachi Junior began to heave. His father reached out to take his hand and he flinched.

"No! Don't touch me! Leave me alone. Dad, just leave me alone. You think I'm strong; I'm smart. I can't deal with this!

I have to go. I have to get out of here." He was on his feet. He grabbed the suitcase with his left hand and was reaching for the sound system he had placed on top the side table next to his dad's bed.

"Junior."

"Shhh. No, I don't want to hear any more. Shh!" Like a pre-schooler shushing his best friend, Malachi Junior's index tapped exaggeratedly against his lips. His raised voice had roused one of the patients in a neighboring bed from sleep.

His heart galloping now, he was beginning to feel funny. The shuffle of feet grew louder as two nurses scurried into the room.

"I'm done here. I'm leaving, Nurse. I'm leaving." He almost tripped on a chair as he backed out of the room. "Sorry. I didn't mean to… I need air. I—I can't breathe," he heard himself mumble, seconds before his world went blank.

CHAPTER TWENTY-FIVE

The first thing he saw when he came to was a wrinkled, old man with a smattering of teeth.

"I told you he wasn't dead," the old man was saying to his elderly friend with the bandaged foot. "Percy here said yuh dead for sure."

It took a few seconds for Malachi to figure out where he was. A quick look around told him that he was lying on a bed directly opposite the nurses' station. His legs were elevated.

"OK, Mr. Singh and Mr. O'Neil, the show is over. Please get back to your beds. Everything is under control. Nobody is dying tonight."

"Sister, with all due respect, that is real stupidness you say there," Mr. Singh, the elderly man of Indian descent, said. "This is a hospital. People dying left, right, and center. What you talking 'bout nobody dying tonight."

"Mr. Singh, I'm glad to see that you're feeling plenty better. I need you to go back to your bed now, please. Don't let me have to ask you again," the ward sister warned.

"All right, all right. I does forget you in charge, yes. But doh vex with me. I was sleeping on my bed good good. Is the boy wake me up, from a nice dream too. But plain talk bad manners, Sister, but ah find yuh should learn to speak to people properly. Gosh man, yuh buff me there like my late wife Pavati. Just so she used to boss me around: 'Sit down here,' 'bathe now,' 'doh eat that,' and with all that she still come and dead before me." The patient snorted out a laugh.

Malachi was sitting up now. He was fully aware of where he was and why.

"How long was I out?" he asked the ward sister.

"Just a minute, minute and a half. Are you diabetic, son?"

"No."

"Your dad told us you're not. Just double checking. Did you have anything to eat today?"

"I had a few spoonfuls of the dinner they served on the plane, but I didn't have much of an appetite." Nurse Roberts wheeled the sphygmomanometer over to the chair where Malachi was now sitting. He slipped his hand into the cuff to get his blood pressure taken.

A female doctor approached the small group. She couldn't have been more than twenty-five or twenty-six. But the look was there. She stood like a gazelle about five feet nine, dark-skinned with cheekbones that most models would kill for. There was an efficient, no nonsense manner about her gait. She greeted the nurses respectfully. Her hair was open but all back and cropped ruthlessly straight by the nape of her neck. He'd never seen a more attractive specimen in white coat and stethoscope. She opened her mouth to say something to him. That's when Malachi noticed the braces.

"Mr. Williamson. Hello, I'm Dr. Tinsdale. Heard you kissed the ground tonight, ouch…I guess you were really happy to be back home, huh?" She reached for his wrist and took his pulse.

"So how are you feeling? Any dizziness? Ever fainted before, Mr. Williamson?"

Where in the world could she have been? He certainly didn't notice her anywhere on the ward when he walked in. Nobody pointed her out when he'd asked to see the doctor. Exactly when had she arrived, he wondered, and how is it that she could know so much about him already?

She looked at him again and misread his silence. "Did he hit his head?"

Her query was directed at the ward sister.

"I didn't hit my head; at least I don't think so." Malachi looked at Nurse Roberts who nodded her confirmation.

"So you just fainted. Let's see. Blood pressure is fine, pulse is fine. Are you diabetic? Any history of heart disease? Are you on any medication?"

"No, no and—no…Doctor," he added after a deliberate pause.

She smirked. "OK...stand up. How does that feel? All right, have a seat. I'll be back in a few minutes." She spoke to the ward sister at the desk and the both of them walked down the corridor. Malachi figured they were going to check on his dad.

Nurse Roberts brought Malachi a cup of water. He accepted it gratefully and drank it.

Dr. Tinsdale returned in five minutes and motioned to Malachi to follow her. He followed the doctor into a small room with an oil painting of scenery on the wall. The striped drapes matched the amber-colored walls. There were three round tables, each with three chairs. Dr. Tinsdale closed the door and motioned Malachi to sit at the table nearest the door.

"Your dad told me you had a bit of a shocker tonight?"

"How is he?"

"He's fine. Resting now. He was a bit concerned about you, but we told him we're taking good care of you."

"Well, what can I say? I found out that my mom slept around, contracted HIV, and from all indication gave it to my dad. Just couldn't hear any more, you know? Guess I exceeded my quota of bad news for the day." A flicker of a smile touched his face.

Dr. Tinsdale studied him.

"Your humor is intact. Good," she said.

"Right."

"I understand you're first year med?"

"Wow, word gets around. Yes I am. Sorry, uh, Dr. Tinsdale, are you the doctor who is treating my father?"

"One of them, yes. There's also a consultant."

That's a relief.

"How could he not tell me? It's probably been like what, close to two years. He never said a word. How do people hide stuff like that? I guess our relationship is worse than I thought."

"Your dad told me to speak freely with you, so I'll start by saying that talking about HIV, even to the people closest to us, can be very difficult."

He noted that she said "us." *Nice touch, Doc.*

"So why exactly is he here? Is he like…dying or something? Please give it to me straight, Doc, I won't faint again. Promise," he added, and prayed that she couldn't see the tremor in his hands.

"Your dad is here as a precaution more than anything else. He was brought in because of a distal radius Colles' type fracture. That apparently happened when he lost his balance and tried to break a fall. He also came in with flu like symptoms, ear pains, and a discharge. He gave a history of recurrent otitis media, which is basically an ear infection. Given his age and medical history, we were concerned about treating with the ear infection. We were also mindful that the fracture, ear infection, and being an HIV patient put him at an increased risk for clots. The good news is that his CD4 count is good, and he's been responding well to treatment. We expect to be able to discharge him, say, day after tomorrow once he continues to progress."

"So he's going to live."

"Listen, Mr. Williamson, your dad isn't planning on going anywhere anytime soon. He's well-motivated. He's been blabbing to everyone about you since he came in. The best you can do is to educate yourself about his condition and what he's likely to face in the years to come. You've heard about Highly Active Antiretroviral Therapy?"

"Yes. I know a little."

"Well get to know a lot more because compliance to HAART, as we call it, will help him prevent viral resistance and basically allow him to stay healthy longer until they find a cure for this thing. But he's also going to have to deal with stigma and discrimination. My humble advice is start with yourself. Even medical professionals and those in training can nurture hang ups and misconceptions about HIV and AIDS. Don't be one of them. The medical facts are clear. Casual contact is safe. He's still your dad, isn't he?"

Malachi took a deep breath.

"Yes, Doctor, he sure is."

****

There has to be something seriously therapeutic about sleeping in one's bed, Malachi thought for the second time as he pulled open the fridge door in his quest to discover something fit for breakfast. He settled on milk with bran flakes. It wasn't his favorite cereal, but it was all he found in the cupboard.

He felt a chill as the cold air jabbed at his bare skin. Strange enough, that made him think of Megan. In fact as much as he hated to admit it, he hadn't been able to shake the woman whom he realized was his first official ex completely from his thoughts. He'd kissed girls, gone out on a few dates, but nothing came close to the level of sharing he had with Megan.

Dealing with the breakup was easier when he was in Jamaica. His elixir was simple: exams. He'd entered the zone—the one that had taken him successfully through most of the major exams in his short life. He prayed it worked this time around.

But it was different somehow now that he was home; now that he had faced the second-worse news he'd ever had to face in his life. Megan Le Blanc was all he could think about—at least when he wasn't thinking about his dad.

He ignored the apples and grapes in the fruit bowl and reached instead for the pomegranate, since it was a locally-grown fruit that he hadn't seen in a while. Come to think of it, he couldn't recall seeing so much fruit in the fridge for quite some time. Mom was the fruits person. His dad had apparently turned into one. He opened the vegetable drawer. Sure enough it was near full, although most of it had begun to wilt.

His father was clearly taking care of himself, eating well. That's good. He made a mental note that he'd have to find an Internet cafe or go to the med library on the local campus and research everything he could find on HIV.

Suppose, he thought, it's all part of the big plan for his life: studying to be a doctor, finding out his dad has HIV. He looked up to the ceiling.

"Is this part of your plan? Hmm? It would be nice if you would consult me now and then."

He dragged out the vegetable drawer, ripped a fresh garbage bag from the roll installed next to the paper towels and emptied the wilted contents into the bag. He held the drawer in his hand and for a moment he was gripped with a strong urge to break something.

The phone rang.

"Hello."

"Hello, Malachi?"

"Abby? Wow, this is a surprise. I can't remember giving you my number for here."

"No you didn't actually. I got it from Caleb. Hope that's all right?"

"Why wouldn't it be?"

He knew that somehow that didn't come out right.

"So what's happening, Mal? When I spoke to Caleb yesterday, he told me you had some kind of medical emergency with your dad. Is everything OK?"

Note to self: Get a new best friend.

"More or less. He had uh, a fall at home and got a distal radius fracture."

"Yikes. It must have been pretty bad for them to keep him."

"Yeah…He should be discharged tomorrow though."

"Thank God. Well, we've got to give God thanks, Mal. It could have been worse. Lucky for him, his son is a med student, huh?"

"Yeah… lucky."

"Well, I knew you were planning to spend the holidays in Jamaica, so I figured it had to have been serious for you to change your mind."

"I had to come and see for myself, you know?"

"Absolutely. I would have done the same."

"So you spoke to Caleb—finally."

"Yeah," she sighed into the phone. "He kinda popped in last night to say his goodbyes, I guess. He heard I was leaving blah blah. Needless to say I was unhinged for the first minute or two of the conversation, but it was civil. Did you know he's planning to get engaged? "

"What!"

"Yep. He and Brandy worked things out. His words. He didn't mention anything to you?"

"Nope. Abs, that's rough. What can I say? I'm sorry. You OK?"

"Yeah yeah. Spilt milk. Sometimes things just don't work out."

He resisted the temptation to tell her that that's exactly what Caleb had told him.

"So you're all packed and ready to go?"

"Off hall? Oh yes. Looking forward to it actually, even though I may have to start over. I'll be spending Christmas at home with my folks and then it's off to Columbia University in January. It's kind of exciting going back to New York to live after all these years. I hope you can come visit me one of these days…or years."

They laughed.

"That would be nice."

"Hey Mal…uh, have you, uh, heard from Megan recently?"

"No. Guess she hopped planets after we broke up. But truth be told, my head's been in the books with exams. There just hasn't been much time for anything else."

Abby bit her lip. This was the one occasion when she'd hoped the rumor mill on hall was working. But it sounded as if Malachi was still in the dark about the rape. She suspected that Megan's dad had used his connections to keep the incident out of the papers. If it wasn't for the call she got from Megan's mom, whom she had met less than a week prior to the attack, she too might not have known.

"Right. Well, she and I are supposed to get together sometime tomorrow. Any messages?"

"No, Abby, and I would really appreciate if you don't say anything about my dad being in hospital. Megan is not part of my life anymore, and I'm not one of those guys who deludes himself into thinking that he can remain friends with his ex. It's not going to happen."

It wasn't the answer she had hoped for. If even he'd said, "Tell her hi," it would have been enough—enough for her to tell Malachi about the rape. Megan had begged her not to tell Malachi about her assault. She felt that he didn't need to be burdened with that kind of news, especially so close to exams—not with all that had happened during the semester. But exams were over.

"Abby, did you hear what I just said?"

"Yes, Malachi. I guess I'll never quite understand how easy it is for guys to switch off."

"You seem to be forgetting that she's the one who wanted out. Guess she figured we're unequally yoked all of a sudden. Wonder where she got that idea?"

There it was. He blamed her for the break up. So she hadn't imagined the frost between them over the last few weeks. It was real; as real as it gets. And it wasn't because he was so focused on exams as she had told herself.

God, give me wisdom, she prayed.

"Malachi, I know you're still hurting, so I'll ignore the insinuation. Sometimes...Sometimes it's just hard to know what the right thing is. One thing's for sure: I have no regrets about meeting any of you and the friendships we've built, neither do I regret sharing my faith. It's who I am."

"That's wonderful, Abs, and I don't regret meeting you either. In fact, I think you're a big reason why my resolve has been strengthened."

"Please, Mal, there's something I—"

"No, Abs. I need to say this. If you haven't noticed, my list of friends is dwindling. But that's OK because I realize now that I can't afford to let anyone or anything distract or derail me again. Maybe it's seeing my dad in that hospital bed last night, but I woke up this morning with laser beam focus. And priority one is finishing med school and honoring the sacrifice that both my parents have made. Now when I look in the mirror, Abs, I see everything and everyone I need to make it happen. Everyone else can take a hike for all I care...This is my time."

Abby cradled the receiver on the other end of the line. His words, painful as they were to hear, told her everything she needed to know.

"Well, Mal, got to run. Happy Holidays. I'll try to call you again before I leave for the States."

"Geeze, Abs, sorry, I forgot you were calling long distance. Thanks for the call anyway, take care of yourself."

"Yeah. You too."

CHAPTER TWENTY-SIX

Malachi met his dad sitting on a wooden bench outside the ward. The bench reminded him of the first set of pews at his home church. Malachi Senior was reading the newspaper.

"Waiting for me?" he asked as he approached his dad.

"Hey. You're here. Good to see you. For a while there I thought you might have ended up in the bed next to me this morning."

"Yeah, well. That was a lot more than I bargained for. Sorry if I scared you."

Malachi Senior shrugged and tapped the seat next to him.

"No IV today."

"No IV, praise the Lord. That was uncomfortable to say the least. I tell you there's something about being in a hospital that reminds a man of his own mortality," Malachi Senior started.

"Dad, I need to ask you some questions before the rest of your visitors arrive. Pastor called. He and Sister Dee are coming. They said they might be late, but they're coming. I guess my first question is do they know?"

"Yes, they were the only people from church I told."

"So you told your pastor and his wife before your own son?"

"Junior, I know that doesn't sound right, but sometimes it's just very difficult to tell the people closest to you. It's not an excuse, I know, but that's just how it is. I guess—I suppose I was afraid of being…rejected."

"Rejected? Dad, I'm your son, and I am a med student in case you forgot."

"So what? Think I haven't noticed that some of them can't even touch me without their latex. I'm not infectious. They're supposed to know that."

"Well I know you aren't…infectious."

"You know last night when everything was tumbling out and I tried to touch you and you pulled away and said, 'Don't touch—"

"That was different I—"

"No, let me finish."

"I know you didn't mean it like that, but that's the physical reaction—the words that every person with this virus dreads hearing."

"Dad, I'm sorry." He placed his hand over his father's and held it there.

"I didn't tell you that for you to start feeling me up all over every chance you get." They both laughed at the comeback.

"How was exams?"

"Tough. But it should be OK."

"Good. How's your girlfriend—the one you're sleeping with?"

"Dad."

"Don't 'Dad' me. I'm in a hospital with HIV. Sex did this, Junior, not dirty needles. Sex. That's as real as it gets, Son, so don't 'Dad' me. I'm going to talk to you man to man from now on, and I'm going to do it till I'm blue in the face."

Malachi sighed and looked down at his sneakers. "We broke up."

"Got tested yet…for HIV etcetera?"

"No."

"Get tested." He looked at the people filing into the ward. "That's not a suggestion, by the way."

"Yes, sir," Malachi said and gave a mock salute.

"Remember what you said when I told you on the phone that AIDS is no respecter of persons."

"It's a bit of a blur."

"I bet it is. Let me remind you: You said that you are au courant with the facts about AIDS. You said I didn't raise an idiot, and you assured me that you're not one of those crazy people who can't control themselves.

"Do you think I'm an idiot, Son? I need to know. Think your grandaddy raised an idiot?"

"Course not, Dad."

"Well I've got AIDS!"

"HIV. Shh and lower your voice."

"HIV, AIDS, the virus, whatever you want to call it. I'm just bringing home the point that based on your reasoning, I've got to be one of those idiotic, crazy people who can't keep it in my pants."

"I can't believe we're having this conversation. Of course you're not any of those things, Dad, but why are you attacking me all of a sudden?"

Malachi Senior took a deep breath and crossed his legs by the knee. He folded his arms high on his chest.

"I'm sorry," he said in a softer tone. "It's just that for years, I'd hear people talk about not wanting to be judged. People see HIV and they make assumptions, and as much as I am a social worker I must confess that I was probably guilty of that. Now I'm the one with the big label stuck on me and suddenly I get it; I truly do." He looked down at the overgrown lawn framing the footpath on the ground floor.

"Don't you think it hurts? I'm a deacon in the church for heaven's sake. It blows my mind that I thought I was safe as Sunday morning. HIV was the last thing I felt I needed to worry about. Those flighty hard-headed teenagers who were out fornicating their little brains out, yeah, maybe. But not me. All I did was love and make love to my wife. My own wife, Son." He thumped his chest. "Now I have all these eager young pups with stethoscopes poking at me and looking at me like I'm some perv who got what was coming."

"They're not thinking that, Dad; that's all in your head," he said while patting his father's hand.

"Is it?"

Malachi nodded. "Dad, listen, I know this is hard but I have to ask, is that why mom...you know?"

"You've asked the million-dollar question, Junior. I really can't answer that."

"I really hope she didn't do that, not in this day and age when people with HIV are living longer than ever before. I wish we knew for sure, but she didn't even leave a note."

Malachi Senior stood up and walked over to the nearby railing.

"Junior, you're going to hate me for this but I lied about the note thing. Your mother did leave a note."

Malachi's voice was still. "What did it say?"

"I kept it from you because it was hard to explain, and I thought, at the time, it would only mess you up."

"What did it say, Dad?" His voice sounded firm and wounded at the same time.

"It was short, I memorized it, but I know you'd rather see it for yourself.

Malachi took the white envelope his father produced from his shirt pocket and now held out to him. He pulled out the folded note. The sight of his mother's penmanship on the sunny stationery was almost too much to bear.

My Darling Husband Malachi,

I'm sorry I broke our vows. As it turns out, living with myself is harder than I thought. It's just not working out anymore. Tell

Malachi Junior that I love him more than life itself, and that this
has nothing to do with him. Take care of our son. Promise.

Love forever,

Lavern

(never Lav.)

Malachi Junior propped up his head with his hands, his elbows rested on his knees. His dad came back to the seat and
sat beside him. They sat in silence for two full minutes as they
watched more lunchtime visitors shuffle in and out of the ward.

"You should have shown me this before."

"I should have done a lot of things. I should have told your
mom that coming off her meds was a bad idea when she asked
me what I thought she should do. I should have confronted her
the very first time she stayed out all night instead of ducking my
head in the sand. There are ten thousand things I should have
done. All I can say is, 'I'm sorry.'"

They sat side-by-side, each lost in his own thoughts. Malachi
Junior broke the silence after a minute.

"I forgive you, but don't hold back on me like that
again. Deal?"

Malachi Senior looked at the younger version of himself sitting beside him and smiled. "You're such a grown-up now. You'll
make an excellent doctor. You hear me? Excellent."

"Thanks."

"And I have one more confession while we're putting it out
there... I told your dean, Dr. Livingston, and the rest of the lot
about my status when they had their big meeting about you."

Malachi sprang to his feet so suddenly that it caused an old lady who was approaching the door to hesitate for a second. "Nooo. Why would you do such a thing? It's bad enough that you tell pastor and Sister Dee before me, now you're telling me that the entire faculty knows?"

"Just the disciplinary committee."

"Wow!" He sat back down slowly, his hands clasped behind his head.

"Hey, to tell you the truth, I'm not particularly sorry about that. Sorry that it embarrasses you, yeah, but not sorry I told them the truth. A guy I met in the clinic I go to—positive for seven years he says—told me that you only get one chance—one chance—to play the sympathy card with the HIV thing, and I played mine, OK. I put it all out there for those big shot doctors, OK. I even faxed the proof. Was it low of me? Probably. Was it worth it? You bet."

They sat in silence until both father and son spotted Pastor Olivere and first lady Sister Dee as they erupted from one of the glass doors on the ground floor and joined the queue of those waiting for the elevator.

"See those two," Malachi Senior said pointing at the couple. "They've been family to me. Treat them with respect. Always. Should anything happen to me—before you finish school, I mean—you'll be taken care of. I've named them executors of my will."

"You made a will?"

"You bet. And I'll tell you something. Being frugal has its benefits. I've saved and invested the equivalent of a small fortune over the years. Thank God I was also insured to the hilt before all this happened. Ironically, your mom was the one who insisted on it. I guess there are upsides to having a wife who was as crazy as bat."

"Dad."

"What? If we can't joke about this between us, what's the alternative, cry like you?" he asked and bumped his son lightly on the shoulder. Malachi squeezed his eyes shut and brushed at the wetness that his father's disclosure to the disciplinary committee, and his rationale for doing so had triggered.

"Love you, Dad. Always have, always will," he mumbled and slung his arm over his father's shoulder.

It was a rare display of affection for them. Malachi Senior took a deep breath. He made a mental note to hug his only child more. Much more.

"Wait till you have a child of your own, then you'll know love," Malachi Senior told his son with a sniff. "I'm glad you're here. You're the best thing that happened to your mother and me. You better believe that," he said, and kissed his grown son on the head.

****

The antique four-poster bed was by far the most impressive piece of furniture in Megan's room. At first it appeared to be king size but Megan said it was just a queen. Megan's bookcase reminded Abby of the wall system bookcase in the family room at her house. Bookshelves were a feature that appeared in almost every room of her home in Forest Hills. Her parents were unapologetic bibliophiles, and she inherited the gene.

Megan's shelves weren't all packed with books though. Her white shelves had an eclectic mix of glass ornaments in unusual shapes and colours, framed family photos, and bronze figurines of ballerinas in various positions.

"Guess nobody has to ask what you're in to?" Abby said as she lifted one of the figurines from the shelf and was surprised to discover that it was lighter than she expected.

"Those were a gift from Sylvie who I told you about. I went wild when I saw them."

Abby walked over to the milky green recliner futon with the chocolate stained hardwood base that matched the stain on Megan's poster bed. She lowered herself unto it and stared out the bay windows that opened up to the pool area.

"The flowers go nicely with my décor," Megan said, to keep the conversation going. "Thanks again, Abby. It was sweet of you."

"I have a thing for flowers," Abby replied, "especially daisies, but I've had to embrace other flowers since I've been here."

Abby fiddled again with the arrangement that was now in a crystal vase on the ultramodern bedroom table that lay to one side of the futon.

"Am I looking that horrid, Abby? You've hardly looked at me for ten seconds straight since you've arrived."

"I'm sorry, Megan. I guess I'm a little nervous for some reason. No, you don't look bad, your wounds are healing nicely compared to what I saw that day in the hospital."

Megan's face was still bruised along the left eye and the right side of her mouth. When Abby had visited her in the hospital the day after the rape, she was still very swollen. The swelling had gone down now, but her skin, which was once flawless, still bore the marks of someone who'd received a beating.

"Abby I fought like a demon that night. I wasn't prepared to go down like that. The police got tissue under my fingernails. I hope that might help them catch the monster. The stupid officer said I must have scratched him up like a cat in heat. And I didn't imagine the smirk on his face when he said it? I mean, why would he say something as insensitive as that to someone who…?" Her voice faded.

"Megan people say stupid things to rape victims all the time. He's a jerk."

"Most of the officers were quite nice, though, very professional. It's just that sometimes, I don't know why, but you remember the bad more than the good, you know?"

"Yes."

"Did you…uh…get through to Malachi?"

Abby took a deep breath. "Yes, we spoke. Not for very long, though."

"Well what did he say? Did you tell him?"

"Megan, you begged me not to, remember?"

"Right. But that was because he was in the middle of exams. Really, Abby, I wouldn't have fussed if you'd betrayed my confidence. You don't have to be Miss Perfect all the time, you know."

Abby bit her bottom lip. She had no idea why people assumed she was perfect when she was so clearly in need of work.

Megan sat up on her bed, her shoulders slumped in resignation. "Abby, I don't know what I'm saying. I'm...I'm really a mess right now. That was uncalled for. It's just that things have got quite desperate since we last spoke."

"What do you mean, Megan?"

"I visited the doctor two days ago and he had the results of my STD screen."

"Yes." Abby willed herself to sound calm.

"He told me everything is OK on that front. He recommended that I repeat the tests in six months."

Abby knew that she exhaled a tad more dramatically than she ought. "That must have been a relief?"

"Yes and no. Abby, the doctor also told me that I'm pregnant."

"What? What!"

"I told him that I hadn't been feeling all that well, and I described my symptoms. I've been having so many symptoms that I just didn't think anything of it. He took blood and a urine sample and then came back with the news. Abby, I threw up there and then all over his floor."

Abby instructed herself to wipe away the stupefied look on her face, but her non-verbals refused to cooperate.

"Megan, I-I don't know what to say. Do your parents know? What did they say?"

"My mom's on sedatives. That's why you didn't see her when you got in. Poor Dad is walking around literally like he wants to kill something or someone. He told me he's going to put in notice at the High Commission; he doesn't want to stay apparently, although I doubt I'm the only reason."

"Where would you all go?"

"I don't know as yet. My dad's ranked as the Envoy to the British High Commissioner, but he's served as the top representative many times before this appointment. He deliberately asked for the Envoy posting after he had a pacemaker installed last year. Once he gives notice we'd just have to wait and see how long it would take to send a replacement and where they would post him next. That takes care of him and Mum. As for me, Paul has been begging for me to come up to New York since—" her voice trailed off.

"Megan, I think you should go."

"You do? But what if…? Abby, I must tell you, there is a possibility that this child is Malachi's. Don't you think I owe it to him to share that possibility? Please, Abby, he must have said something. Did he even ask about me?"

It was the moment of truth, and Abby was torn. She didn't need a PhD to figure out that one word from her was all her newfound friend would require to convince herself that Malachi might be up to the task of raising a child—one that might not even be his—while finishing med school. But to get that hope, Abby would have had to feel it first, and as much as she wanted to, she didn't. The Malachi she spoke to yesterday was chillingly indifferent. He has even begged her not to say anything about his dad being in hospital for fear that Megan might feel obliged to contact him. But what if the child is his? Doesn't he have the right to know? He'd been in so much trouble this semester. What would this do to his plans of becoming a doctor? Was Megan even thinking about that? Abby felt she was enough of a realist to know that she and Megan were not in the same boat as Malachi financially. This was his big chance; his ticket to the future he dreamed about.

"Abby, please. Your silence is killing me." She couldn't conceal the quiver in her voice.

"The truth is Megan, Malachi…"

"Yes?"

"Malachi was on Malachi… in a big way, if you know what I mean?"

Megan broke eye contact and crunched down a little harder on the cham-covered pillow she nestled between her arms and legs.

"I do," she said and exhaled. "Unfortunately, I do. Right. I better get on with it then. Abby, I can't hide this from you. When I spoke with Paul last night, he hinted that I should come up now. He didn't say the words, but I think he's hoping to persuade me to terminate the pregnancy."

"Hmm… That doesn't surprise me at all."

"Abby... I must confess I'm a bit confused about the timing of all this. I mean, I just gave my life to the Lord. Aren't there supposed to be legions of angels and such?"

"There are, Megan. There are. I...I'm not even sure what to say to you, except that bad things happen to us at times, but God is still good, and His love for you hasn't wavered. Megan you must believe that."

"Well... I spoke to Him last night." Her voice was small. "It was hard. I couldn't for a while, but I did last night."

"OK."

"I've already made a decision about the pregnancy, and since there's nothing to hold on to here, I'll go to New York to stay with Paul."

"I see."

"I guess on the upside, I'll have a friend in New York." Megan used the back of her hand to swip at the moisture that was pooling on her eyelids.

"That's great." Taking her cue from Megan, Abby's voice sounded chipper even though her heart was anything but.

"Abby, I'm talking about you, silly? Or have you forgotten that you're going to New York too?"

"Right. Of course." She smacked her forehead playfully. "I'll be there for you, Megan... as best as I can," she added and swallowed hard. And she told the truth as she still wasn't quite sure what she was consenting to when she made the promise. She hoped and prayed that Megan knew her well enough not to expect her to compromise her principles on the sanctity of life.

"Look at the both of us," Megan said suddenly, a weak smile on her face. "We've both been dreadfully unlucky in love this semester: you with Caleb; I with Malachi."

Megan tilted her face and raised her left hand to shield her eyes from the spray of sunlight that had invaded the room she'd hardly lived in. After a few seconds she pushed the pillow aside and slipped both hands one above the other over her midsection.

"Looks like it's just you and me kid…And Godmother Abigail?" she added and glanced up at Abby, the petition naked in her eyes.

"And Godmother Abigail," Abby confirmed with a smile that sprinted across her face.

PART 2

New Beginning

CHAPTER TWENTY-SEVEN

Some people never get used to the contrasts and contradictions of New York. Malachi knew that he would be one of them. Even on the most ruthless of summer days, the memory of his first winter just six months ago still had the knee-jerk effect of making him hunch his shoulders and arch his back ever so slightly.

His Jamaican friends told him he was certifiably insane when he broke the news that he was accepted to do his residency at a teaching hospital in Queens and was planning to join the winter cohort rather than wait for spring. Malachi had tried his best to prepare physically and mentally for his first trip to America. He'd purchased second-hand winter gear—enough to get by until he was able to raid the nearest department chain. He started

watching the international weather report daily, paying attention to the winter vocabulary and accompanying advisories.
He even went online and listened to the anecdotes of those
who had faced winters before and lived to tell the tale. But
absolutely nothing could have prepared him for the reality:
the taste of ice as it nibbled at his bones, or the mockery
of layers covering his frame as he waddled his way to the
subway to get to work on time.

"People actually live here?" he had said with a burr in his
voice one sub-zero morning, more to himself than to the old
lady with the gigantic green ear muffs that stood on the plat-
form blowing into her gloves. That day he studied the com-
muters as they descended the subway steps. Daylight hadn't
even punched in as yet for the long haul and there they were
already queuing up like ants preparing to surrender to their
daily rituals.

As a doctor, he knew he had an appreciation of the human body that was more than romantic. But days like those
reminded him of why he choose medicine—it was the same
cocktail of awe, privilege, and excitement that threatened to
overload his system the day he practiced on his first cadaver.

Those were the memories that were dancing around in his
mind when the phone rang in his apartment. He picked up on
the second ring.

"Yes," he grunted into the receiver.

"My man, Mal!" The salutation came from a familiar voice.

"It's eight o'clock in the morning on my day off. You're killing me, Pete," he said to the caller and yawned into the phone.

"Hey, you said that like one of us. The accent is coming in nicely, Mal."

"Pete, bad words are forming in my head."

He heard a hearty laugh from the other end of the line.

"OK, just buzz me up, man, I'm downstairs. When are you going to get your super to check this intercom. This is America. They fix things here you know."

Malachi hung up the phone. He crawled out of bed and pressed the buzzer to release the ground floor gate. Pete would be at his door in a minute. Malachi took a glance around his second storey Queen's apartment. He was fortunate to get a two bedroom. He could've gone for something cheaper, he knew, but he liked the fact that there was a place for his dad to stay whenever, if ever, he decided to visit. Pete had asked about the extra room the first day he visited. He laughed when Malachi supplied the rationale and asked why he didn't just buy a fold-out couch.

"That's how it's done, Mal. Do I have to teach you everything?" Pete had said.

He had to admit that there was still so much to learn about how it's done in the Big Apple.

"You obviously forgot," Pete blurted out when Malachi, dressed in boxers and a T-shirt, pulled the door open and stepped aside to allow the six foot three man, who looked more like a linebacker than a doctor, to enter.

"Forgot what?" Malachi yawned and covered his mouth quickly as he remembered he hadn't yet brushed his teeth.

"The shelter where I volunteer? Remember, I told you about the clinic we started? You said you'd put in some hours with me?"

"That's today?"

"That's today. Hey, I just came off duty. I smell ripe. Can I take a fresh? You do have hot water, right?" Pete had the fridge door open as he scanned the shelves for a quick fix breakfast.

"Course."

"The place looks nice. Something's different. You got new curtains or something?"

The place did look nice, Malachi had to admit as he surveyed the apartment. Dr. Pete McGregor was one of two persons from the hospital who'd seen his apartment. The second was Dr. Brenda Busby, another resident whom Pete dated for a little while. The night that Brenda saw his apartment was a red letter day in the couple's budding romance. Malachi had invited Pete and Brenda to hang out at his place. It was one of the rare nights they were all off at the same time. After the visit, Brenda had apparently gone about spreading the word around the hospital that Dr. Williamson had a two-bedroom Queen's apartment all to himself. Malachi had made it clear over dinner that he wasn't interested in a roommate. The message was apparently lost on Brenda. The next week, Malachi had been bombarded with enquiries from interns, residents—even a receptionist—all wanting to know how much he was asking for the room. Malachi had been cool about it. Pete saw it as a deal breaker.

"C'mon, Doc, you need to be more observant than that," Malachi called from inside his bathroom as he spat mouthwash into the sink.

"Look hard. All I can say is 'God bless America.' There was this sweet garage sale over in Cambria Heights. The rug and those two accent lamps were calling my name. What could I do? I had to rescue the poor things."

"So you've turned into a regular Martha Stewart now," Pete said, scooping a spoonful of dry cereal from the bowl, into his mouth. "Next time I come over I just might see slipcovers and hardwood flooring."

Malachi alighted from the bathroom and dropped down on his black leather couch. He placed a navy blue towel next to him. "Towel's for you by the way. Nah. This flooring's a keeper, but the slipcovers. Now that's an idea." He wagged his finger.

"You're scaring me, Mal."

"So what did you say we're doing in this place again?"

"We're volunteering our time. That means no money," Pete said between chews.

"Why you have to say it like that, man? I can volunteer my time and expertise. I can give back. It's just that, as I explained before, I need to make the paper right now. I have plans."

"Yeah yeah, I know, I know—the plans." Pete made air quotes. "Lemme see if I remember: your own home in a nice, upscale neighborhood by thirty. The wife and three kids—two sons and a daughter. The English Bull Terrier, although I don't get the English part. We have perfectly respectable pooches in America, and, uh, oh yeah." He snapped his fingers. "Was there a ranch in there somewhere?"

"That was just an idea I was toying with. But I don't need to be in the hinterlands to get some greenery in my life. I'll settle for nice landscaping in the suburbs."

"I don't know, you might want to reconsider. I grew up in Michigan, and my family has a summer home in Bushkill Pennsylvania, so I know that there's something to be said about acreage." Pete had placed the empty cereal bowl on Malachi's coffee table and had begun disrobing on his way to the bathroom. He dismissed Malachi's offer of a plastic bag for his clothes with a wave of the hand.

"Plastics are the devil man."

"I'll tell the chief to shut down the hospital immediately."

"Can you just put it with your stuff. Please Mal, I know I will get it back from you in no time. The laundry back at my place is just piling up, man."

"Which baffled me since the laundromat is just downstairs in your fancy Central Park apartment complex."

"It's three blocks away from Central Park. Hey, hope you haven't told anyone that I have an apartment overlooking Central Park. What can I say, I'm a country boy; I need to be near something green, you know. Man, if that comes out, it's all over for me at the hospital. I'll be branded as some rich doctor brat."

"Two out of three." He raised his hands. "I'm just saying."

"Dr. Williamson."

"Dr. McGregor."

Malachi shook his head and watched his slightly overweight friend head to the bathroom. He'd often wondered if their friendship surprised Pete as much as it had surprised him. They met while on rotation in Med/Surg. The day they met, the two residents were nearing the end of a twenty-four hour shift when they were both given the opportunity to assist an attending in an appendectomy. Malachi noticed Pete was falling asleep in the middle of the procedure and kicked him under the table. Pete said afterward that he'd never been more grateful for being kicked in his life since that attending had a well-known reputation for kicking residents out the OR for much less.

Malachi saw right away that Pete's "patient-centered" approach to medicine mirrored his own philosophy. Pete cared about his patients and it showed. He'd found many of the other residents aloof and sometimes mechanical when it came to the patients, especially the minorities, who accounted for a significant percentage of the hospital's intake. He wasn't totally surprised by the treatment meted out by some doctors. Malachi had long disabused himself of any notions of the profession being the bleeding heart band of brothers and sisters that would give their plasma for each other and their patients. He had also learned, when it came to new people in his life, it was better to deal with folks as they come. That policy seemed to be working out for him, he felt. It certainly brought him an unlikely friend. A blue-eyed, white boy from Michigan.

The only downside: he was a pastor's kid.

"I hope this is not some salvation-for-soup joint you're taking me to. We have an agreement, remember."

"I agreed that I would respect your disquiet with all things Christian right now. So let me level with you. No. It's not a salvation-for-soup thing as you call it. Sure, there are people there who love the Lord and are in his service. Anything wrong with that?"

Malachi couldn't miss the edge in Pete's voice—the one that meant that the respect he insisted on had to be mutual.

"Not a thing. How are we getting there, by the way?"

"Uh—subway, duh," he said, triggering raised eyebrows.

"Don't look at me like that, Mal. I've got your back."

"In the Bronx? Right. I'm sure you'll blend in just fine."

CHAPTER TWENTY-EIGHT

The Weinstein House had all the trimmings of a typical shelter with one exception—nobody was called homeless. Everyone who wasn't a volunteer was considered a guest and was expected to be treated accordingly. The walls were a cheerful canary yellow with the south side being a mural that blended the abstract with the literal. The place had an open floor plan which made it feel like one giant living room with designated areas for pool and table tennis, television viewing, reading, and dining. There was even a stage where Malachi was told recitals were held.

"Cool huh?" Pete nudged Malachi, the excitement in his voice akin to a child showing off his new bike.

"Very—um, homey. Didn't expect that."

"See the mural over there? An ex-guest painted it. The master bedrooms are behind those walls."

"Master bedrooms?"

"That's what Herb calls it."

"Maybe we should check him out first—medically speaking," Malachi said and tapped his right temple with his index. "Before we move to the other...uh guests."

Pete chuckled. "Here's your opportunity. There he goes with Linda. She's on Herb detail."

"Herb detail?"

"I don't think I mentioned this but Pastor Herb's blind. Has been for almost twenty-five years."

"What happened?"

"Aw, he'll fill you in himself. He likes to share his story."

"OK. Hey isn't that the nurse from pediatrics coming toward us?"

"Yep. Nurse Greta," he said under his breath. "How's it going, Greta?" Pete called out amiably to the older nurse.

"Great Pete. I see you've brought more hands for the clinic."

"You bet ya. This is Dr. Malachi Williamson. Mal, this is Nurse Greta Forrester."

"Seen you around a couple times. Pleased to make your acquaintance," she said with an extended hand. "Hope you like it here."

"What's there not to like?" a voice boomed from behind. Pastor Herb had arrived.

"Eavesdropping again, Herb?" Greta chided mildly with a chuckle.

"Can't help it, Nurse G. Those senses I've left don't give me a rest. But hey, I ain't complaining, got bionic ears and my nose never failed me yet. Keeps the air quality in here at an acceptable level."

Malachi shifted, suddenly conscious of how he smelled after the long subway ride.

Did I remember to put on deodorant?

"Dad, this is my friend Dr. Williamson, first name Malachi. Remember I mentioned that he wanted to help."

Pastor Herb extended his hand and pulled it back suddenly. "Your hands clean boy?"

"Yeah. Well. I was on the sub—"

Pastor Herb, Greta, and Pete started cackling at Malachi's earnest response.

"Works every time," Pete said.

"I'm just playing with you, son," Pastor Herb said as he stretched out his hand again. "But seriously, this is a homeless shelter. All kinds of people are gonna want to shake your hands, unless you want to keep having to wash them, better come up with something. I ask them outright, 'your hands clean?' When it's not, they usually let me know."

"Pete here didn't tell me that he was bringing me to meet his dad?"

"Oh he didn't? What's wrong boy, shamed of your old, blind pa or something?"

Everyone laughed harder. Malachi knew he'd have to get used to this.

"Well, now you know. I didn't tell you because we came here to work, and I wasn't even sure if he would be here today. Honestly."

Malachi wasn't upset. He wasn't even annoyed. His relationship with Pete was one where they were in each other's lives, yet they weren't. Malachi knew the basics about Pete in terms of where he was from, where he lives now as well as a few of his likes and interests, and Pete pretty much knew the same about him. But Malachi was not oblivious of the fact that they'd both omitted lots of details about themselves. Pete never asked him how his mom died or what his dad did for a living. And today's revelation was just confirmation of the need-to-know policy they both seemed to have subscribed to.

"It's all good, man," he said and gave Pete a manly pat on the shoulder. "It's a pleasure to meet you Pastor Herb."

"Call me Herb if you like. That's the little privilege I give to the volunteers. Can't pay you squat, so you might as well call me Herb."

"Well you can call me Malachi, sir…Herb."

"There we go, quick learner. I like that. Malachi, what's say I release Linda here from Herb detail and you and me walk a bit. I like to get to know a little about the volunteers, if you don't mind."

"Don't mind at all."

Linda put on her pouty face and then gave Herb a gentle pat on his hand. She then proceeded to give Malachi a quick lesson in the proper way to walk with Herb.

"Thanks, darling." Herb beamed behind dark brown shades, his generous smile revealed a well-cared for dental display. Malachi couldn't tell if it was all natural or veneers.

"Talk to you again sometime, Lady Linda. Remember what I said now."

"Of course," she replied with a girlish ripple of laughter.

Greta and Pete disappeared in different directions—she toward the kitchen, and he walked over to where one of the guests with a sling on his arm sat reading.

"Pretty girl isn't she?"

"Hmm. Linda? I guess she is," Malachi said with a chuckle.

"She told me today that she likes Herb detail more than anything else. Know what I think?"

"Haven't got a clue."

"I think she's sweet on Pete."

Malachi chortled.

"Don't get me wrong, everyone who has to do Herb detail at first thinks, 'I came here to volunteer not to waste time shuffling around an old, blind man.' That's before. Soon everyone is practically fighting for Herb detail."

"If you say so," Malachi replied, the laughter still in his voice.

"Aww, you don't believe me? I'll give you a month if you stick with us. Then you'll be like, 'Hey, where the old man's at?'"

Malachi laughed harder.

Herb's laughter faded suddenly. "Sorry, didn't mean to offend with the ghetto stereotype. Sometimes I mess up on the political correctness sensitivities."

"I wasn't offended. It's cool."

"So Pete tells me you're from the Caribbean."

"Trinidad—a beautiful island."

"I'm sure it is. Nice accent too."

"Thank you."

"Man, wanna hear something? You know, I never set foot outside of this here United States of America?"

"Is that so?"

"Always wanted to but never had the opportunity. Now that I could afford it, well, there's just so much going on here. Guess you want to know how I ended up a blind pastor huh?"

"Only if you want to share."

"What kinda half-baked answer is that? Is either you do or you don't wanna hear it. Now which is it?"

"I do, sir. I guess I do," Malachi said, and recognized the same edge in Herb's voice that pops up in Pete's when he's bent on making a point.

"That's better. Sometimes you got to stop beating around the bush in life and come out and say what you mean and mean what you say. Understand?"

"I think so."

"Why don't we sit for a while and have a cup of coffee or something. You had something to eat this morning?"

"Just toast."

"That won't do. Just shoot your hand up and wave at one of those ladies in the blue T-shirt. They'll hook you up with a nice breakfast. That's another perk of volunteering here: free breakfast."

Malachi and Pastor Herb sat at one of the tables in the dining room section and chatted as Malachi ate breakfast. He saw no strong resemblance between father and son. Pete was basically big-boned as they say back home, but Herb, though far from frail, was average in build. The similarity, however, could not be denied in their mannerism: both had the same way of cocking their heads to the left when they were listening intently. Both had the same way of raising their voice and sounding slightly miffed when they were bringing home a point. And, above all, they both had the same endearing way of making you feel like you belong.

Over breakfast, which consisted of pancakes, eggs, sausages, and orange juice, Malachi learned that Herbert Ignatius McGregor grew up on a farm in a small town in Michigan and married the local librarian—who he described as "a peach of a girl" named Maggie. When his father died, Herb and his older brother Ken entered into a property dispute, and Herb walked away with the short end of the stick. With a quarter of the inheritance he was meant to have, Herb and Maggie decided to start over and move to New York to seek out better opportunities.

"Within a week of coming, we seriously considered packing our bags and heading right back where we came from."

"I know the feeling," Malachi said, remembering his first few days in the Big Apple.

"Maggie got a job in a library in Brooklyn, and I worked at a green grocer. That's when I met Greg and Fran, the beautiful couple that owned the place. Apart from being madly in love, they were also wild about Jesus and it showed. Well, I've always been a curious one, and I started asking questions and before long I became a Christian too."

"That's great, Herb. I grew up in church, so I know all about it," Malachi said, hoping to scuttle any perceived need on Herb's part to dilate on the subject.

"Do you now?" Herb replied.

"Yes, sir."

Herb smiled. "Anyway, back to my story. Naturally, I shared my faith with Maggie and sure enough she accepted Christ too."

Malachi had the sudden urge to yell, "Well, Praise the Lord," but he bit his tongue and glanced at his watch.

It's not like the old man could see me and take offense.

"Well, I can go on and on, but I've got guests to see, and I know you have work to do."

Malachi released an inaudible sigh. The chair creaked slightly as he eased himself up from his seat.

"So I'll hurry up and see if I can cut to the chase," he heard Pastor Herb say. Malachi plopped back down in his seat.

"The grocer started to expand. I was promoted to assistant manager. About that same time Maggie found out she was pregnant. We were so happy, we thought the good Lord just picked up a big old bucket of happiness and poured it on us."

Pete was first, a fact that Malachi already knew, followed by Nathan, who, Pete told him, has a flair for languages and has his heart set on becoming a missionary. Herb talked about how after Nathan was born, he felt the call of God into full-time ministry. He enrolled in a seminary part-time and on the day that he graduated, Maggie found out she was pregnant again.

"That's when my eyes started to go bad. At first I thought it was some kind of eye strain from all that studying. I finally listened to my wife and got the eye doctor to see me. After poking around a bit, they gave me the news that rocked me to the core. I had something called retinitis pigmentosa, and I was going blind."

"That's a pretty rare genetic condition."

"They say it affects one in four thousand Americans. My old man always had a little night blindness, but nobody ever mentioned anything like that. Oh well. Pretty soon, it was lights out for me."

"Must have been rough."

"Rough doesn't even begin to describe it, son."

Pastor Herb told Malachi that he didn't handle the news very well.

"I started drinking, believe it or not—beers at first, which we all thought was harmless enough, but then I graduated," he said with a chuckle. "We lived a block away from a bar, so it wasn't that hard. Maggie didn't say much about the drinking at first.

Guess she figured I was dealing with things in my own way. But then I started staying away for longer hours after work. They even called her couple of times at the bar to get me. She was about ready to pop by then. She was upset. I was mad. Mad with God, life, Maggie. I couldn't figure out 'why me?' you know?"

Malachi shifted in his seat.

"I wish I could tell you I just went home one day and Maggie and I kissed and made up, but it didn't happen like that. I called my wife from a pay phone one Friday after work and told her I wasn't coming home. Told her I couldn't bear for my child to be born and I not see what he or she looked like. She was devastated of course." He sighed.

"Am I boring you?"

"No. Go ahead, Herb."

"Well, I ended up in a homeless shelter, if you can believe it. The pastor who owned the shelter was a genuinely nice guy named Tom Weinstein. He had a church out there in Long Island, but he said the Lord led him to buy this old building when it went into foreclosure and open up this here shelter in the Bronx. Ain't God something?"

Malachi nodded.

"Anyway, there I was jobless and homeless by choice. I bounced around to a few more shelters, but somehow I just kept coming back here to Weinstein House. Got mugged couple of times. Still called home now and then. Poor Maggie would cry and beg me to come home, but I just didn't feel like I was of any real use to anybody, much less a wife and three kids. Little Rachel was born by then."

"Then I got arrested." Herb told the young doctor that getting arrested for sleeping in the wrong place was another wake-up call. After Maggie bailed him out, he confessed that he still couldn't go home, but he asked her to drop him by Pastor Weinstein's shelter. He shared his story with the elderly pastor and asked him for a job. He got one doing odd jobs. Days later in one of the voluntary Bible Study sessions the pastor held with the men, Herb ended up in a verbal spat with one of the guys from the shelter who was going on about God being a figment of man's imagination.

"I guess I impressed the socks off of Pastor Weinstein that day or something. Before long I was promoted to Bible Study coordinator at the shelter, could you imagine? The pastor said I had a way with folks. At first, I said to myself, 'I wonder if this man has all his marbles intact, trusting someone like me to speak to people. I'm just as down on my luck as the rest of them.' Looking back at the whole thing, young Doc, I'd say that that old guy was the smartest man I've met in my life."

"Why's that?"

"You see the old geezer knew that if you're a real Christian, it's hard to spend so much time in the Word and not be changed. And that's exactly what happened. The Holy Spirit spoke to me about my life, my family, and before long I was back home."

"That's a great story, Herb."

"That's not a story, son; that's my life."

There was that impetuous tone again, Malachi noted.

"Let me tell you this last thing before I release you from Herb detail. This'll tickle you."

"OK"

"One day at the shelter, I was preparing a Bible Study listening to those Bible tapes the pastor got me. I decided to share something on giving with the folk, so I turned to your namesake, Malachi. I was planning to slam them with the bit about robbing God. You know that part?"

"Certainly."

"Well it's a short book so I listened to the whole thing. That's when I came across the passage that the Spirit used to reel me back in."

"OK."

"You see old Malachi was a messenger, and the Lord used him to tell his people stuff. After the bit about the tithes and offering, the Lord told the people that their words have been harsh against Him, yet it's like they're playing dumb and saying, 'What have we said against You?' And what struck me was when God said through Malachi: 'You have said it is useless to serve God; What profit is it that we have kept His ordinances...' Imagine God's people saying that?"

"Imagine," Malachi said flatly and closed his eyes.

"But, son, that's exactly what I was doing. I wasn't saying it to Tom, Dick, and Harry, but I was thinking it alright." He tapped his temple. "Man, I got so convicted that day when I heard that.

I kept pressing repeat, and I played that part over and over, crying my useless eyes out."

The silence between them lingered a few more seconds.

"So how did you...ur...I mean, what did you—"

"The question I guess you're asking is if I got my answer from God as to how this could happen to me."

"I guess that's what I'm asking."

"No."

"Sorry? You said—"

"I said 'No.' I didn't get some divine revelation as to 'why me' but I got a word—a promise really."

"OK."

"Later in chapter four of the book of Malachi, he said...Now where's that Bible? I want to read it to ya." Herb stood up and shouted to someone named Rhoda to bring him his Bible.

He took it from her and rewarded her with one of his smiles. Malachi thought he would have asked her to find it for him. But he found it for himself.

"I resisted this Braille business at first, but then the Lord spoke to my heart about it. I'm an independent person, young Doc, and this allows me to study the Word for myself—like how I used to when I just got saved. Anyway, let me read the passage for you." Pastor Herb then read verse two of chapter four.

But to you who fear My name
The Sun of Righteousness shall arise
With healing in His Wings;
And you shall go out

And grow fat like stall-fed calves

Malachi stared at the man who couldn't stare back and asked: "So you believe that you're going to be healed, is that it?" He refused to mask the cynicism in his voice.

Pastor Herb smiled.

"I've already been healed, son, that's why I'm here. The healing on the inside took place years ago in that shelter. If it hadn't been for the Lord who was on my side, I don't know where I would have been today. Might have given up."

Malachi nodded as an image of his mom flashed before him.

"As for the stall-fed calves bit," Herb started. "That's a promise fulfilled. Things turned around for me after that. My brother and I reconciled. He never married, never had kids, and so when he died, he left his entire estate to me. Let's just say it was enough for me to help my family in the way I always wanted to."

"Is that when you took over this place?"

"Naw. That was long after. Pastor Weinstein and I became very close, and months after I moved back home, he invited me to share at his church in Long Island. In a year, I was made the assistant pastor, and when he passed away eight years ago, the board voted me in as pastor."

Malachi saw Pete approaching.

"Sorry to break up the party, Dad, but Dr. Fiedler and I need the extra hands. Almost everyone wants to see a doctor today. Don't worry, I brought a replacement. Rhoda says she'll take over Herb detail today."

Pastor Herb smiled.

"Now that's a girl with vision," he said as Malachi got up.

"Thanks for sharing your story, Herb. It was…It was real."

"Thanks for listening and for your help today. As you can see, you're needed. I hope you come again."

"I'd like that…Really," Malachi told the pastor. Herb extended a hand to him.

"Are your hands clean?" Malachi asked. The old man cackled and turned a shade of pink.

"I like him, Pete. He has a sharp mind…and a good heart," Herb added, before turning to the direction of Rhoda.

"Rhoda, my dear you smell lovely today if you don't mind me saying so," Pastor Herb said as he took the young woman's hand and started walking toward the kitchen.

Pete waited until they were safely out of range.

"My dad's trying to set me up with Rhoda. I've been trying to tell him she's not my type. She's gorgeous, I'll give her that, and she cooks almost as good as my mom, but she's way too mousy for me. I see you survived Herb duty. Sorry about that. He gets carried away at times."

"That's cool."

"So I'm here twice a week. I can put you down for once a week depending on how it goes today. We get some interesting cases now and then. I've learned a lot."

"Sounds like a plan… and Pete."

"Yeah?" Pete turned to face his friend who was two steps behind.

"You can…uh slot me in for half an hour of Herb detail when I come next, if that's all right with everybody."

"Consider it done," Pete said as he tossed his friend a sterile pack of gloves.

CHAPTER TWENTY-NINE

The walls in the waiting area outside of Dr. Rodriguez's office was a funny blend of brown and gray, which, for some reason, reminded Abby of the rum and raisin ice cream she fell in love with in Jamaica. She picked up one of the three magazines from the glass top coffee table with the wrought iron base that was twisted into some abstract artistic sculpture.

Dr. Rodriguez's door was ajar and Abby could hear the controlled tone of the lecturer as she talked with someone on the phone. Probably thesis stuff, she thought. Abby had heard that two of her colleagues had submitted late. Missing deadlines was a big deal at Stanford. She was grateful that she'd got hers in on time, and based on feedback from her supervisor, she was heading for a distinction. Which is why she was baffled by the summons.

Abby replaced the magazine on the table and placed her hands palms down in her lap. She closed her eyes, took a deep breath, and exhaled slowly.

This is nothing. I will not panic. I will trust. Lord, I will trust.

When she reopened her eyes, Abby was startled to find the petite frame of Dr. Rodriguez staring down at her, hands clasped at the front.

"If you need a minute," Dr. Rodriguez started.

"No. I'm great; I was just waiting on you, actually." She smiled and sprang to her feet.

"I'm ready for you. Shall we?" Dr. Rodriguez extended a hand toward her open door.

There was a hint of jasmine in the air. Abby wasn't sure if it was coming from some plug-in or Dr. Rodriguez herself. Abby once had a shampoo with the floral fragrance, and Dr. Rodriguez did have a bouncy head of curls. It was by far her most flattering feature. Her face was not what one would readily describe as pretty. Her eyes seemed beady—at least that's how it appeared from behind her red frames. Abby couldn't recall seeing her with makeup. She obviously was one of those women who were content with a dust of powder and dab of gloss. But there was something about her smile that, though slightly crooked, gave her an air of sincerity that Abby was quite sure was an asset in her profession.

Abby took a seat in the center of the chocolate brown leather couch that leaned against the eastern wall of the office. She'd seen the office before—had admired the vintage mirror on the eastern wall, the sculptures, and artifacts that added character to the flaking built-in shelves. Abby had asked about the artifacts during her first visit to her supervisor's office and was told that they were Mayan in origin. A coconut tree grew from a gigantic clay pot in a corner of the room. It tilted desperately toward the streams of light that peeped through the blinds behind Dr. Rodriguez's chair. For some reason Abby felt sorry for the tree—for the fact that it was denuded and being forced to survive where it clearly didn't belong.

Abby shifted her gaze back to the sculptures. She crossed her legs at the knee and unconsciously started to bounce the one that touched the floor.

"Comfy isn't it?" Dr. Rodriguez said, as she took her seat in a black, high back office chair behind her walnut-stained desk.

"It is," Abby responded, her poker face fixed.

"Abby, why do you think you're here?"

"To freak me out?" she replied, with a chuckle. Dr. Rodriguez's unsmiling face stared back at her.

"I brought you in to talk. I know you probably had your fill of it between all the empathy training and the sessions with Dr. Harper, but there's something about the reports of those sessions that bothers me. A bit."

"Oh?"

"Yes." She flipped through the file on her desk and stopped on a page which had been tagged by a fluorescent orange tab.

"Abby, let me say from the start that Dr. Harper thinks you are going to make an excellent therapist. He has no doubt you will do this institution proud, and you would be a credit to the profession. So relax," she added with her first smile.

"He had some concerns, though. He felt that you might be carrying some baggage."

Abby hiked her eyebrows and then relaxed her facial muscles in the controlled way she'd been taught. The thing about her profession, she had to admit, is the way some practitioners never let you forget your past. She had shared about her eating disorder back in the day when she had self-esteem and body image issues. But that was old news. She couldn't believe a trained professional had dredged that up. Talk about overkill.

"Who is..." Dr. Rodriguez continued, unfazed by the lack of verbal response. She took off her spectacles, placed the tip in her mouth and then put them back on. She then circled something with her pen. "Yes. Tell me about Megan?"

Abby eyebrows furrowed. She'd mentioned Megan once or twice during the sessions with Dr. Harper, and as far as she'd recalled, it was all very light.

"What about her?"

"She's your friend, isn't she?"

"She is. I'm godmother to her daughter Alexandra."

"Dr. Harper seems to think that your friendship with her is shrouded in guilt."

"What!"

"Are you denying this? Did Dr. Harper get it wrong?"

"I'd say. Dead wrong. With all due respect." Abby instructed herself to lower her voice and soften her tone.

"So you're not feeling guilty?"

"No."

"But you are angry?"

"I am a little. Yes. I guess this is what a misdiagnosis feels like."

Dr. Rodriguez peered at the open file and reclined in her chair. "Dr. Harper said you'd be...defensive, if not angry."

"I'm angry because that's not an issue in my life. I thought that whole psychotherapy for yourself requirement was meant to unearth issues so that we don't transfer them to our clients—issues that can actually stand in the way of us giving quality care."

"Perhaps this is yours. Dr. Harper certainly felt so, and you haven't given me a reason to believe otherwise."

"I can't believe this."

Abby sat at the edge of Dr. Rodriguez's couch. Her gaze shifted to the door. She felt cornered and she didn't like it. She knew she had options: she could excuse herself and walk out, or she could stay and...talk."

"I told Dr. Harper that I loved Lexi, that's Alexandra's pet name. I said that her mother and I met as undergrads and something bad happened. I said Megan had to make some tough choices, and sometimes I question whether I gave the best advice back then. I was just sharing. Wasn't that the point? If I wasn't... free, I wouldn't have brought it up."

"What if I say to you I don't think you are free, as you put it— that I think you feel responsible in some way for how Megan's life turned out."

"That's ridiculous. How can I be responsible? I wasn't a professional then. I didn't know anything, really. How could I be responsible?"

"Indeed. But you do feel responsible, don't you?"

"How could I? She was raped, she got pregnant. She didn't know who the father was. It could have been...this guy I know that she was seeing, who is my friend, too. They broke up just before... But she wasn't sure, it could have been the rapist's child. I was sworn to secrecy. Alright, so sometimes I wonder if I should have told him about the possibility that this child was his. Or I could have told her to get off her high horse and tell the guy what happened. Maybe he wouldn't have dropped out of med school as I...we all feared he would do if he'd found out. Maybe Lexi would have had a daddy. Yes, maybe I do blame myself. Is that what you want to hear? Maybe it's all my fault, Dr. Rodriguez—that this beautiful, brilliant child is growing up without a daddy to bounce her on his knee, to tuck her in at night, to see her dance like an angel. Maybe that's why I call him every year on his birthday but can't seem to talk. I mean really talk. And talking is supposed to be my thing!"

Abby sniffed. This is where she would have offered tissue, had she been the therapist.

"You kept in touch?" Dr. Rodriguez wanted to know.

Abby's voice was small now.

"Yes." She smiled up at the doctor, her eyes unable to mask her emotions any longer. "He recently moved to New York." She swiped at her tears before they could fall. Still no tissue. "I call him every year. Yep." She placed her hands face down on her lap. "Every year on his birthday. I call and all I can say is, 'Hi, how are you? Good. How's your b-day so far? And your dad's doing OK? Great, well it was nice talking to you. Take care now.' And you know what, Doc? I'm just sick of it." The falling tears were outpacing the swipes now. Abby was using her sleeve in lieu of tissue.

Dr. Rodriguez nodded and scribbled something in her file. She put her pen down.

"Abby, you do realize the need to deal with this? If you don't, it will consume you, and, yes, it can ultimately affect the quality of care you give to your clients. I can't tell you what to do here, but you need to go get your freedom."

Dr. Rodriguez extended a box of tissue to Abby.

Took you long enough, Abby thought.

Abby sat back on the couch and stared at nothing in particular. She knew Dr. Rodriguez, like Dr. Harper before her, was right. The only question that remained was, What did she intend to do about it? The power to change the status quo, she knew, was hers. Some way, somehow, she had to find her freedom.

****

The orthopedic mattress was the only item of furniture—the only evidence that someone lived in Redding Flat. The mini fridge and the bookcase were the last items of furniture to be snapped up by the bargain hunting undergrads who'd responded to her garage sale ad. The mattress that she purchased, that had served her well over the last year, would be donated to charity, giving way to a return of the original mattress, now in storage, that came with the room. It took two nights on the single bed for her to realize it wasn't going to work. Her back pains had been near crippling. She had similar challenges while on hall in Jamaica, which is why the floor became the preferred spot for sleeping. But she wasn't prepared to take another day of it and she had invested in a mattress specially designed for troubled backs. But she couldn't take it with her; it was simply too costly to ship.

Her books, pillows, laptop, clothes and personal effects were the only items Abby decided would make the journey to New York with her. That and her blue pre-owned Chevrolet cobalt wagon. It's the reason she'd chosen to live in Brooklyn. Apart from the lower cost, she would be able to keep the car and have an alternative to the subway whenever she felt like it.

Abby glanced around the room which she had called home for the last two years. In two days it would be some other post-grad's crash pad. Someone else's curtains would flutter in the breeze when the dormer is opened during summertime, some-one else's knick knacks would line the built-in shelves near the window which Abby had used for her potted plants and framed family photos.

The tip of the burnt orange pillow with the red and gold tas-sels poked up from the box at the foot of the bed. The pillow had been with her since junior high and if it were possible for a pillow to be all hugged out, this one would qualify. She grabbed a pencil from her hair and scribbled a note in her day planner to call her new landlord to remind him of the day she would be arriving. She was looking forward to returning to New York, the place she called home for most of her life. Everything was in place for a smooth transition. At least that's what her checklist told her. She scrolled the legal pad with her pencil tapping the page with the eraser end at each check mark. It was all done. All, that is, except one.

She picked up the receiver on her phone and punched the numbers. He answered on the third ring.

"Hey Mal. It's me."

"Abby? Hey yourself."

"Is this a bad time? You sound a bit weird."

"I just got in, practically ran to the phone. I thought it was my dad. He normally calls on a Thursday."

"Oh, how is your dad?"

"He's good. Better than me in some respects. Gosh, I can't get over hearing your voice. Guess I sort of got used to my once-a-year call." He chuckled.

Abby closed her eyes and nursed the sting of his truth. She couldn't hold it all in any longer. Her lecturer's words echoed in her head. If the assessment of her tutors was correct, her entire professional career was in danger of short circuiting before it even got off the ground. She had to find a way to redeem the situation. Her prayer was that it wasn't too late.

"Yeeeah, Mal…about that."

CHAPTER THIRTY

Malachi could have kicked himself as he slid across the leather sofa of the booth that the waitress had directed him to. He'd been escorted to the couples section of the restaurant where partitions were higher and the booths cosier. It was the only spot that had opened up when the guest pager had gone off, and given the line of patrons after him, he thought it best to grab it rather than extend his wait indefinitely for a different kind of spot.

Pete, he thought, was right about one thing: the ambience at *Joy* was amazing. It was classified as casual dining, but the sleek lines, gleaming table tops, and semi-Asian backdrop offered up a facade that was far more upscale. Malachi felt for his wallet, pulled it out and checked that he had all the cards that mattered.

The service so far was acceptable. The wait was what anyone might have expected on a Saturday evening in a Manhattan restaurant. He imagined it increased the restaurant's stock for patrons to relay that they had to wait twenty, thirty minutes to be seated. Pete also told him that the food was something to write home about. Based on the aromas that greeted him so far, he couldn't wait to make his own assessment. What his good friend failed to mention was that if ever a restaurant screamed "you're the love of my life" it was this—and that wasn't the message he wanted to communicate to his long-time friend.

Maybe he was overreacting; maybe all New York restaurants felt like this. He certainly had not dined at enough to judge. He was on Ob/Gyn rotations these days. This meant he hardly left his apartment on his days off. Between reading up on procedures and volunteering at the shelter, Malachi knew that his social life had taken a nose dive.

He was lost in his thoughts when he heard it.

"Oh Zack!" The woman, who could have been his age, gasped, as tears welled up in her eyes.

"Yes, yes! Of course I will marry you!" she screamed and lunged into the arms of the proposer who was still on his knee. The poor guy let out an audible sigh.

Patrons clapped. The waiter, in a well-timed move, popped the Champagne.

You've got to be kidding.

As if on cue, Stevie Wonder's "Overjoyed" floated from its mysterious source. Even the tea lights on the table seemed to blush with the moment.

"Dr. Malachi Williamson!"

"Abi-Gail Shaw. Wow, you—you look great." He got up from his seat and grabbed the friend he hadn't actually seen in seven years in a tight embrace that practically lifted her off her feet.

"I wondered if I would recognize you, but you're basically the same except that you're bigger somehow and even more handsome, if that's even possible."

Abby was glad that she made the extra effort to please her reflection. She wore a stylish sleeveless black dress that fell just above the knee. The cowl at the front dropped elegantly, while preserving her modesty. She asked André, her hairdresser, to pin her hair up, but to give her a soft bang which fell more to one side. For once he obeyed. She chose not to wear a neckpiece but to accentuate the dress with her diamond studs—a graduation trinket from her parents, one that she planned to reserve for special occasions. This, she felt, qualified.

She scanned him from head to toe. He was indeed not as lean as she'd remembered him in Jamaica, and it wasn't because of his tailored black jacket and crisp white shirt that opened up at the collar. His head was low, though not completely bald, and he had a six o'clock shadow, which, together with the jeans, added something dangerously rugged to what she always felt were above-average features.

"Well, it's a good thing you recognized me because I certainly would have had a hard time picking you out. Abby, you're a woman!"

"Shh. Stop it, just stop it!" She threw her head back and giggled girlishly at the compliment. Abby knew exactly what Malachi was talking about. When she'd returned to New York after her time in Jamaica, Abby had decided that a drastic change in venue warranted an equally radical new look. She'd kept her virgin tresses, but she started experimenting with products that would give her more styling options. She'd even dropped a few pounds and toned up by taking advantage of the campus gym. She started paying more attention to her skin-care regimen and even had one of her girlfriends teach her a thing or two about makeup. But those were her secrets to tell…or not.

"No, I mean it. You have to be a man to understand what I'm seeing. Something or someone is definitely agreeing with you."

"It's the joy of the Lord," Abby replied, without missing a beat.

"Uh-huh," he said, and they both laughed.

"Did I walk in on a proposal a minute ago?" Abby asked, as she spread her napkin on her lap.

"Fraid so. Abby, I must apologize for the overdose of romantic vibes in here. A friend recommended the place. It was meant to be a dinner to celebrate your PhD, your job, and return to New York. That's it." He put his palms up.

"You mean you're not going to propose?" She mimicked a sniff and heave of the chest before waving her hand in the air to dismiss his concern. He got a whiff of her fragrance. It was spicy; just like the person who wore it.

The waitress approached the table to take their order, and they asked for two more minutes. After discussing the menu, Abby settled on the mini egg rolls, the seared salmon teriyaki with oriental fried rice and Szechuan vegetable stir-fry. Malachi ordered stir-fried shrimp appetizers, ginger beef with jasmine rice, and shanghai style vegetables. They both ordered non-alcoholic wine with their appetizers and entrees when the waitress returned.

"So you made it; you survived med school. How does it feel, Doc?"

"It feels great, though I'm beginning to realize that all that means is that I'm a well-qualified work horse. But it hasn't stopped feeling good, I must admit."

"Your dad must be proud."

"He is. He made it up to Jamaica for my graduation. That really surprised me. And what about you? Doctor Shaw!"

"Oh my, isn't that something?" She fanned herself with her hand. "Gosh, it feels like just yesterday we were sitting in my room talking about our dreams and now look at us. We're living the dream!" She raised her hands in the air.

"Or at least we're off to a good start."

"A pretty good start, I'd say."

"So…how's the new apartment?"

"Hmm. I love it. The neighborhood's great, and I have more space than I need at the moment. But, hey, after living in dorm rooms and student housing for the last eight years of my life, I'm not complaining. I might take in a roommate; haven't decided yet. It's a great space, really. Can't wait to go all HGTV on it."

"You should have a house warming or something, Abby. Bring the New York clip together. Heaven knows I need to meet some people who don't wear white or scrubs all the time."

They laughed and it felt like old times. The waitress approached and placed the drinks they ordered on the table.

"You know, you're giving me ideas," Abby said with a wag of her finger. "I just might do the house-warming thing."

"You should."

"So Mal…are you, uh, in touch with anyone from school?"

"Yes. I email and do the social media thing with a couple of my former classmates when I find the time. I—uh—I also hang out with Caleb every now and then."

"Really? He's here?"

"Yep." Even as he responded, Malachi noticed the sudden dip in Abby's eye contact. He wondered if she still harbored feelings for his best friend.

"He lives in New York now. Haven't seen him much since his new job as an investigative journalist or something like that."

"Investigative journalist? Wow."

Malachi nodded.

He was trying to read her. Certainly, there was more he could say about Caleb if he so desired, but the blank expression on Abby's face made him question whether she was truly interested in hearing it. Besides, his best friend's life choices should not be on the "small talk" menu for the evening, he reasoned. Brothers' code.

Abby sipped her water. "So what about you, Mal? Any serious relationships lately? How many hearts have you left strewn all over Jamaica or New York for that matter?"

She held her breath. Everything she was planning to tell him hinged on his response to that question. What if he was in a serious relationship? What if he was engaged?

"Minus one," he said with a chuckle.

"What does that mean?" There was an earnest texture in her voice. She caught a glimpse of herself in a nearby wall-mounted mirror. Her face looked too intense. She reminded herself to smile—look casual and breezy.

Yes, casual and breezy, Abigail Shaw! What am I doing, Lord?

"It's like sub-zero," he replied, interrupting her noisy thoughts. "It's a joke. My goodness, Abs. They made you surrender your funny bone in the PhD program, huh? Wow."

She laughed; they laughed. She laughed harder.

"Seriously, after the scare of almost being kicked out of the program, I turned into a super nerd. It was all about the books. I mean, I played a little volleyball and badminton now and then. The hall was grateful I suppose, especially since I was living off campus, but I couldn't afford the distraction of a serious relationship."

"How dull."

"Yeah, I guess it was," he said with a chuckle. "It paid off, though—literally. I made the Dean's List every year. Got some real nice bursaries, and Dr. Bruno even hired me as a research assistant for six months in my fourth year. I'd like to feel it was a mutually beneficial experience. Her recommendation certainly came in handy on my residency application."

"Good for you. Well, school's out, my friend. It's time to get you back in the social circuit," she said and thumped her fist playfully on the table.

"I've been out a few times. I've got some calls, pokes on social media, some numbers… from girls mainly."

Abby almost choked on her water. "Excuse me," she said, and patted her chest. "Why am I surprised? Of course you got hit on by guys. Hey, welcome to New York!"

"Ent."

"And what about you, missy? I hope you're taking your own advice. Abs, listen to me, some people are called to the single life."

"What?"

"Shh. Don't interrupt. You and I are not among the called."

"How do you know that?"

"Hey, I'm a doctor. I know these things."

Abby placed one hand over her stomach and the other over her mouth. It's been a while since she had one of those rib-tickling laughs that picked away at her decorum.

"Besides, Abs, I won't have it. In fact, I feel I have just the guy for you. How do you feel about interracial relationships?"

"Hello, let me not remind you that the last friend you introduced me to…" She twirled her finger in the air.

"Right. Gosh Abs, don't remind me." He covered his face with his palms to show contrition.

"Sorry you got your heart broken," he said, pensively, after a pause.

She shrugged. "I don't hold it against him. He made his choice. That's ancient history. Now…" She lightened the mood with a smack of her lips. "There was a guy I met through a classmate at Stanford."

Malachi bounced in his seat and rubbed his hands in boyish glee. "Yeah? Tell me more."

Abby laughed.

"You're too silly. He's from California. A dentist."

"Nice."

"Believer of course."

"Of course."

"A little older, but that wasn't the problem. There just wasn't any… sizzle, you know. I need a little sizzle in my life. It felt a little too academic—like I was just matching degrees or something. Anyway, I called it off before it got too serious."

The waitress arrived with appetizers. Abby said a quick prayer and they dug right in with their chop sticks. Each transferred samples of what they'd ordered on to the other's plate.

"So what are you looking for, Mal? I have quite an impressive network of girlfriends in New York," she said before biting into half an egg roll.

"Well, let's see. She must be intelligent. Funny without being a clown. Must love the Lord, and it would help if she wasn't too hard on the eyes."

Abby almost gagged on her egg rolls. "I'm sorry, did you say 'must love the Lord?'"

"Of course. My wife-to-be must share my faith in Christ." Malachi smiled slowly.

"You're not toying with me, are you?"

"Nope. Abby, I'm sure you'll be happy to know that I rededicated my life to the Lord about...hum...three months ago."

"Get out of here! That's fantastic. Man, do I want to cry!" She fanned her eyes with her hands.

"Get a grip, Abs," he said jovially.

"What happened? I mean...Tell me everything." She placed her elbows on the table and cupped her chin.

Malachi puffed out a breath. "Where do I start? Let's just say the Lord sent someone in my path who'd been through a kind of Job experience, in my book, and yet he had so much love and gratitude in his heart that he put me to shame. I guess God just used him to remind me of His goodness and mercy toward me... and my dad. Even being a doctor has a whole new meaning. I literally wake up in anticipation of what God is going to do next."

Abby slumped back in her chair. She wiped the edges of her mouth with her napkin. This was her big cue.

"Malachi, as I told you on the phone, there's something I need to tell you. It explains why I've been so... distant over the years."

"Listen Abs, we both know that our friendship took a different turn when you left Jamaica, but I want you to understand that I don't hold anything against you. Things change, people change; it's just a fact of life. We've both been busy accomplishing our goals. Besides, some of it is on me. I definitely went into a kind of zone myself."

"OK but—"

"No 'but' Abby... Just let it go." He said it softly but firmly. "You know, just recently my pastor was sharing from Philippians where Paul talked about forgetting those things which are behind and reaching for those things which are ahead. Abby, one thing I've learned is that life is about pressing forward. The past is the past. It's sunk. That's the term my accountant friend from Bible Study introduced me to. My gaze is ahead, and we're in New York!" He lifted his hands triumphantly. "This is the place where dreams still come true."

He was happy. It was all behind him. Abby didn't need a bunch of degrees to see that. She allowed a smile to pinch the disappointment from her face. The evening's plan had failed, and she, once again, was forced to concede defeat—for now at least.

"A place where dreams come through. It is, isn't it?" she said without conviction, and pushed aside her last egg roll.

He lifted his flute. "To new beginnings."

Abby raised hers thoughtfully.

"And old friends," she added, to the clink of glass.

CHAPTER THIRTY-ONE

If there were a perfect month, it had to be September. Abby was convinced that if life were filled with Septembers, all the reasonably-minded people would be happy. It wasn't as scorching as July and August, with their sub-human heat waves. And those who hated the cold would be spared the nip that tagged along with late autumn, spring, and the winter months. That's why it was so perfect.

"The perfect. Month. For a. Perfect. Party," Abby said in a huff that forced the final burst of air out of her lungs. She'd pushed and pulled the rug that she'd bought for her living room half-way through the front door and had begun taking quick breaths in preparation for the other half.

"Abby, what are you doing?" Megan scolded. "Why didn't you call me to help you? I thought that's why I'm here."

From the minute she had told Megan about her decision to hold a housewarming, her friend had gone into event-planning overdrive. Megan told her that she'd picked up a thing or two from observing her parents plan numerous soirées over the years, especially when the whole family got together in the summer or at Christmas. Abby figured that Megan's know-how would come in handy, and it had. She'd given brilliant advice on catering and décor. It was Megan's idea to hire a mixologist who specialized in non-alcoholic drinks for the event. Her friend had even gone through the trouble of sourcing one and paying for him out of her own pocket. Megan had refused Abby's offer for reimbursement, suggesting that she considered it a "house-warming/congrats-on-your-doctorate" gift from her. And when Abby had thought of pulling the plug on the event out of worry over how bare the place was, it was Megan who suggested that they scan the newspapers for garage sales in her neighborhood to acquire key pieces of furniture. Her friend had even dismissed her suggestion of hiring a professional cleaning service to detail the apartment. Instead, Megan had made the prodigious offer to give up work for a day to help her clean, which is why Abby felt like Judas's twin sister right about then.

She'd accepted as much of Megan's help as her conscience would allow, but had remained secretive in one key area: the guest list. That one, she figured, was better kept close to her chest. She'd invited Malachi to the party, and given the history between himself and Megan, she knew that by doing so, she was taking the ultimate risk: her most treasured friendships.

Megan grabbed the other end of the rug and pulled as Abby pushed. "You sure you don't have a body wrapped in here. This is far too heavy to be an ordinary area rug."

"This is no ordinary rug, I'll have you know. It's a hand-woven prairie rug from India. I got it for half price at that warehouse sale I told you about."

"You didn't? Is it damaged?" Megan wanted to know.

"Nope. Per-fect."

"You got to love this country."

"No place I'd rather be right now."

"Have you made up your mind about whether you're catering out the whole thing or doing some stuff yourself?"

"I took your advice. Catering all the way. You were right, chips and dip wasn't gonna cut it, and those canapés recipes your mother emailed were going to kick my butt big time. Besides, I want to relax and mingle with my guests. And good old Mom came through with the money for the catering. She said if I were stuck in the kitchen whole night fussing and fretting, I'll never find a man. As if it were that simple."

"Tell me about it. I'm starting to feel like one of those Dance Moms you see on TV. It's worse than a soccer mom, I tell you. Lexi's obsessed with ballet."

"Wonder where that came from?"

They laughed.

"Abby, I must confess that as the days draw nearer, I'm getting more and more excited about your party. Paul, Sara Lee, and the kids are coming—they asked me to confirm with you. Are you sure you can handle the whole squad? Really Abs, they're not the type to be offended if you say no kids."

"Relax, I wouldn't have told you to invite them if I felt it was too much. Besides, my goddaughter must have someone to play with. Who better than her cousins. Have you picked out a dress yet?"

"I don't know. I was thinking of wearing my nice peach cold shoulder shift dress. You know the one with the tiny flowers by the hem. Simple and elegant."

"No-ho. No. No. No. C'mon Megan, you need something new; something that says: 'See me 'ere. I'm available,'" Abby said in a perfect Jamaican accent.

"Are you mad? You want me to look like some kind of hoochie?"

"Of course not. Besides, you are much too stunning for that label. It's just that I really want everyone to dress up. This is New York. Do you see how those girls dress to go clubbing?"

"Yes? And your point is?"

"Well, think of this as our night out, only…we're in," she said with a wink. "You know what I mean. Listen, the goal here is to look hot…but saved. I'm telling you, Megan, I have a good feeling about this party."

"Fine. I'll go shopping later," she said, before collapsing on Abby's couch. "The apartment is shaping up nicely by the way. Your colors rock. I was a bit nervous at first. Your taste is border-line bohemian. You know that, right?" Abby opened her mouth in protest. Megan's hand stopped her. "Buuut…you pulled it together. I'm genuinely impressed."

"Well thank you, Your Royal Highness," Abby said with a curtsy. "It means the world to know you approve." She clasped her hands in mock adulation.

They laughed good-naturedly.

"What time are you going shopping later?"

"About fourish I guess. Why?"

"I think I'll tag along," Abby said, and perched herself on the arm of her couch. "Just so you don't mess this up. Maybe I'll call André, see if he can hook you up with a chic new cut, maybe some layers and definitely some highlights."

"Hmm. Abby, what are you up to? Seriously, you've guarded that guest list like it's the Colonel's secret recipe. Who are you trying to set me up with this time? I know you're up to something. I'm just praying it's not one of your psychologist friends from the center. Really, Abby, I'd sooner volunteer for a root canal."

"Oh don't be so dramatic." She flung one of her pillows at Megan and missed. "I'm not trying to set you up, per se. I just think…never mind." Abby dismounted the arm of her chair, stooped and started positioning her rug.

"No, say it. What?" Megan got off the couch and stooped to help Abby with the rug.

"I just feel that you may be forgetting that life is more than about being Lexi's mom. Don't get me wrong, she'll always be priority number one, but don't forget that you're a woman—a young, single one at that. A social being—a sexual being when the time comes. Don't lock yourself into a one dimensional view of yourself. Motherhood is not all there is to Megan Le Blanc. Am I wrong?"

"You're not wrong," Megan said, her voice tinged with emotional lassitude over the subject. "Truth? I don't know...I've been feeling kind of low lately, you know, about the lack of eligible prospects? The last guy who was interested, as I told you, turned out to be such a disappointment. He wanted to jump my bones on the first date for crying out loud."

"Eh-eh, don't even bring that up, Miss Thang. I asked you straight out, 'Megan, is this guy a believer?' And what did you say? You said—"

"He's between churches."

"'He's between churches.' Now what kind of mess is that? And I said it then and I'll say it again: girl, a man tells you 'he's between churches,' that's code for 'run for the hills cause I'm in no man's land and I want company.'"

"As usual, Dr. Abby, you're right. When are you going to start that radio talk show, again? I know you were waiting on the PhD."

"Oh, you have jokes, huh?" Abby's grin faltered when she saw the faraway look in Megan's eyes.

"Seriously, Megan, you need to watch the fortress you've erected around your heart. The Word tells us to guard our hearts with all diligence, but if you have it all barb wired with sharp shooters like it's a maximum security facility, ain't no man gonna work that hard. Look how many people, even people we know, are into the online dating thing. It's not my cup of tea, but hey, to each his own."

Megan sighed.

Abby walked over and shook her friend's shoulders. "Hey, it's gonna happen for both of us, you'll see. Meanwhile, let's remind New York that Megan Le Blanc and Abigail Shaw, two fine sisters, are in the house. Hello?"

"This apartment warming shindig better be worth it. Four o'clock is good for you?"

"Works for me."

"Fine. I'm overdue for some retail therapy anyway."

"Now that's the spirit, and don't forget, the therapist is in the house!"

CHAPTER THIRTY-TWO

By seven thirty in the evening, the first two guests had arrived. Deejay Gary, who was technically not a guest, had arrived since six and had commandeered a spot from which he would release his digital offerings. Abby had met Gary in the laundromat located in the basement during her first week at the brownstone apartment. Gary had told her that he was a part-time disc jockey and full-time undergrad at NYU. He was rooming with two other students. When Abby decided to have the party, he was one of two neighbours she'd invited. Gary had asked if she had a deejay, and she'd said no. He'd told her she now had one. Three days ago, she'd knocked on his door with a collection of some of her favorite CDs in a paper bag. Gary had smiled and assured her that he had more songs on his devices than all the songbirds in all the grasslands across this beautiful country. Gary provided Abby with a playlist, and she selected a mix of contemporary gospel, jazz, and a few old R&B hits in case anyone wanted to dance.

She didn't see the need to broadcast the fact that it was a Christian party and that no alcohol would be served. She did, however, tell the folks that she called to let the person that they invite know, just in case they had other expectations. She'd catered for thirty, forty at most.

And here they were trickling in.

A pang of panic clutched at Abby's throat as she mulled over the implications of having told neither Malachi nor Megan of each other's possible presence. Was she doing the right thing? Or was this quest for liberation of sorts merely a self-serving attempt to quiet her conscience? Ever since that meeting with her supervisor, she'd resolved that inaction was no longer an option. But was her action too soon, too drastic? Sure, it was seven years since the events that unfolded that first semester, but was she making the right move? She couldn't figure out why her certitude felt no surer than the flaky pastry she'd be serving.

Megan had dropped Lexi to the party early, since she, along with her younger cousin Andrew, was tasked with finding out, through the intercom, who was at the door and buzzing them in once their names appeared on the list.

"Sorry, I'm not seeing your name on the list. Did you come as someone's guest?"

"Yes," the person was saying on the other end of the intercom. "May I have that person's name, please?"

Abby looked on in awe at the little girl in the yellow and white sun dress with the white leggings and butterfly clips in her hair. She was often taken aback at just how articulate her goddaughter was at six. It should not totally have surprised her considering who her mother was. And Lexi had turned out to be the spitting image of Megan. She'd got her mother's sleepy eyes and coloring, but was blessed with a smile that was safely described as entirely her own. And Abby knew she wasn't the only one who had taken stock of the child's undeniable brio. It was only two months ago while shopping with Megan that Abby recalled the slick corporate brunette claiming to be an ad agency talent scout who had approached them and slipped a card to Megan saying "she liked her daughter's look." And that wasn't the first time.

There were times, Abby had to confess, that she'd caught herself staring long and hard at Lexi—searching for a flicker of resemblance or mannerism that would connect her genetically to the man who she desperately hoped was her father. But apart from her curly hair, her smile, and a slight dimple in her left cheek, all that could be said was that her phenotype left little doubt as to who her mother was. Abby suspected that Megan was relieved about that.

A tall, white guy who looked like a pro athlete strolled into the apartment. Abby's eyes met his.

"You must be Abby? Hi I'm Pete—Dr. Pete McGregor—Malachi's friend. This is for you." Abby took the gift bag with the box which was beautifully gift wrapped.

"Handle with care now. It's fragile... and a little heavy," he said to Abby who pivoted as gracefully as she could in her four-inch designer stilettos. Pete kept his eyes on his hostess as she sashayed across the room toward a round table which was ear-marked for gift bags and other housewarming presents.

Abby noticed her newest guest was staring at her openly as she walked back to him. She had chosen to wear a beaded V neck bodice with a blue chiffon skirt with tiers that fell on the knee. Her hair dropped in playful ringlets which, though girlie, managed to look sophisticated. The look on Malachi's friend's face gave her that extra bolt of confidence her ego had craved.

"It was sweet of you to bring me a present, Pete," she said when she'd returned to where he stood. "And where is your friend tonight? I hope he hasn't stood me up?" She released a nervous titter at the thought.

"Not at all. He got off a little late tonight. Got the opportunity to scrub in on a laparoscopic surgery, I think. Hey, when we get it, we grab it. So he called and told me he'd meet me here. He said, 'Pete present yourself to Abby. She'd be the most beautiful woman in the room; she'll take care of ya, and I must say, the man was spot on.'"

"Oh my," Abby said and blushed without shame. "Well I'll have to take extra good care of you then, Pete. So you're a doctor as well? Not a pro athlete."

Pete laughed. "I get that all the time. It's interesting, though. I'm a huge sports fan, and I want to get into sports medicine as it turns out."

"Sounds exciting," she said with a grin that sounded a bit girlish even to her own ear.

Abby chatted with Pete for ten minutes before the next stream of visitors arrived. Megan's brother, Paul, walked in with minimum interrogation from his niece. He arrived with his wife, Sara Lee, and their children Andrew, five, and Lily, four.

Abby looked around and spotted Summer, a childhood friend, who, Abby noted, gripped the arm of her fiancé Tyler as though, if she didn't, he might bolt. Abby introduced them to Pete.

Asha and Shauna, two close girlfriends from her days at Columbia University, arrived and before long the place was humming with laughter and music. Deejay Gary was playing Mary Mary and the room was abuzz with all the ingredients for a good time.

A game of Pictionary had begun over by the coffee table. A few guests had sprawled off on Abby's new rug. Some talked animatedly. Nothing was off limits: the economy, world affairs, religion, politics. They talked, laughed, and argued all the while cradling cups of non-alcoholic wine and concoctions courtesy the hired mixologist.

Abby almost jumped and spilled her drink when someone suddenly poked her on the side. It was Stacy, a lead soloist from her old home church which she started back attending as soon as she returned to New York. Nyron, the head of the music department, was right behind her. Abby and Stacy hugged and rocked and immediately started catching up on what she'd missed during her time away in California. Abby learned that Nyron and Stacy had started dating. Abby squealed at the news and dismissed a fleeting pang of regret that she didn't take Nyron seriously when she'd suspected that he had a little crush on her.

Abby sipped her virgin piña colada and scanned the room. Everyone was talking to someone. Most of the guests had brought presents: flowers; wine; a fruit basket, and a number of gift-wrapped packages which she planned to open tomorrow. She looked at her watch. It was 8:45 and neither Malachi nor Megan was in sight.

Where are they Lord? Where are they?

She tapped on Sarah Lee's shoulder. "Has anyone seen Megan? I thought she would have been here by now."

Sarah Lee's smile changed to a scowl. "Didn't Paul tell you?" She gently jabbed her husband who was standing with his back turned to her. "Hey buddy, weren't you supposed to give Abby a message from your sister?"

Paul slapped his head. "That's right. Sorry Abs. Megan called us while we were on the way here to say that one of her students did one of those jumping things—uh, what's it called, honey?"

"It's called a grand jeté."

"Right. Anyway the poor thing landed badly and Megan went with her to the emergency room. She'd called from the hospital to say that she was waiting on the girl's mother to arrive and to tell you not to worry, she'd be there to serve the canapés. Don't serve the canapés without her."

"Wow, OK. I hope the girl is OK," Abby said to Paul.

"She said the x-ray showed that nothing's broken so…" He shrugged.

"That's good news."

"Sorry Abby, Andrew and Lily were fighting in the car, Sara Lee was trying to direct with GPS, and it just got crazy. We almost turned and went back home."

"I understand, and I'm glad you're all here."

Abby suddenly became aware that everyone in her immediate circle had stopped talking and was now smiling at someone who, she assumed, had snuck up behind her.

"Happy apartment warming, Abby."

The timbre in his voice made her break out in a grin as wide as the Amazon. She turned around and stared up into the face of Malachi, who was smiling back. He lowered his head and kissed her on the cheek.

"This is for you."

She took the gift bag that Malachi extended to her.

Mercy Lord. He's actually here!

"It's very practical; I hope you like it," Malachi said.

"I'm sure I will," she replied and tiptoed into a hug while giving the room a scan over his shoulder.

"Let me put this with the rest of my loot. And I need to pop in the kitchen for a sec. It's time the second batch of Buffalo wings come out. That batch has a nice twist with a mild version of jerk seasoning. Couldn't help my Jamaican self. Don't want to be left with too much food on my hands. Speaking of which, what can I get you? Let's start with a drink. We have a mixologist on spot who specializes in non-alcoholic drinks….Sooo."

"Surprise me."

"Oh, I will."

She turned to Pete who was helping himself to a shrimp cocktail.

"Pete, I have to run to the kitchen to check on things. Why don't you do the introductions? You can start with Malachi and Paul."

Pete closed in. "Sure Abby. Dr. Williamson, this is Paul, his wife Sarah Lee, and they have a bunch of kids somewhere around here. Dr. Williamson and I work together at the same hospital."

Malachi chimed in. "Oh, is the little girl at the door one of yours because she sure grilled me. I had to stifle a laugh when I came through the door and she said: 'You know your face matches your voice? Isn't it something what children say these day?'"

"I think it's something in the water…either that or the breakfast cereal," Paul said.

They all laughed.

"That's my super intelligent niece, Alexandra. Lexi for short."

"OK."

"Those two rugrats over there are mine and—"

They all heard the crash. Everyone's eyes darted to the direction of the sound. Malachi saw a woman in slingback stilettos and a stunning black dress that fell just shy of her knees, stoop. She was now scooping up the finger foods that had fallen from the tray back onto the platter.

In seconds, Abby was at her side with paper towels helping her to clean up. The little girl, Paul's niece, had run up to her with a broom and hand shovel and was now stroking the lady's hair saying: "Mommy, don't cry. Aunt Abby has plenty more in the kitchen. Please don't cry."

Then the lady in the black dress looked in his direction and their eyes met and locked. It was Megan.

For the next few seconds, or was it minutes, he wasn't sure, Malachi saw the scene unfold as if he were beholding a suspense movie in slow motion.

The guy who was introduced as Paul walked over to Megan's side, with his wife at his heel. Pete's medical instincts also kicked in. He too darted across the room to figure out if a medical emergency had arisen.

Malachi, it seemed, was the only one who did not move— could not move. He just stood and stared as Megan whispered something, apparently reassuring in nature, to her daughter and then excused herself to the bathroom, he assumed.

Daughter. Megan has a daughter.

"She's fine," Abby announced, a shrill in her voice. "Just a little upset about the platter. We paid good money for those canapés."

Her guests laughed.

"Mal, man what just happened there? Have we stepped into the twilight zone or something?" Pete was talking to him. The chatter in the room started to rise again to the level before the platter incident.

Malachi didn't answer.

"Earth to Malachi, come in Malachi."

"Pete, hey listen, I think he needs a minute." Abby had hooked Pete's arm in hers and was leading him into the kitchen. "Are you good at dip, Pete? Think you could help me mix some more dip for the wings? I always put too much of something." She practically batted her eye.

Malachi stood glued to his spot, waiting for what, he wasn't sure. His thoughts were muddled, and the questions were downloading to his head faster than he was capable of processing them.

Is she upset? Is she in shock? Does she live here—in New York? When did she get married? Is her husband here? Does she have more than one kid? Is she a diplomat?

Did she know I was going to be here?

It wasn't the first time that he'd wondered about Megan and how her life had turned out. Her name had appeared under a photo of a ballerina on Abby's Facebook page. He couldn't tell if it were a picture of her or some other ballerina. When he'd clicked on the photo, he was prompted to send a friend request.

Friend request: The words gave him an instant headache.

Someone placed a hand on his shoulder. It was Paul.

"So you're Malachi. Small world huh? Paul Le Blanc." He decided to supply, owing to the dazed expression on Malachi's face. "We met a few moments ago. Megan's brother?"

"Paul. Sorry man. I'm just uh… Is Megan all right?"

"She's fine. Just taking a moment in Abby's room. Actually, she wants to talk to you. You up to that or should I…" His voice faded. "Because if you're not feeling it, I can just tell her—"

"She's in Abby's room, you say?" He ran his hand down his face and started in the direction of Abby's room. Paul's sturdy palm gripped his shoulders.

"Whoa, slow down. Wait a sec, man. Listen, I have nothing against you. I don't even know you, but that's my sister in there, and there's a lot you don't know, so…take your time." Paul gave him a nod. Malachi noted the family resemblance.

Malachi bit his lip and dug his hands in his pockets. Paul released his hand suddenly and stepped back, allowing Malachi to proceed to his destination.

****

Megan was surprised to see that Abby had found the time to transfer so many of her house warming gifts to the foot of her bed.

Her heels off, she found a spot on the beige carpet she'd helped her friend pick out just three weeks ago.

Her friend.

She hugged her knees and adjusted the plaid rayon chenille throw blanket that was covering her body from the waist down. The air conditioning was off, but she felt cold. She knew that the chill was probably psychosomatic. But it felt real to her. She didn't look up when she heard the door open and Malachi enter the room.

"That Abby is just full of surprises, isn't she?" She said the words without making eye contact.

"You all right?" he asked. His voice was remarkably steady, calm.

She cocked her head to one side and finally looked up at him to see him staring back at her. He was standing—hands in pocket—mere inches away from the wall behind the door. He looked good. His features had not changed drastically, except that he looked like he'd gained a few in all the right places, and he had that air of confidence—the one that sometimes came with making a good living. The crew neck sweat shirt he wore had two contrasting shades of gray. The black corduroys were just the right fit, and the outfit went perfectly with his boots.

All of a sudden she was back in boarding school, ultra-conscious of her appearance. Only this time there was nothing awkward about the way she looked. Her make-up, she was grateful, wasn't totally ruined, though her eyes were still a bit puffy from the tears that flowed earlier, mainly on account of shock. The black strapless cocktail dress with the side broach and asymmetric skirt that Abby helped her pick out, was flattering in every way. Abby's hairdresser André was a genius. When he was finished with her, Megan hadn't recognized herself in the mirror. It's amazing what a little haircut and a few highlights can do. André had been pleased with the result, and had told her that she wasn't just chic; she was New York chic.

"I'm fine. I guess the shock of seeing you again made me lose my balance. A bit," she added.

"It was a shock for me as well. How long have you been in New York?"

The questions had begun.

Megan sat up straight; her back found support against the side of Abby's bed.

"I've lived here seven years now. Since I left Jamaica."

"You left Jamaica shortly after we… you know. Why?"

Megan took a deep breath. She twirled the fringe at the edge of Abby's throw.

"Something really bad happened to me, Malachi?'

"Something like what?" There was a catch in his voice.

"I, uh. I was raped."

Malachi squeezed his eyes shut. He removed his hands from his pocket, laced his fingers over the top of his head, and began to take deep breaths.

"Are you alright?" She wanted to know, her voice full of concern.

He shook his head. "Megan I…This is the last thing I expected you to say. I mean, my gut told me something was wrong. You just disappearing like that, but…nobody mentioned anything."

The reasonable part of his brain told him that the contrition he felt had no business being there, yet he felt it: the unshakable need to apologize for his absence on that awful day and the days that followed. He stepped back and found the wall. A groan escaped his lips, and his face contorted with raw emotions as the reality of what happened back then set in. Megan couldn't tell if it were anger or pain that furrowed his brows. Perhaps it was a mixture of both.

Suddenly, he turned and pounded the wall with his fist. She jumped.

"When did this happen? Megan, do you know who…" His voice sounded hoarse. He cleared his throat.

"I don't know. It—it wasn't anyone I knew. As for the when…" she shook her head. "That's ancient history…I suppose it doesn't even really matter anymore."

"When, Megan!" He stepped closer.

"Are you shouting at me?" There was a quiver in her voice as she asked the question.

"Megan, please. I'm feeling pretty…I can't even describe how I feel right now. I—I didn't mean to raise my voice at you. I can't begin to…" He took a breath. "Please, I just need to know." His eyes pleaded for her truth.

"It happened about a week after we broke up…On my way to the library. It was late. I shouldn't have been walking by—"

"It's not your fault," he said interrupting her. His voice sounded like that of a wounded animal left to die at the side of the road. He walked to the end of the wall and slid down until he too was sitting on the floor, his head between his knees.

"I can't believe I let you…If I…." He winced again and looked up to the ceiling. He then transferred his gaze to her. "Megan. Why didn't you tell me?"

"I didn't know how to. If to. Exams had started. You had just barely escaped expulsion. I guess… I figured it would have been too much of a distraction…I'm sorry."

The tears flowed noiselessly from his eyes now—unchecked, unhindered. He didn't care.

The door opened and Lexi walked in. She looked across at Malachi and then ran to her mummy.

"Are you OK, Mummy? Aunty Abby said you're OK, but I wanted to see for myself."

"That is so kind of you, Lexi. I'm fine," she said in as jolly a voice as she could muster and pulled Lexi into a tight squeeze.

"I'm fine. Really, sweetheart," she repeated having tried harder to steady her voice. She prayed that her little girl had found the second act more convincing.

"Then why are you crying?"

"It's a long story, baby. Sometimes people need to cry to get stuff out."

"OK, but if you're not feeling well, Abby's friend over there is a doctor." She turned to Malachi.

"You can fix my mommy if she has a tummy ache or a broken leg and stuff like that, can't you?"

Malachi wiped his face with his hands, cleared his throat.

"Of course I can. You're a very bright girl," he said and sniffed. "How old are you, Lexi?"

"Six."

He smiled, nodded, and closed his eyes.

"Big girl," he said in a voice he hardly recognized.

"Lexi sweetheart, Mummy needs you to run along now. Go and let Aunty Abby give you a cup of hot chocolate. Grown-ups are talking. Remember what I told you about that. Be a good girl now. I'll be out soon."

"OK."

They were alone again. He waited.

"Megan."

"I don't know, Malachi. The truth is I don't know who the father is. It could be... him. And yes, she could be yours."

"Soooo, what you're saying is that for seven years you hid the existence of a life that could possibly have been conceived by us? Is that what you're telling me?" He was on his feet again, though he had not moved from the wall.

"I didn't want to ruin your life—your plans!"

"My plans?" he barked, derision in his tone. Malachi nodded. "You mean, that's all the faith you had in me? Wait a minute. Did Abby know about this?" His voice was accusatory. His finger pointed toward the door.

Megan didn't answer.

"Oh, I see," he said and released something that sounded like a laugh. "So you two got together and decided what was best for poor Malachi."

"It was my decision. Don't throw this on Abby. I asked—no in fact I begged her not to tell you anything. It was my decision. So if you're looking for someone to blame, blame me."

"Oh, I'm not disputing that. Megan, after all we went through; after all we shared. How could you not let me in on something

as important as that? You may have robbed your child–no, cor-
rection–our child, of six years of a father's presence. Does that
sound as messed up to you as it does to me?"

"There was no 'we.' We had broken up, in case you forgot.
You had no obligations to me and the sad reality in this case—
one I'd rather forget—is that the key word here is 'may.' You may
be Lexi's father, but you may not. In which case, the whole point
about you having the right to know, is moot."

"You know what. Listen. Provide me with a swab. We'll get
a DNA test. I'll get someone to do it tonight, and by tomorrow
we'll know one way or the other."

"No."

"What do you mean 'no'?"

"No. Lexi will not be having any such test."

"How else would we know, Megan?"

"Malachi, I want you to listen to me carefully." She closed her
eyes. "I. Don't. Want. To. Know!"

"That doesn't work for me."

"Well, too bad!" she practically shouted the words. Taking a
deep breath, Megan willed herself to lower her voice.

"You know, you have no..."

The tears began to flow again.

"You have no idea whatsoever of what I've been through; how
far I've come. You know what has kept me going these past sev-
en years? The fact that while I was never sure who Lexi's father

was—I always knew one thing—there was never a doubt that she is mine. Do you hear me, Malachi? Alexandra Jean-Marie Le Blanc is mine!"

"This is not over." He shook his head and grabbed the door handle. "Put yuh pot on the fire, it is not over. You better get your court clothes ready, Megan, because this is not over." Malachi yanked the door open and slammed it behind him.

Megan sat staring at the closed door. She had thought of the possibility of this moment many times over the last seven years, but now as she squatted on the carpet in Abby's room, she had to admit that the reality was a hundred times worse than she ever imagined.

CHAPTER THIRTY-THREE

Malachi Williamson Senior dropped his bag on the living room couch and headed for the fridge. It had been a long evening. The lecturer had gone over his time, and the group that he was a part of insisted that they stay back for two hours to put the final touches on their presentation.

Going back to school at age fifty-five was not all it was cracked up to be. Malachi Senior still had moments when he questioned whether the rigor of late night studying, group sessions, non-stop assignments and projects, was the smartest way to spend his time, given the circumstances. But getting his master's degree had given him something to do—something positive to look forward to, and to him, that was priceless.

His son had been against it at first.

"It would put too much strain on your body, Dad," the boy had said in his most doctorly voice.

But what was the alternative? Think and worry about his status whole day? Not to mention the laundry list of opportunistic infections any one of which could do him in. Compared to that mental stress, getting a second degree would be a breeze.

He started to whistle "How Great Thou Art" as he scooped out some of the stir fry vegetables from one of the containers that Sister Mark had brought over for him. The only thing better than not having to worry about meals on Sundays, was not having to worry about them on Mondays. He licked his finger, saw the flashing light on the answering machine on the kitchen counter, reached over, and punched it. The voice filled the room:

Dad, it's...Of course you know who it is. How many sons do you have after all? I uh. Something has happened and...well I need you. I need you here with me...in New York. Don't panic. I'm OK—physically. I'll explain everything when you call back. I'm sending money for the ticket. This is not optional, Dad. Please.

****

Malachi Senior always wanted to see the leaves change color as they did in fall. All of his previous visits to the United States had taken place during summer. In fact, his most memorable visit to New York had been the summer trip when Malachi Junior was conceived. He'd practically grounded himself the last few years before his wife's death. He'd broken the dry spell to see his son collect his certificate in his cap and gown. It had been worth the extra expense. And here he was again. Traveling. Flying. Living.

"It's too early to see the leaves change, Dad; it's not cold enough," Malachi Junior told his father as they sat on the sofa in what his son liked to refer to as the den, which to him was a plain old living room.

"Not cold enough? Are you joking? I'm freezing."

"Dad, seriously, are you cold?" He scooted over to his dad's end of the sofa and without warning placed a hand on his forehead and neck.

"What are you doing? I don't mean now. Outside, especially at night. Gosh, give me a break. I can't even tell you I'm cold now. Relax, I'm OK—really."

"You uh…taking your meds like you should?

"Yes. Don't I look, you know, healthy to you?" He made air quotes.

"Yes. Sorry…I worry sometimes. You've been doing well, but I still—"

"Well don't… You make me nervous when you go into that doctor mode of yours."

Malachi Junior sighed and placed his hands over his head.

"Ready to talk about it?" Malachi Senior took up the remote on the coffee table and found the mute button.

"Nope. But I need to. Dad, what am I going to do?"

"I don't see that you have too many options, Son?"

"You see, that's where you're wrong. This is America. I've already made a list of some law firms that might be able to help. I could start by getting a court order to have a paternity test."

"Son, you're not even a citizen. Who's going to take your case? And even if you find a lawyer who actually thinks you have a leg to stand on, do you really believe this is the right approach… considering."

"Considering what?"

"You know what. What if she's not yours?"

"What if she is? Dad, I'm well-acquainted with the odds here. I know Lexi may not be mine, but let's be real and honest. If it were you, regardless of the circumstances, are you telling me that you can just walk away; pretend it didn't happen—that there's no possibility that you might have fathered this child? I'm sorry, but my father didn't raise me to walk away from responsibilities. It's not in my DNA."

Malachi Senior smiled at his grown son.

"I accept that you feel the need to do something. I accept that but—"

"Dad, remember what happened when I was ten or eleven thereabout and Mom was having one of her manic episodes, I suppose. She got it in her head that I needed to see Disneyland, and she tried to take me out of the country without telling you. Remember that?"

"We never talked about that. I'm surprised you remembered." He folded his arms and played with the imaginary goatee on his face.

"You know what stuck with me? I will never forget the look on your face when you ran up to us in the airport terminal soaking wet like you just stepped out of the shower. I heard you tell Mom that if she ever tried anything like that again, you'd have her committed. I had to look up the word, so it kind of stuck with me. Remember that?"

Malachi Senior nodded.

"You told me later that night that it was God who gave me the good sense to find a pay phone and call you to tell you what was happening. You said if Mom had stepped on that plane with me you would have made it your life's mission to find me."

Malachi Senior chuckled. "You've got a memory like an elephant. I always said that. Your mom and I always had to be extra careful what we said around you."

"Some things should never be forgotten, Dad, and I consider children to be one of them."

"Fair enough. Just remember this. You don't know what it was like to be violated the way Megan was. I have worked with many victims of rape over the years, and it's an uphill journey for most of them. Some women in her shoes would not have hesitated to terminate the pregnancy. She didn't. That makes her a bona fide superhero in my book. God knows how much therapy she's had to have just to be functional and sane for that little girl under the circumstances. Don't mess her up; don't try to undo all that."

Malachi sighed. He lifted himself slowly from his seat on the sofa and began pacing the room.

"Have you prayed yet?" His dad was asking.

He stopped and stared at his dad. "What? No...Not really."

"Well, what are you waiting for? None of this has taken our Lord by surprise. We might have been in the dark on this, but He wasn't."

"I know that."

"Well then. Why don't you have that chat with your Heavenly Father. We can do it right now if you like. I've come all this way, I might as well make myself useful and agree with you in prayer. I'm not your Deacon Dad for nothing yuh know?"

Malachi forced a smile. He sat back down on the sofa and bowed his head, his elbows resting on his knees.

"I'm glad you're here, Dad. You have no idea."

"Well, it's like you always say, everyone can't be doctors. Some of us just get to be fathers to them." He smiled and bumped his son's shoulder.

Seconds later, Malachi Williamson Junior lifted up his voice in a prayer that he knew, before he even began, would change his world forever.

CHAPTER THIRTY-FOUR

"So, he hasn't called."

"Are we having a bad connection, Abby? How many times do I have to repeat myself?"

"Sorry, it's just that I was so sure he…Never mind."

"So, he blew you off when you called him?" It was Megan's turn to ask the questions.

"Worse. He hardly said anything to me. He said he was disappointed in me for not telling him all these years. I asked him what kind of friend or confidante would I have been if I had gone against your wishes."

"And what did he say to that?"

"What could he say? He knew I was right. It's not something I can ever feel smug about, and I told him as much."

"Well, if he feels that way about you—disappointed—as he put it, then he must be throwing darts at a picture of me on his wall." Megan propped her head on her hand.

"Seriously, Megan, I really think that deep down he understands why you made the choices you did, and if he doesn't now, he would eventually."

"You still have faith in him, I see. How can you be so sure, Abs? Really, when you pulled this little stunt, did you stop for a moment to think of the legal implications for me? What if he tries to sue me for custody or something? And what am I supposed to tell Lexi about all this?"

Abby was silent.

"Listen, I'm sorry. I know you meant well and part of me is actually relieved that it's all out in the open. I just wish you'd given me a little heads-up."

"I couldn't risk you not showing up."

"If it's worth anything, I don't think he'll hold this against you, Abs. It's not in his nature. Give him time."

"I guess I'm not the only one who has some faith left in the old Mal, then," Abby said, the smirk in her voice detectable through the phone lines. "He does look good, doesn't he, Megs?"

"Bye Abigail."

"Nothing's wrong in admitting that much. It's good for you... and that's my professional opinion."

"You're a piece of work you know that. Ta-ra."

Megan stared at the textured gypsum above her bed. Abby was right: Malachi did look good. The years they've been apart had been kind to him. He was much bigger than she remembered, and a tad more rugged. But the changes had worked for him. Moreover, as much as she hated to admit it, her attraction to him had not waned. If Abby was right, and he was not seeing anyone currently, she imagined it wouldn't be long before that changed. Young, straight, eligible doctors, she imagined, were as loved and longed for as caffe lattes in New York. And she knew some women who would rather be fired before they missed their latte.

****

Back in the day, Malachi recalled that he and Megan would talk about their future dreams and goals. Details were sketchy, but two things were always part of the plan: medicine for him, and a dance academy for her. She told him that she wanted a studio of her own, which she would later turn into a full-fledged dance school. She had described the nonskid floors, the mirrored walls, and the barre that never seemed to end.

"She did it," he mumbled to himself. "She actually went out and did it."

"Can I help you, sir?" A woman in her forties with a French-accent was asking.

"Yes, ah, I would like to see Ms. Le Blanc please."

"Is she expecting you?"

"No. It's an impromptu visit. I am...uh Dr. Williamson." He hardly ever referred to himself by his professional title, but if it helped him to gain access to Megan, he had no qualms using it.

"Well have a seat and I will try to get Mademoiselle Le Blanc's attention. She is finishing up a class. You can help yourself to coffee or tea while you wait."

"Thank you."

"Pardon me, but where are you from, if you don't mind me asking? I thought I was au courant with many of the accents in New York, but this one eludes me."

"Oh. I'm from Trinidad and Tobago, a twin-island state in the Caribbean."

"Trinidad and Tobago. Sounds delicious. So does your accent," she said with a wink before disappearing into an adjacent room.

Her posture was just about the only thing that had not changed. But in so many ways, Megan Le Blanc was not the same person he knew in Jamaica. She was wearing a blue leotard and a black skirt which ended two inches under her knee, white tights and pointe shoes. Her hair was open, cropped sharply at the neck and tucked neatly behind her ears on one side. The cut accentuated her neckline and added an extra layer of sophistication to a woman who was already dripping with class. He caught her in instructor mode as her class was still in progress. Her voice rang out with authority, yet it was clear from the way the students approached her, how enamored they were with her.

"Malachi, hi. This is a surprise," Megan said, slightly winded as she pat her face with a towel.

"Life is full of them these days," he responded and regretted it. He reminded himself that the plan was to keep the conversation light. Nonthreatening.

"Please. I'll take you to my office where we can chat." She gestured to a blond young woman who might have been around twenty-one or twenty-two.

"Katherina, can you take over for me. I'm going into a meeting in my office. I need not to be disturbed for the next twenty minutes or so."

"Certainly. I'll take care of it," the young woman said.

"Nice socks," Megan said, looking down at his feet.

"Thanks. Happy to oblige to your no footwear policy. These socks are actually my favorite pair. It was either these or ballet slippers."

The comment earned him a tight smile.

Megan led the way along a long hallway which led to lightly-tinted French doors. When she opened them, his eyes honed in on Lexi sitting behind her mother's desk using the computer.

Lexi looked up and saw the doctor from the other night. Their eyes met and held. Malachi smiled. The little girl didn't smile back.

"Lexi, you remember Dr. Williamson from Aunty Abby's party, don't you?"

"Yes. Hello."

"Hello Lexi. Nice seeing you again." Lexi turned back to the computer. She wore a private school uniform: a blue shirt with a rounded collar, a plaid skirt, navy, knee-high socks, and black shoes.

"Lexi sweetheart, are you finished with your homework? All of it?"

"Yes Mummy, would you like to see it?"

"Yes. I will take a look at it in a few minutes, but right now I need you to go with Aunt Katherina for a bit. Tell her to give you a task."

She looked from her mother to Malachi. "OK."

"You like computers, Lexi?" Malachi flashed one of his broad smiles—the one that all the kids he treated seemed to love.

Still no teeth.

"They're OK, I guess; this one's a bit slow. The one at home is faster, more games and stuff."

"Were you playing scrabble again, love?" Megan took a swig from her water bottle.

"Yep, and I'm getting better." Lexi made one final swivel in her mother's chair before jumping off.

"Scrabble huh," Malachi tried again. "You know, in my day, I could hardly handle a mouse."

"Kids today are much smarter," Lexi said matter-of-factly. "That's what my teacher, Mrs. Scott, keeps saying. She's having a baby."

"Is that so? Well, Mrs. Scott's probably right, Lexi," Malachi returned, with a chuckle.

Lexi looked at Malachi again.

"I know you're a grown up, and you're just trying to be my friend and that's kinda nice but..." She glanced around to confirm that her mother was listening. "You made my mommy cry the other night, and I didn't like that. I think you should apologize."

"Lexi!" Megan warned.

"But it's true. You tried to tell me it wasn't his fault, but you were happy until he came and—"

"That's enough, Alexandra. Now I told you I... I cried a bit because I had not seen Dr. Williamson for a long, long time. We were good friends back in college, and I was a bit... emotional. That's it. There's no need to be rude."

Megan looked from Lexi to Malachi. He was biting his lip. He didn't trust himself to speak.

"Sorry, Mommy. I didn't mean to be rude. I just never saw you cry like that except for when Grandpa got the heart attack and was in the hospital."

Megan bent down and kissed her head.

"Well, my crying days are behind me, OK? So scoot," she commanded and pat her daughter's behind playfully. "Let the grown-ups talk a bit. OK, pumpkin?"

"OK," she said, in a voice that sounded a tad more upbeat, and bounced out of the room without a backward glance.

Malachi sat on the chair opposite Megan. Slowly, a smile crept up on his face.

Boy, I'm in trouble.

"Wow."

"Yeah. She's a little overprotective where I'm concerned, and just a little more precocious than most six year olds. At first I thought it was the telly, but I have to conclude that it just seems to be her personality. She speaks her mind."

"It's not necessarily a bad thing."

Megan sighed and started rotating her neck. Malachi clenched his hands shut as he resisted the urge to get up and help her massage her shoulders.

"Your dad had a heart attack?"

"Yes. It was awful. He had a pacemaker installed a year before he went to Jamaica. The heart attack happened when he was on vacation in Paris. He had triple bypass surgery, but he's a hundred percent recovered now. Thank God. Finally made the lifestyle changes he should have made all along."

"And your mom, how is she?"

"Great. She's so much happier now that Dad has retired. They're back in England most of the time. She finally planted the garden she always wanted to. How is your dad?"

Malachi looked at Megan and allowed a few seconds to elapse.

"My dad is…" He shifted in his seat. "My father is HIV positive. We found out when I was an undergrad. Long story."

Megan's mouth remained opened for a few seconds. She caught herself. "I'm sorry. That must be very tough on you both."

"I'm just glad to be of some use to him… medically. He's basically fine, thank God. He's even gone back to school to get his master's."

"I have two friends who are positive. One of them found out just two months ago when she ser...Oh what's that word again?"

"Seroconverted."

"Right. She's only thirty. Could you imagine that?"

"I met some of Dad's friends from his support group. Half of the group is under thirty-five. He's in New York for the week. I hope you can meet him before he goes back."

"I'd love that."

They sat and stared at each other for a few more seconds than was expected of polite company.

Megan broke the eye contact first. "So, Malachi, to what do I owe the pleasure of this visit?"

"Well, I feel we have some unfinished business. Namely Lexi."

"OK. Should I get my attorney in on the conversation?"

"I don't think that's necessary. Megan, I've decided that I'm not going to push about the paternity test."

Megan sighed noticeably. "Well. I can't pretend that I'm not happy to hear that."

"I do, however, want to be part of Lexi's life."

"Malachi I don't think that—"

"No, hear me out. I've had the benefit of a mother and a father when it counted the most. I think it's part of what has made me who I am today. Their influence."

"Sure."

"Not having a father is going to leave a gap, whether you care to admit it or not."

"That's why I live so near to Paul. He's a big part of her life."

"Your brother is great, but he has two children of his own. What's wrong with having another male that can be there for Lexi? I've thought this through and I believe that I can be there for her. I want to." He shifted to the edge of his chair. "Please Megan, that's all I'm asking."

"I don't know, Malachi. Your career is pretty demanding. What specialty do you want to pursue?"

"Neurosurgery."

"Like Dr. Ben Carson. *Gifted Hands*—I read the book."

"I read his books and saw the movie. Look, I know I have a long road ahead of me, and some of that is going to take me out of New York. I'm pretty sure of it, but I'm not a quitter. I believe you know that much about me."

"I do."

"When I rededicated my life to God, I asked him to show me how and where I can make a difference in this world, and I believe that he's directing me every step of the way. I'm not going to tell you 'God says' where Lexi's concerned, but I feel strongly that my making a difference is also meant to include her."

"Are you cool with not knowing?"

"I won't lie to you. I wish you didn't feel that way, but you do and I respect that. Megan, you made a decision seven years ago that you thought was best, not just for yourself, but if I'm to be brutally honest, I have to admit that you were probably thinking of me as well. I can only conclude that you didn't trust me then. I don't know, maybe you had good reasons not to. But I'm asking you to trust me now."

Megan looked out the window. There was an enviable view of the city's skyline from her office. It's why she decided that blinds weren't necessary.

"Let me think about it, and I'll give you an answer soon. I promise."

"OK."

"Dr. Williamson. That sounds good. Malachi, I can't tell you how happy I am that things worked out for you."

"Thanks. And you…" He tipped his hand toward her.

"You've been rolling over in success as well from what I've read online. You opened the studio, which is very classy by the way from the little I've seen. Graduate of Juilliard, no less. In fact I heard through the Abbyvine that you even have a waiting list to get in here."

"The Abbyvine? Oh she would strangle you if she heard that moniker."

They laughed like old friends.

Malachi reached into his shirt pocket. "So, Ms. Le Blanc, I have these two shiny tickets to the New York City Ballet for Sunday night, and since I haven't had chance to go to any shows since I arrived in New York, I was hoping that you can go with me."

"You have NYC Ballet tickets?" She was powerless against the smile that overtook her face. "I see," she said and ran her hands through her hair.

"Yes ma'am. And I was thinking it would be nice to have someone to explain things to me while everyone's jumping around and pointing their toes. A little island boy like me can get easily confused. Easily. So what say you? And don't worry, it's not like it's a date or anything. It's just…ballet. You can handle a little ballet, can't you?"

Megan threw back her head and laughed in a way she hadn't in months—possibly years.

"You know what, Malachi? I think I can."

Author's Bio

Natasha Coker Jones is a communications professional who has no qualms breaking ground. She started her career as a reporter with a leading daily newspaper in her home country, Trinidad. She left journalism to become the co-founder and managing director of Upstream Publications Limited (UPL). The company's first product was *Upstream*, a lifestyle Christian magazine that circulated as a glossy before being converted to an online magazine. Through UPL, Natasha has led the creative team that has helped her clients to produce collateral as part of their marketing, public relations, advertising, and behaviour change communications strategy. Her formal training and experience allow her to speak authoritatively on various aspects of publishing. *When the Poui Blooms* is her debut novel. Natasha sees writing fiction as a natural extension of her creative expressions over the years. She has been scriptwriter and director of major productions for her home church, Daybreak Assembly. Passionate about writing creatively, Natasha hopes to inspire others, especially from the Caribbean, to take the steps necessary to become published authors. She lives in Trinidad with her husband and son. Look out for Book 2 of the Good Seeds series.

Like Natasha on Facebook and follow her on Twitter

Visit her website at natashacokerjones.com